THE PRINCE'S WING

AMBER R. DUELL

THE PRINCE'S WING

AMBER R. DUELL

THE PRINCE'S WING
© 2021 Amber R. Duell
www.amberrduell.com

Published by Crooked Heart Publishing

Cover Design by Artscandare Book Cover Design

For everyone who helped
my family after the fire

PROLOGUE

Twenty-Three Years Ago

The carriage rattled toward the palace gates, jostling the little boy inside. Saer had never ridden in the rear-facing seat before and his stomach churned with every bump. Cheeks pale, sweat dripping down his forehead, he clutched at his middle.

"You *cannot* be ill, do you hear me?" Lady Sol growled. The middle-aged woman's harsh warning brought tears to Saer's eyes and her piercing gaze only made him feel worse. "And you will *not* cry. Ever."

Saer drew in quaking breaths. "I want Mama."

Sol's cane cracked against his knees and he cried out. "She's dead and if you don't wish to join her, you'll never mention her again."

It had only been five days since soldiers dragged his parents away and he didn't understand why they hadn't come back. Didn't understand what *dead* meant. He was only four, after all. Saer clung to his mother's skirts with all of his strength when the king's men shoved her into the carriage bedside his father. He was ripped away from them. Flung into the mud. Left cold and sobbing until a man found him and passed him to Lady Sol.

"We've arrived," she said. "Keep your mouth shut, do as you're told, and remember your what your parents fought for. You owe your *life* to the Asters and will answer to their every demand. If the king discovers any of this, you will be killed. Understand?"

Saer sniffed and nodded. The king was bad, his parents said. Evil. That everyone needed to fight against him. But Lady Sol was taking him to see the king now … Saer clutched his hands in his lap.

The carriage came to a stop and a man in a red uniform opened the door. Lady Sol took his hand and stepped down, snapping her fingers at Saer for him to follow. He shuffled to his feet and hesitated—it was a big step. Too big for him to take alone.

"Hurry, boy," she snarled as she strode forward.

The servant gave him a smile and lifted Saer by his under arms, setting him on the fine gravel pathway. He gasped at the sight of all the splendor around him. Flowering trees, sparkling fountains, white stone buildings. Men wearing rich velvet and women in beaded gowns.

Pain exploded on the side of Saer's head— another crack of Lady's Sol's cane. He fell to his knees with a yelp.

"Stop dawdling. Do you think the king will wait all day?" She grabbed him by the back of his jacket and hauled him to his feet, grumbling.

Between the blow to the head and the brimming tears, the palace blurred. Saer rushed to keep up as the lady dragged him by the arm, her sharp fingernails digging into the sleeve of his gray jacket. His feet slipped on a set of smooth stone steps but he managed to correct himself just in time to pass through a massive carved door.

Inside, everything smelled like rain and flowers. Saer blinked until his vision cleared enough to make out the grand entrance. Gold shone off almost every surface, reflecting again and again in mirrors that faced each other. A chandelier dripped with crystals between a massive double staircase. He twisted his head, taking in all the details. The scrolled molding and the mosaic flooring. Flowering baskets of roses and ivy.

Lady Sol tugged him through a side door and into a new hallway. The walls there were exposed brick with wooden planked floor—the servant passages, just like his own home. Only, these hallways had more twists and turns and staircases. By the time he was led back into a gilded hall, Saer was completely lost.

"My Lady," a man with a hooked nose greeted. He wore blue silk lined with fur and a pointlessly small hat. "You're late. You're lucky the king hasn't canceled this meeting."

"He knows the importance," she insisted.

The man scowled and ushered them into a small, yet opulent room. Textured white paper on the walls, thick fur rugs on the floor, and deep red curtains. A handful of adults stood, talking, at one of the arched window. Saer tensed, his feet slowing, but Lady Sol's fingernails bit into his arm even harder.

"Bow," she hissed as she dropped into a curtsey. Saer obeyed, the eyes of everyone in the room weighing against his small body. "Your Majesty. We humbly apologize for—"

"Is this the child?" the king's deep voice demanded.

"Yes." Lady Sol stood up straight and shoved Saer forward a step. "Lord Saer Tufaro, son of Lord Henrik and Lady Eloise."

"The former Lord and Lady of Bragoss?" he asked, incredulous. The king was a short man, stocky with a pronounced brow and squared jaw. Saer felt himself wither under his gaze. "Their heads are on pikes in the middle of the capital. Why would I ever entrust their son with the safety of my own?"

What's a pike? he wondered to himself. And why are his parents putting their heads on them? Lady Sol must've lied when she said his mother was dead if she was in the capital. Maybe if he was really good, the king would let him go home today.

"He's of fine noble blood," Lady Sol insisted. "While his parents were traitors, he's young enough to mold in whatever you want."

A soft tug on Saer's sleeve drew his attention away from the king. He found a boy around his own age with auburn hair, dressed in white satin, beaming at him. Saer gave him a nervous smile back as the adults quarreled over Saer's existence.

"Play?" the boy asked and held up a wooden block.

Behind him, a lopsided tower was already half built on a low table. The blocks were unevenly stacked, ready to topple over. Saer had blocks too. His father bought them for his birthday three months ago.

"Play?" the boy asked again.

"Look." Lady Sol released Saer's arm and spun him to face the other child. "They already get along. Go on, child. Play with the prince."

Saer hesitated, glancing between Sol, the king, and the offered block. This felt like a test. Like he would be in trouble no matter what he did. But the boy giggled and shoved the block against Saer's chest. He caught the wood before it could fall to the floor and followed the prince to the table.

"Bastian would play with anyone his own age," the king snapped. "He's three and there are no other children in the palace."

"That could work to their advantage," one of the other men said. Saer carefully stacked blocks without looking back to see which adult spoke—not that he knew any of them by name. "The boy will have no one else to grow attached to except the prince."

"Not even a second Wing," another said.

"Only one Wing?" Lady Sol asked.

The king grunted. "No bird flies without two. My son will stay on the ground until I die of old age."

Sol's laughed as if the idea were ridiculous. "But Wings are meant to be raised alongside the royal. It will be too late for the prince to get a second if you wait."

The king snapped his fingers and Prince Bastian froze. He looked past Saer at the king, at the sudden flurry of movement, and crept to stand behind the older child. Saer turned, letting the prince hide behind him as the guards grabbed Lady Sol.

"Your Majesty?" she cried.

"I'll keep the boy. If he doesn't do well, he can join his parents," the king announced. His soulless eyes met Saer's from across the room. "Would you like to see what happens when you question your king?"

Saer tensed, unable to reply as his father's words echoed through is mind. *The king is a bad man.*

"Your Majesty, please. Forgive me. I didn't mean any disrespect," Lady Sol pleaded.

With a flick of king's hand, a third guard stepped up behind her.

And sliced her throat.

Saer winced and squeezed his eyes shut while the prince clung to the back of his jacket. But a moment later, rough fingers pinched his chin.

"*Watch,*" the king ordered.

Saer looked at the woman who had beaten him with her cane almost every day since he was thrust into her care. Watched as the blood seeped from her throat, stained her bodice. Watched as the guards released her and she slumped to the floor. Watched as blood soaked into the carpet beneath her.

He wanted to cry. Scream. Run. Find his mother, his father. Hide under the blankets on his bed. But he couldn't do any of that. Deep down, he knew the wrong reaction would put him in danger—*the king* was dangerous. And Saer? He was young and scared and alone. But he understood self-preservation. Knew instinctually how to survive.

With silence.

With obedience.

The king twisted Saer's face to look him in the eye again. "Do you understand what a Wing is to a royal?"

Saer felt his bottom lip quiver, but he refused to let himself cry. "Yes," he answered, his voice quaking.

"Tell me."

"Wings protect the king or prince," he whispered.

"It's more than that, but you'll learn." The king stood, patted the prince on the head once, and motioned to the other men. "My son has his Wing. I want him training with a sword first thing in the morning."

"Yes, Your Majesty," they said in unison.

"And dispose of the Lady Sol," he shouted once he'd exited the room, almost an afterthought.

Saer's whole body shook as the other men followed the king out. Left him alone with the prince and a dead body. The prince's hands unfurled from the back of his jacket. Saer turned and gave him the best smile he could manage. Trying his very best not to let Bastian see the corpse, he angled himself between the two.

"Do you want to finish building the tower?" he asked.

Bastian simply lifted a block and stared at it with teary eyes.

"It's all right," Saer said, partially to himself. He understood then that he was never going home again. That his parents' death *wasn't* a lie. He reached up and gingerly touched the lump Lady Sol had left on his head. It didn't hurt so much anymore. In fact, he didn't feel much of anything. Picking up a block, he added it to Bastian's crooked tower. "I'll stack them and you can knock it down, okay?"

ONE

Twenty-Three Years Later

Some risks were worth taking.

Escorting Crown Prince Bastian of Eradrist through the capital without an entourage wasn't one of them, however. The citizens hated the royal family more than… well, everything. Not that I could blame them. After murdering the beloved King Jonty and stealing the crown, Bastian's father drove the country into the ground. The people were hungry. They were tired. And they were furious.

So, no. The risk was too high.

But what did I know?

I was only the Prince's Wing. While the prince studied politics, I learned to fight. To kill. But, at the

9

end of the day, when lessons were done, Bastian and I had only ever had each other.

"Smile, Saer," Bastian mumbled from the corner of his mouth.

I narrowed my eyes, never daring to stop scanning the cobbled streets for danger. Ora Et was relatively quiet this early, but the sun was barely over the sloping roofs. Any number of would-be assassins could be lying in wait. An archer pressed behind a chimney. A swordsman lurking in an alley. Hell, the baker currently loading his vendor stand could've hidden a crossbow beneath his loaves. The man's ruddy cheeks grew a deeper shade of red as our horses clopped by.

Probably wishes he had *hidden a weapon.* Nothing would turn him into a martyr faster than murdering King Edric's only heir.

"*Saer,*" the prince whispered.

"There's nothing to smile about," I snapped.

Bastian shifted in his saddle. "There could be *less* to smile about if you don't try."

I exhaled sharply. No amount of false cheer would soften the people to our presence. "You know what would put a smile on my face? Heading back to the palace."

"I told you—"

"I know what you told me, *Your Highness.*" It was the late queen's death day and, as religious custom dictated, Bastian had to offer a gift to the temple on her behalf. It was an obvious scheme by the priests and no one could convince me otherwise. The priests had no sway over the quality of a person's afterlife; that was between them and the gods. Bastian shared the sentiment, but not publicly. Why give the citizens another reason to call him a heathen?

"*Oooh*," Bastian said light-heartedly. "I love it when you throw titles around."

"I don't know what you mean, My Prince." If anyone happened to overhear me use Bastian's given name, a shit-storm would follow. King Edric wasn't a forgiving man, and there were eyes and ears everywhere. Some reported to the palace. Others to the rebel group—the Red Asters. The closure of the private royal temple only yesterday seemed like a way to draw the prince out. The fact that Bastian refused extra protection when we left the palace was infuriating. He didn't want to draw attention, which I understood, but being murdered in the streets was bound to attract a crowd. "I'm only one person, you know. If the people decide to riot, I'm *one* person."

Bastian's smile grew wry. "What are you trying to say about my swordsmanship? We are very clearly *two* people."

I whipped my head toward him. "Take this seriously."

Bastian's blue eyes lacked the humor his voice held a moment ago. Slowly, his gaze locked onto mine and he repeated, "Smile."

Fucking politics.

I forced the corners of my mouth up into my best attempt at compliance. I was sure it did absolutely nothing to make me look more pleasant—in fact, it likely had the opposite effect. Regardless, the people gawking at us from their windows wouldn't care how approachable we looked when their bellies were hollow. A fact that haunted me every time I sat down to a full meal at the palace.

A single thread from the gold embroidery on Bastian's jacket would feed a family for a month. Longer if they spent it wisely. The royal horses below us would feed them too. As would the massive ruby on the hilt of his sword and the silver circlet braided tightly beneath his auburn hair. Or, if I *really* wanted to embrace my pessimism, a prince's ransom. A prince's *head*, delivered to the right people.

"If you die, I die," I reminded him. "There's no scenario where I return to the palace without you and survive."

"No one is dying, Saer." Bastian motioned to the end of the street where the Temple of Igeris stood, foreboding. "Look, we're almost there."

I glared at the once-white exterior, now blackened with mildew. Its twisting spires and open bell tower pierced the sky. Inside, the most judgmental men in all of Eradrist waited. And, personally knowing both the king and the Red Asters, that was saying something. "Great."

We passed through the iron gate surrounding the temple with only the sound of our horses' hooves to accompany us. After a quick visual sweep, I slid from the saddle and urged Bastian up a short staircase in the fenced courtyard. The thick wooden doors were wide open, a permanent invitation for anyone to enter.

Inside, rich cherry wood lined the walls with scenes from the Book of Gods carved by expert craftsmen. Matching pews ran in two rows along the main aisle and an altar stood at the front of the temple. A large cauldron for offerings sat right beside it. White velvet circled all of the pillars that held the thirty-foot ceiling up and, where they met the rafters, the fabric swooped down, tying together at the top of a massive iron chandelier in the center. With fresh white roses stuffed in every nook, the priests had clearly given the prince a proper welcome, but... where *were* the priests?

"I thought they were expecting us." My whisper echoed through the room.

"They are," Bastian said. The smile finally fell from his face as he called out, "Hello?"

Silence rang back at us—the kind that raises the hair on the back of a person's neck. Still and heavy. *Motherfucker.* Aster plot or rebellious citizens? One held significantly more danger than the other.

I unsheathed the sword at my hip and angled my body in front of the prince. "Stay behind me."

Trusting Bastian to do as instructed, I eased down the center aisle, eyes scanning back and forth for the inevitable attack. The breeze coming from the open doors rustled the bouquets. Made the velvet sway. My senses ramped into high gear, making the cloying scent of roses overpowering. Even the air felt thick against my exposed skin. My clothes were suddenly too constricting. My bracers too tight.

Where are you?

I caught a glimpse of red as we neared the altar. *Blood.* Another step revealed a bald priest in white robes sprawled across the polished floor. Throat slashed. Dead.

With an aster flower sitting on his chest.

"Asters," I breathed and felt Bastian tense behind me.

No. It couldn't be.

But it was. There was no denying the red flower on the priest's chest. So why hadn't Faramond warned me? The leader of the Red Asters *always* told me of planned attacks so I could be prepared. Extra assurance that I wouldn't fail—though I didn't need it. I was the best. Between the Asters and the royal training, there was no choice but to excel. My life was chosen for me. No questions allowed. No deviations tolerated.

I was a fucking pawn, forced to betray the one person I cared for with every breath I took. The sole person who gave a shit about me. My only solace was that the Asters still wanted Bastian alive so they could use false assassination attempts to fuck with King Edric's head.

The soft hush of moving fabric drew my attention to the ceiling. The velvet swayed. A shadow leapt from beam to beam. Then everything went still, as if the wind itself were waiting. My heartbeat settled into a steady rhythm, my body using it to remain calm and clear-headed.

A scratch of metal on metal. The shadow moved again. Dropped. Landed behind Bastian. I shoved the prince aside, and he stumbled into the pews, safe. He knew how to fight well enough, but that wasn't his job. It was mine.

The attacker rose from her crouch. Black, textured material covered her from the neck down, a diagonal smudge of red paint across her left cheek, marking her as an official assassin for the rebels.

She spun—her long, black braid whirling around her—and struck out with dual short swords. I met them with my longer one, and swept out with my leg at the same time. She fell backward, rolling into the motion, and sprung back up, swinging.

Each stab, every swipe, I met them. There were three chances to end her life in the first two minutes of the fight, but was I meant to? Perhaps the message informing me of the attack was lost. If I killed an Aster assassin, Faramond would be livid. But I couldn't keep this up. Not when Bastian knew the way I fought and undoubtedly saw the same three openings I had.

Fuck.

The assassin let out a furious cry. Brought both blades over her head. Swung down.

I spun, ducked, sliced.

A squelch replaced the scream and, seconds later, a new wail filled the temple. One of pain. Of death. I raised my sword. Finished the job. The assassin collapsed, intestines spilling from her abdomen to the floor, my sword buried deep in her chest.

"Are you hurt?" I asked Bastian between heavy breaths.

He stood between the pews where I had shoved him, sword out, and shook his head. "Are you?"

"No." I stepped over the dead assassin and slammed the temple doors shut. "Stand against the wall. We don't need you to be attacked from behind again while I check for more Asters."

Bastian listened, keeping his sword at the ready, as I worked my way through the temple. I hated stepping into the vestibules and priests' quarters, leaving the prince completely alone. But I had to be sure there weren't more. Attempts on the prince's life weren't uncommon, but they were mostly for show. A threat to the king, a reminder that the Asters were still there, a distraction from their true plans. Plans that included me being inside the palace. Close to the crown. Among other spies, but none of us knew the others. It kept everyone safe, unable to turn on each other, and stopped us from betraying the cause. No one was trustworthy.

Least of all me.

Because I would die for Bastian. We'd grown up together, sharing every up and down, every mistake and achievement. He was the prince I was meant to hate but, in truth, there was no me without him anymore. We were too intwined.

And the rebels would kill me for it.

The people of Eradrist deserved better and the Asters claimed they wanted to give them that. Bastian *was* better though. He wasn't his father. The old royals were dead—there was no going back—and the country would prosper once the prince sat on the throne. A familiar pang of regret and guilt hammered inside me as I returned to his side. I was lying to my best friend. My *only* friend. In the worst possible way.

"All clear," I said in a weary voice. The assassin had been skilled—too skilled. They were usually puppets posing as professional killers. Criminals headed to a noose anyway. Something was wrong, but protecting Bastian was all I could do right now. "The priests are all dead."

Bastian let out a breath and slid down the wall, sitting. Blood had sprayed his white tunic and jacket, his face paler than usual. He stretched out his long legs in front of him. "I suppose we should head back to the palace."

I sighed and sat down beside the prince, resting my elbows on my knees. My head thunked against the wooden wall. "We should."

But neither of us moved to leave.

"Want some?" Bastian asked after a few tense moments of silence.

I looked over to see a small pouch of dried fruit in his hand. "Why do you have that?"

"In case I got hungry," he said as if it were obvious.

"You're a prince, not a squirrel." I pushed his proffered snack away with my forearm, my hands coated in wet blood.

"Suit yourself." Bastian plopped a piece in his mouth and chewed slowly. Then, after he swallowed, dragged a hand down his face. "This probably isn't the best time to bring this up, but I have some news."

"It's definitely not the best time," I agreed.

"I spoke with Father this morning before we left."

I was aware—I'd walked him to the Main Palace for the meeting. "What is it this time? Another tax hike? A decree to sacrifice all first-born children to the fire god?"

He released a humorless chuckle. "I'm getting married."

"You're…" My jaw dropped. "Sorry, *what*?"

"Getting married." Bastian swallowed. "To King Jonty's daughter."

King Jonty—the king that Bastian's father had murdered—didn't have a daughter. Not a *legitimate* one anyway. *Oh, shit.* "His bastard? With Countess Odelia?"

"The one and only." He gave a stiff smile.

The countess was known for her many affairs. There was no telling if the child was truly the old king's daughter, and that wasn't to mention how dangerous the woman was. Her vile nature was even more infamous than her numerous bed mates. It was rumored that she'd poisoned any woman that caught the king's eye, including her own sister, had servants killed for the slightest offense, and snapped the neck of the queen's beloved bird out of spite.

"What is your father thinking?" I asked.

Bastian shrugged. "That I'm twenty-six and far past marriageable age? As the only heir to the throne, he wants to secure the line with many grandchildren."

"You could marry *anyone*. Pick a princess from any nation."

Bastian rolled his head to the side and looked at me with resignation. "Yes, but only one bride will help ease tension with the Red Asters."

Because King Jonty's bastard daughter was of the old royal blood. Therefore, Bastian's children would be true heirs. Unless the girl killed him on their wedding night so the Asters could place the crown on *her* head.

Ah, fuck.

TWO

Heavy clouds hid the waxing moon as I navigated the streets of Ora Et for the second time that day. This time I had no horse, no uniform, and no prince to protect. Bastian was safely in his residence with two dozen guards outside, so no one would miss me until morning. It was my time to sleep, to rest, so I could properly protect the prince once he woke.

Hidden beneath a natural, rough-spun cloak, I turned right. Boisterous laughter drifted from a tavern in the center of the street. Through the large window, men and women drowned their sorrows with money they didn't have. But they were happy for the moment—something no one could begrudge them. I quickened my steps before jealousy over their freedom caught hold of me. What wouldn't I give for a night of smiles and laughter without an undercurrent of guilt and fear?

I'd give too much.

I shook the thought from my mind and darted down a dark alley that smelled like piss. Rats scurried along the uneven brick wall to my left and disappeared through a hole near the cobbled footpath. Above, a low, slate roof covered a doorway. I leapt and gripped the edge, swinging onto it. From there, I scaled the bricks and threw myself onto the second story roof. A small attic window arched from between pieces of slate with a handful of candles burning inside. I held my breath as I rapped a gloved knuckle against the warped glass.

Faramond's head snapped up from where he sat behind his desk. Stubble grew along the Aster leader's thin face, and his salt-and-pepper hair fell from his usual-slicked back style. Even from outside, I could tell his clothes were wrinkled with days of wear.

"What the fuck are you doing here?" he growled, gray eyes narrowing.

I opened the window and slid, feet first, into the warm office before anyone on the street noticed me. "Hello, Faramond."

He threw his quill down and scowled. "This better be good."

"Would I take the risk otherwise?" I shifted toward the small fireplace to get rid of the late-night chill and gave a small, belated bow. Faramond *was* a lord, after all. But so was I. A fact Faramond seemed to forget. *Lord Saer Tufaro.* I was born to the title, but Faramond was the reason I was allowed to keep it after my late parents supported King Jonty during the rebellion. He suggested to the right people that I train as Bastian's Wing. Sometimes I resented it. Resented what he made me—a liar and a spy. Growing up in an orphanage couldn't have been a worse fate. At least I couldn't carved out an honest life for myself.

Faramond snapped his fingers. "Speak, boy. I'm a busy man."

"An assassin attacked the prince today," I said without preamble.

"Yes," he said slowly. "It wasn't an order, or you would've been warned. A damn shame she acted on her own. She was one of our best."

I wasn't sure how to feel about that. If the Red Asters couldn't control their own people, bigger problems were brewing.

Faramond's chair creaked as he leaned his elbows onto the desk. "Is that why you're here? To whine about being taken unaware?"

"No." I gritted my teeth at the accusation. "Although, I can't say I'm happy about it either."

Faramond combed one ink-stained hand through his hair—he lifted his quill with the other. The papers piled on his desk were covered in scratched out words and illegible scribbles. "You have intelligence to share, then? Something that couldn't wait?"

"The prince is getting married." I said it as if it should've been a shock to him, but I knew, deep down, it wasn't. Not when King Jonty's bastard was involved. "He's engaged to Countess Odelia's daughter."

Faramond smirked.

I balled my hands into fists. *Conniving bastard.* "You had one of your other Asters suggest it, didn't you?

They convinced King Edric that it would help ease tensions."

"It won't help the false king, but it will certainly help us."

Us. Because I was an Aster too, whether I liked it or not. I hated the king, but I didn't like Faramond either. There had to be a middle ground, but neither side was willing to come down from their mountaintop to find it.

"Is she going to kill Bastian?" I asked. "Marry him, kill him, and take the throne herself? Be your puppet monarch?"

"*Bastian*?" His smirk grew crueler as he scratched the quill through the parchment, leaving a large hole. "I've warned you repeatedly not to get attached to the pretender prince. He'll die just like his father will, otherwise this was all for nothing."

My eye twitched in an attempt to keep my face expressionless. Bastian *wouldn't* die because I wouldn't let him. "He—"

Faramond stood so quickly that his seat clattered to the floor. "Don't you dare try to defend him again. You're walking a fine line, Saer. If I can't trust you to do what the Asters need you to do, you'll be dealt with just like any other traitor. Am I understood?"

Dealt with. *Murdered.* No matter the unique position an Aster held, fuckups weren't permitted. Wavering loyalty wasn't permitted. And leaving the Red Asters was *definitely* not permitted. I would like to see him try to kill me, though. If the assassin at the temple was one of their best, I dared him to send someone after me. There was Bastian to think about, however. His safety. So, I swallowed my pride and said, "Understood."

"Good." Faramond pointed to the window. "Now get out." I was halfway onto the roof again when the Aster leader added, "Return next week. I have a job for you."

In my twenty-three years as Faramond's marionette, he'd never given me a job in addition to being the Prince's Wing. I'd pushed him too far tonight, asked him too many questions. There was no free thought allowed within the Red Asters, no walking away from their cause—there was only obedience or punishment.

A shiver ran down my spine. "Yes, sir."

THREE

While King Edric's concern that Bastian would one day steal the throne was absurd, it saved me from sitting through meetings all day at the prince's side. Faramond nearly had a stroke when I told him that I was barred from the Main Palace years ago. I should've known better than to best both of the King's Wings at a public exhibition.

"Enjoy your morning," Bastian said as we approached the gate. "I know I will."

"Such cynicism," I muttered. The two guards at the entrance pounded their staffs once on the ground, signaling the others inside.

Bastian drew in a deep breath and squared his shoulders. "I'll be late today."

"Your Highness." I bowed and waited until the metal gate parted enough for Bastian to stroll in.

Once it shut behind him, I sighed and headed for the royal gardens. There were bigger things for me to worry about than the king's vanity. Like the job that Faramond had for me, if the future princess came with a murderous agenda, and whether more Asters would go rogue. I sighed a second time. Everything would be fine—I'd make sure of it. No one was killing the prince, even if it meant I had to start sleeping at the foot of his bed.

Viscount Jarsdel stopped abruptly in his tracks when I rounded a bend. His stringy beard practically quivered with distaste as he escorted his daughter past the rosebushes. The brunette was still in her first year of husband-hunting—all wide-eyed and inexperienced. She'd likely heard her father's musings about why I wasn't trusted inside the Main Palace, but was still curious enough about me to bat her lashes.

"Good morning, Lord Tufaro" she greeted when I passed.

I offered a small, quick bow. "My lady. Viscount."

"Where is the prince?" he snapped.

"With the king and governors," I answered, forcing my voice to remain even. "As he is every morning."

"And where are *you* going?"

While I was used to the questioning looks and rumors about my parents, I didn't subject myself to it unnecessarily. Most nobles had the manners to at least pretend to trust me to my face. I smiled at him, then the woman at his side. "If you'd like me to escort your lovely daughter somewhere, I'm more than happy to oblige."

"That won't be necessary." The Viscount grabbed his daughter's hand. "Come, Elany. I'm taking you to your mother so she can explain *again* how a handsome face doesn't equate to honor."

Anyone else might've taken offense to his insult, but he wasn't wrong. I had as much honor as a man in my position could possibly have. A spy. A liar.

Slipping into an overgrown, forgotten nook of the garden, I stretched out on my favorite bench. It was perfectly situated beneath a large oak, the seat comfortably curved. I tipped my head back to watch the morning sun shining through the foliage. The leaves danced, creating patterns of light with branches that broke across the entire canopy. A sense of calm accompanied the soft rustle, and I closed my eyes to let the warmth soak in.

"My lady?" came a woman's voice from the other side of the large hedge. My eyes flew open and I held my breath, listening. "My lady, where are you?"

Damn. Running into some lord's lost daughter was not on my agenda. All it would take was for someone to find us alone—that sliver of honor I had would be called into question, and I'd be at the center of a shit storm. But not only would I never touch a woman against their wishes, I wouldn't touch them if they begged me to. I'd visited the royal brothel when I was younger because I was curious and stupid, but I wasn't allowed to start a family. Why risk the scandal of consorting with a lady or, worse, the heartache? So, I stayed on my bench, waiting for the trouble to pass by.

A twig inside the hedge wall snapped behind me, and I tensed. No one came here—that was the point. The royal gardens were immaculately groomed, full of fragrant flowers, and elegant sculptures. All things that drew nobles in, unlike the weeds and family of rodents living at the base of the oak tree. This tiny square of chaos was *mine*. The crack came again and I swung my legs over the bench, sitting up.

The far hedge shook, then a woman fell from between the wide leaves.

The hell...?

I darted forward to catch her before she could land in the dirt, ruining her gown. The intricate pattern sewn into the gray fabric and strands of gemstones swooping down to decorate her upper arms were worn only by high-ranking nobility. When she looked up, my breath caught. She was absolutely stunning with delicate features, honey brown hair, and amber eyes. I couldn't recall seeing her at the palace before, and I would have. The dress highlighted her narrow waist and perfect breasts in a way that would draw the eye of every man in the room. *Even those who shouldn't be looking.* I cringed as I steadied her and took two steps back.

"Thank you," she said, sounding breathless.

I clenched my jaw. Her voice was as pretty as a songbird, and I hated myself for wanting to hear it again. "Your ladies are looking for you."

"I'm sure they are," she mumbled, examining a scratch on her forearm.

"If you wait here, I'll direct them—"

"No!" She grimaced. "I mean, no. Thank you. I'm... trying to get a moment to myself."

I met her gaze and lifted a brow. While I understood the desire to be alone in a place where *alone* didn't exist, she couldn't stay here. Not with me, and definitely not without a chaperone.

"They'll find me soon enough," she reasoned.

"Undoubtedly." I caught myself before I could grin at her attempt to smooth her hair back into place. With the number of beads woven through the locks, it was going to take an expert pair of hands to fix. "And once they do, which of us do you think will feel their wrath?"

She paused, looking me over, and I couldn't help wondering what she saw. My dark hair, swept back and tied with a leather cord, my light green eyes, and sharp jawline. Or was it the black pants, tunic, and jerkin with the silver wing pinned over my left collarbone. The bracers on my arms and the sword at my hip. Did she see me or did she see a Wing? I hated myself for caring about the answer. After years of never being seen as a person, it shouldn't have bothered me anymore.

She shrugged. "No one has to know you saw me."

"There are no secrets here," I warned.

It wouldn't be surprising if the entire palace knew we'd met before midday. She flashed a brilliant smile that hit me like an arrow right in the chest. *Fuck no.* I had to get away from her *now*. No good would come of this.

"Do the birds speak?" She made a show of looking around. "The ants?"

"Only the flowers," I said, hinting at the Red Asters. Her easy laugh told me she didn't comprehend the warning. My eyes narrowed. "This is your first time visiting the palace, isn't it?"

She sobered. "Is it that obvious?"

Extremely. She was too unbothered to be a regular visitor. Getting lost and avoiding the maids was bound to get her in trouble if her family found out, but it was the careless way she treated the repercussions that gave her away. That, and the fact she'd seen the Wing on my chest and not reacted. "It is," I assured her. "You're not wary of me."

Hesitation flashed through her large, beautiful eyes. "Should I be?"

I lifted a brow. Should she be? No. Not unless she was planning to track down the prince and threaten his life. "That doesn't make a difference."

"Doesn't it?"

"Give yourself a few days and you'll have the answer on your own."

She cocked her head, her waist-length hair catching in the beads on her arm. "I would've thought you were popular."

I huffed. "What gave you that impression?"

"Because…" Her cheeks blazed red and she stood straighter, giving me a clumsy curtsy. "I haven't introduced myself yet."

"You're not supposed to," I told her with a touch of humor. Had she not been taught any court etiquette before her parents brought her here? It was refreshing, but not wise. "A mutual acquaintance is meant to make introductions or they're not to be made not at all."

She waved a hand through the air as if the idea were ridiculous. "I'm Karina."

Karina. As in the bastard daughter engaged to Bastian? No—it was one of the most common given names in Eradrist. At least half of the ladies at court were named Karina. And no daughter of Count Odelia would be this… unrefined. The engagement wasn't public knowledge yet and Bastian's fiancée was still in Port Black.

"And you are…?" she prompted.

I cleared my throat. "The Prince's Wing."

The smile immediately fell from her face. *Ah. There it is.* The suspicion. Perhaps I should've given my name instead, but this was for the best. The unfamiliar thread drawing me toward her needed to be brutally cut—something my title was sure to do.

"I thought you would be older," she said after a long moment.

My eyes widened. "Older?"

"A seasoned guard," she clarified, cheeks pink.

Experienced, she meant. But I had my fair share of that in my twenty-seven years. While I hadn't seen a battlefield like most of the older men in the army, I'd been slaughtering would-be assassins since I was thirteen. Before my first kill, I'd fought Bastian's assailants off long enough for guards to arrive. And I still wore the scars to prove it.

"If I didn't know any better, I'd say you're underestimating me," I said, half-questioning.

She gave me a lopsided smirk. "Stories about you are well-known throughout all of Eradrist and beyond. You singlehandedly defeated both of the King's Wings at an exhibition so, no. I believe you're as dangerous as they say."

I tilted my chin up, pulling my shoulders back, in some sort of unconscious desire to *make* her afraid. To give her a reason to be cautious.

"Multiple people have warned me to keep my distance," she continued. "But perhaps they're simply jealous of you."

I snorted. "You really *are* new to court."

"You mean I'm a breath of fresh air?" She gave a stilted curtsy. "Why thank you, Lord Wing."

Her eyes gleamed with amusement as she smirked and, for a moment, I forgot the point I had been making. I was too caught up in her essence. The light that shone from within her, unreserved. Then I blinked. *I was dangerous.* That was what I had wanted her to understand. But maybe *she* was the dangerous one.

"Stay here," I told her in a gruff voice. "I'll fetch your ladies."

"No need," Karina said and hurried through the opening in the hedge before I could stop her. She looked back just before she disappeared and called, "You never saw me."

I plopped down on the bench and let out a heavy breath, staring at the place she just stood. If only she would be that easy to forget. Especially when I wanted to see her again already. After having spent minutes in her presence, I knew that was ridiculous, but I'd never experienced such an instantaneous draw to someone before.

Pull yourself together.

Women were off limits to me unless they worked in a brothel. And I had another woman to be concerned with. One who was currently living in Port Black with the Countess, where she was likely hatching plans to murder Bastian. A murder I had to prevent without guaranteeing my own death at Aster hands.

FOUR

Soft footsteps drew my attention from the sunlit patterns above me, the oak leaves slowly thinning as cooler weather blew in. Swinging my right leg over the bench, I sat up, ready to react as necessary. To bow or duck behind my tree to avoid doing so. I flicked a glance at the wide trunk. Hiding was definitely the preferable choice.

"You're here," a woman said as I sat on my hidden bench.

That voice…

I held my breath as my gaze slid to the entrance in the hedge. Karina picked her way through the overgrown grass, golden hair twisted with strings of pearls that matched the strands cascading off her light blue gown. My pulse leapt at the sight and I jumped to my feet.

"I wasn't sure you'd be here again," she said when I was silent. "It doesn't look like anyone visits this place much."

"That's why I like it," I said with a clenched jaw.

Was she trying to test me? Or, maybe use me to get herself sent back home? Seven days ago, after supplies started being delivered to the empty Women's Palace, gossip had spread like wildfire. No one knew if Eradrist was getting a new queen or a princess, but the idea of either was enough to drag power-hungry lords from their personal estates. It seemed as if her father was ahead of the chatter and likely came to make her a lady's maid. But, if she didn't want the position, it would only take the slightest whiff of impropriety to get herself rejected.

I scowled at her. "What are you doing here?"

She stopped beside the bench, tipping her head back to look up at me. There was at least a foot difference in our height which was twice that of most Eradristian women. "I wanted to see you again."

"Why?"

"I felt bad about the last time we met." She swung her silk skirts to the side and perched on the bench, patting the spot beside her. "Sit with me."

"I'm fine standing."

Her smile fell slightly. "I'm sorry for running off. My mother warned me that you were dangerous." She looked pointedly at the sword on my hip.

I raised a brow. "You didn't seem the least bit frightened."

"Right, well…" She blushed slightly. "After meeting you, I thought about my mother's warning and realized that your skillset is something to be admired."

"Oh?" I crossed my arms, staring pointedly at her.

She nodded, smiling again. "You're not your parents, so the people who distrust you for that reason are small-minded. And the king trusts you to protect his son so you're clearly not a bad person."

Except, technically speaking, I was a trained assassin—just like the Aster I killed in the temple. A murderer for hire for both the Asters and Bastian. Not to mention that the king *doesn't* trust me. "I would love to know how you came to that conclusion."

"Instinct," she said, half-questioning.

I held back a snort. "What else does your instinct tell you?"

"Don't trust people who *say* you can trust them," she said, using her fingers to count. "Leave the turtles alone. Stay away from the edge of cliffs. Treat all snow as if it were yellow, at least in a city."

"What's wrong with turtles?" I asked, though for the life of me, I wasn't sure why I latched onto that.

"I don't know." She grinned sheepishly. "Something."

"And you don't feel that *something* about me?"

"You're obviously not going to kill me." She rolled her eyes. "If anyone wanted me dead, you would be overkill. Someone far less skilled could easily end my life, and if swordsmanship defined whether I should speak to a man, I would be in a convent already."

I stared at her, mouth parted at her boldness, then a laugh burst from me. A real one—one that only Bastian had ever heard. And rarely. It shook through my chest, rumbling. "Perhaps you *should* consider giving yourself to the gods. Running your mouth like that will get you in trouble here."

"*Hmm.*" She shifted on the bench. "They would make me cut my hair though, and I rather like it long. Besides, I've never been religious."

"Neither have I." Sitting on the far end of the bench, I left plenty of space between us. "But never say that. Not when you're visiting court."

She picked at the pearls hanging over her shoulders. "So many rules."

Perhaps she *should* use me to get herself out of here. Create a false scandal. Return to whatever country estate her family owned and marry a lesser lord. Or… I could use her inexperience to my advantage. Recruit her as my spy. "Tell me," I said carefully. "How old are you?"

"Twenty-three."

"And you're hoping to be a lady's maid?"

She scoffed. "I am not."

"Oh?" I chuckled. "Do you have better prospects to consider?"

Karina glanced at me. "I suppose that depends on your definition of *better.*"

A good answer. "If not a life at the convent and not a life serving the crown, what is it you want, then?"

She shook a finger at me. "That sounds like a dangerous question. Perhaps my mother was right about her third warning regarding you."

"Third?" I tilted my head and watched her from the corner of my eyes. What were the first two?

"She said that you see too much," she whispered conspiratorially.

"Is there something you don't want me to see?" I studied her, watched her tense, squeeze her hands into fists. There was—she had a secret. A lover left behind, perhaps. She wouldn't be the first lady to pine for a man they couldn't have. The thought of her loving anyone irked me. "Keep your secret, my lady. I'm sure it poses no threat to the prince and that's all I'm concerned with."

"Why aren't you with him, then?"

"Because I defeated the King's Wings," I reminded her simply.

"And the prince…?" She bit her lip and peeked at me from the corner of her eyes. "What's he like?"

The prince. Was that why she came back? Not to see me but to learn about Bastian? It wasn't that shocking but it didn't stop the jealousy from pricking my insides.

"He's a respectable man," I offered. "Generous, good-natured, and women seem to find him handsome. One day, he'll make a great king."

Karina nodded, glancing away. It bothered her. Why? No part of that was disappointing, unless she was looking for something more personal. I wouldn't give that information to anyone, let alone this strange, mysterious girl.

"Some advice?" I asked. "Train your expressions."

"Yes, yes. I've already heard that my face will get me in as much trouble as my mouth," she mumbled.

The dejected look she wore now made me regret saying anything. Who was I to snuff out the light radiating from inside her? If she'd managed to hold onto it for over two decades, perhaps the court wouldn't beat every ounce of it into the dirt. I reached out, lifting a lock of her hair before I realized what I was doing. As soon as I felt the softness against my skin, I lost track of rational thought.

What would it feel like against other parts of my body? Skimming over my chest while she rode me? Wrapped around my hand as I sunk into her from behind? "I like your hair too," I said in a low voice, letting the soft strands slip through my fingers.

Karina stood, giving a small curtsy, cheeks red. "I should return before they notice I'm gone."

Had she seen the lust on my face? Felt the same tension between us that I'd felt? The inexplicable pull. *Fuck*. I had to get it together and remember who I was—*what* I was. "You shouldn't come here again." I gave her a half-hearted smile. "Not that I mind, but it's asking for trouble."

"I've never minded a little trouble," Karina whispered. Then she left me there to consider our interaction. To wonder why I claimed not to mind her visits. And why it was the truth.

When I met Bastian after his morning meetings, we went straight to the archives. He'd said nothing, not to me nor the caretakers when they asked if he needed assistance. A tightness had lined his normally gentle features as he searched for the books alone. The look still remained, all these hours later.

I grew tired of watching him flip through pages and turned my attention out the window. The coolness of the glass soaked through my sleeve where

I pressed against it, settled onto a padded bench that was boxed in with shelves where I could still see the prince in my peripheral. The smooth stone wall that surrounded the Main Palace blocked the view of the garden. Perhaps I shouldn't return to my secret nook for a while. It seemed wise to avoid Karina in case she foolishly decided to sneak away again.

Or I should use her for information.

Why didn't I want to? It was a golden opportunity. But she'd made me feel things I'd never felt before. Almost hopeful, though the realist in me knew better. It was a simple infatuation—nothing more. I'd barely spent any time at all with her, and yet…

"You look as happy as I feel today," Bastian said, breaking the silence.

I twisted, putting the garden and the Main Palace behind me, and crossed my arms. "You're speaking to me now?"

Bastian glanced up from his stack of research. "I wasn't *not* speaking to you. I was busy thinking about something the governors' decided today."

"What is it this time?" I asked, weary.

Bastian looked around the large, dimly lit room. "Not here."

"That bad, huh?" I stood and stretched, cracking my back. "It's getting late. Are you joining your father for dinner?"

"Not tonight." He shut the book in front of him and rubbed his eyes.

I hesitated, waiting for Bastian to move onto the next volume, but when he didn't, I motioned to a caretaker. If I waited on the prince to call for someone himself, we'd never leave. Not when he was in a mood to research.

The man that scurried over wore a red belt cinched at the waist of his brown robes, identifying him as the head caretaker. He bowed, gaze down, speaking to the floor. "Do you need assistance, Your Highness?"

"He's finished," I answered for him. "If you could put these away for us?"

Bastian sat up straighter, setting his palms on the mess of papers. "I should keep going."

"No, you should eat," I insisted. "And don't tell me you're not hungry."

"Fine." Bastian leaned back in his chair and waved the caretaker forward. "We'll come back later."

Not if I can help it. He always did this. Buried himself in history and law as if it had changed since the last time. He'd memorized it all, likely word for word, at this point. "After you."

"Look at you, giving me orders around in front of people," he joked as we made our way outside.

I snorted. "I dare them to say something to your father."

Bastian grinned, elbowing me hard in the side. I scowled, knowing he was aware that I couldn't strike back. Not until we were safely alone in his private rooms.

"Please have someone deliver two servings of dinner," Bastian told the guard standing at the gate of the Prince's Palace.

The prince stopped just outside his private residence and waited between two other guards while I did a quick sweep of the interior. The tall windows were shut, dark blue curtains drawn back with gold ties, and someone had reset our unfinished game of game from earlier. A handful of steps took me to the doorway from the sitting area to his bedroom. The four posts of his bed jutted up toward the ceiling and the cream bedding was perfectly made. No one was beneath it, nor were they hiding inside the large armoire. The small private bathing chamber with its round copper tub was also free of threats.

"All right," I called. "It's clear."

Bastian dismissed the guards at the door and joined me inside. The second the doors shut behind us, I slapped the center of his back.

"Ah!" He leapt sideways, arching his back. "Asshole."

I shrugged. "You started it."

"You're still an asshole."

I grinned and sunk into a soft, velvet chair. "Someone has to keep your ego in check."

"Who's going to check yours?" he grumbled.

"*Please* find someone to give me a decent fight." I loosened my bracers and shifted to pull the sword from my hip, propping the scabbard against the arm of the chair. "What was the research for this time?"

He scratched beneath the braids holding his crown in place. "Taxes. The Governor of the People insisted they need to be lowered or citizens will starve this winter."

"And the others decided to raise them anyway?" I asked, though it wasn't really a question.

"I'm trying to find an alternative."

The answer was yes, then. Because of course they did. The governors didn't give two shits about the citizens.

"If we cut a few other expenses, it could be avoided, but they're not going to be happy about the options." Bastian sighed and sat down across from me, glaring. "But enough about that. What's gotten under your skin today?"

I shifted uncomfortably. "I don't know what you mean."

"You're a fucking liar," he said with a laugh. "Someone giving you a hard time? I saw Duchess Fransabelle in the Main Palace today."

Ugh. The Duchess was as hard as they came. If I had a smudge of dirt on me as a child, she raised hell. It didn't matter if I was coming from training or not. And if I so much as spoke in the wrong tone of voice, I received a smack on the back of the head. Beneath that though, she had a sweet side. Sneaking Bastian and I sugared candy, telling us stories. She was something like a part-time mother when she visited the palace—more than anyone else here had been.

"Thank the gods, no." I needed my hair trimmed and probably a shave if I was going to see the duchess. A quick glance down told me I needed to order a new jerkin too. The leather was comfortably worn, but that only meant she wouldn't approve.

"Then what?" Bastian pressed. "Don't lie. I can tell the difference between your normal sullenness and when something is on your mind. You look like you did when the commander banned you permanently from training with his troops."

My scowl deepened. I was fourteen and the *permanent* ban only lasted a week before King Edric demanded I return. Not because I was sulking, of course, but because I needed to learn how to defend his son. Besides, it wasn't my fault the had misfired. The bolt didn't even hit anyone. "Why did they make me your Wing again?" I grumbled.

"Because you were conveniently dropped in my father's lap?"

And because he killed any adult he thought might split my allegiances.

I huffed. "Fuck you."

"Well?"

"I…" *Ah, damn.* I couldn't lie. "There was a woman in the garden today."

Bastian's eyes widened. "A woman?"

"Fuck. Yes, Bast." Groaning, I rubbed my sweaty palms against my knees. "A very pretty, very *noble* woman, in fact. And she spoke to me like a normal human being." *Because she wanted to know about the prince.* I hung my head. "Shit."

"You could—"

"No," I said, cutting him off. False hope wouldn't do me any good. It was best if I accepted my limitations with women and drove Karina from my head completely. My life was already complicated enough without adding heartache. "Don't encourage anything. We both know I can't."

Bastian was quiet for a long moment. I felt him staring at me, disappointment radiating off him, buzzing in the air. "Saer… I'm sorry."

Me too. It was the price I had to pay to be his Wing—the price I deserved to pay for being an Aster. I didn't want my friend's pity nor did I deserve it. "Don't be."

"If it wasn't for me, you—"

A knock came at the door, saving me from the rest of the conversation. I slid to my feet, lifting my sheathed sword in case it wasn't our dinner. It was, though. A servant girl gave a small bob of her head while holding what had to be a very heavy tray. I stepped aside to allow her entrance. The smell of roast meat, savory gravy, and tangy fruit followed her through the door. Once she set the tray on the small dining table in the corner, the servant backed from the room while maintaining a bow.

"Let's eat," I grumbled.

Bastian moved to the table and lifted the lid off his plate, motioning for me to do the same. My stomach was in knots thinking of Karina. The way the sun caught the golden tones of her hair, the mischievous glint in her eyes when she joked, the scent of her. But it there was no point in torturing myself. I had to forget her, not because I wanted to, but because I *needed* to. So I willed away the image of her beautiful face. Then I sat and I ate. And neither of us spoke about taxes or women again for the rest of the night.

FIVE

The fact that two lady's maids in white and blue uniformed dresses were buzzing around the gardens should've made it obvious that Karina was nearby. And yet, when I slipped into my private little corner to find her already there, words failed me. How did she keep sneaking away like this without getting caught? Even I didn't tempt fate this much.

"Are you haunting me?" I asked in greeting.

Karina jumped at the sound of my voice, but a smile quickly spread over her face. She shifted down to the far end of the bench, leaving plenty of space for me to join her. Sapphires adorned her arms and the bodice of her bronze gown. Her hair fell, loose, with three strands of matching gemstones looped across her head. A splash of bronze covered her eyelids, making the golden hues more prominent.

"I wasn't sure what time you usually came," she said when I didn't immediately sit down. "You were already here when I came before, so I had to guess."

I sighed, resigned, and sat at the very edge of the bench. "I escort Prince Bastian to the Main Palace in the morning and, when the weather's decent, come here to wait for the end of their session."

"This is decent weather?" she asked.

My eyes wandered down her body before I could stop myself, and I noticed her goosebumps for the first time. "You would likely agree if you'd taken your cloak when you snuck out."

"They confiscated it to try and dissuade such excursions," she mumbled, rubbing her arms.

If I had worn my cloak, I would've been tempted to wrap it around her. Even if it was for the few minutes she stayed. But my jerkin, the tunic beneath, and the leather spalders covering my shoulders kept me comfortable. In another month, I would need to wear more layers, but now, it was enough to keep the chill away.

"I see their plan is working." I grinned.

She shrugged, sapphires clacking against each other on her upper arms, and looked down at her lap. "As it turns out, I'm not very good at being a proper lady."

"I've met plenty of *proper ladies* at court."

"You don't need to agree with them," she grumbled under her breath.

My smirk grew. "They're exhausting."

"But they're safe," she scoffed—a distinctively *un*ladylike action.

I shrugged with one shoulder, not having the heart to tell her she was right. "No one is ever completely safe."

"You are." Her eyes met mine and it felt as if she were staring straight into my soul.

A nervous laugh fell from my lips. "Me? My job is to take a blade for a prince universally hated outside of these walls. And inside them, everyone hates *me*. I'm surprised I made it to adulthood." And that wasn't counting any of my Aster dealings. That easily doubled my chances of being assassinated.

"The way everyone talks about you, I don't think you have anything to worry about. You're practically a legend. I've overheard the maids talking about the things they'd do to you if you weren't so intimidating." She glanced at my sword. "They're only afraid of you because they don't know you."

I snorted. "If they knew me, I think they would be more afraid."

"I don't." She studied me, her tone and gaze serious.

Her words twisted inside me, squeezing the permanent ball of guilt I kept locked away. I deserved the hate and sideways glances. The distrust. The wariness. Nobles didn't know the real reason I shouldn't be trusted, but they were right about me nevertheless. "You don't know me either," I whispered. "Just because I haven't told your ladies where to find you or tried to kill you for interrupting my private mornings doesn't mean I'm not a monster."

"You're determined to believe that." Karina took a deep breath. "Nothing I say will make you believe me, but that doesn't make me wrong."

I gave a small *hmm* in response. Neither of us would be changing our minds today so, instead, we sat in oddly comfortable silence for a handful of minutes. Before now, I hadn't thought that was possible. Bastian and I spent plenty of time together without speaking, but I'd never experienced it with anyone else. It was … nice.

"Can I try that on?" Karina asked.

I jumped at the sudden question, having been too lost in the ease of the moment, and my hand went straight for my hilt. "Try what on?"

"This." Her fingertips landed softly on my bracer.

My eyes slid between hers and the thick leather protecting my forearm. Metal studs held the black cowhide to the softer material beneath. "Why?"

"Why not?" she countered.

I slowly unbuckled my right bracer and slid it off. Despite the long sleeve of my tunic, the cool air immediately prickled the skin that the extra layer had kept warm. "Give me your arm."

Karina twisted toward me to offer her right forearm. I wrapped the bracer around her slender wrist and fit the straps back through the buckles. Though my fingers never once grazed her skin, they tingled as though they had. Would she be as soft as I imagined? Unlike the pads of my fingers that were rough from years with a bow. I hurried with the buckles and pulled my hands away to grip the edge of the bench.

"It's heavy," she mused, flexing her fingers. The straps were as tight as I could make them but the bracer was still too loose on her. She twisted her wrist and it slid halfway down her hand. After quickly adjusting it to her forearm again, she slammed the side of her hand down on top of it.

"What are you doing?" If she returned with bruised arms, her lady's maids would search for a reason. Then, after they found out that we were meeting along, they would tell her father and I'd be fucked.

"Testing it," she said simply.

"Okay." I took her arm again and made quick work of removing the leather. "It's perfectly crafted, but thank you for your concern."

She wrinkled her nose. "You're no fun."

"I never claimed to be." I tightened the straps around my forearm until the bracer was firmly back in place. "I'm not interested in explaining how you hurt yourself to your maids."

Karina rolled her eyes. "If I was worried about them, I wouldn't keep sneaking out."

I glared at her from beneath my lashes. It wasn't *her* I was concerned with. If anyone thought I abused a noblewoman, I would be whipped. "How do you keep evading your maids long enough to come here?"

"Why? So you can cut off my escape route?" She waved a finger back and forth. "No. If I told you that, I'd have to kill you."

"Oh?" I laughed. "You could try."

Flicking a dismissive hand, she struggled to contain a smile. "I'll just keep my methods to myself and save us both the trouble."

"I won't tell anyone."

She gave me a stern side-eye. "No, you won't. Because I'm not sharing the information."

"Fine," I conceded. She didn't need to tell me—I could find out on my own if I really wanted to. All I would need was her family name to learn where she was staying. But I couldn't bring myself to ask. It would make her too real and, deep down, I enjoyed the mystery.

A proud smile spread across Karina's face before melting away. She rubbed at her arm where my bracer had been. "Hopefully you'll be as understanding the next time we meet."

My eyes narrowed, all sense of humor gone. "What do you mean by that?"

She shrugged. "You said as long as I wasn't planning to act against the prince, you didn't care."

"I don't believe those were my exact words. In my position, I have to take an interest if you plan on hurting *anyone*." Especially now that she'd said that. I could be considered an accomplice. Even if she did the country a favor and murdered the king, that would put Bastian in a vulnerable position.

"My only plan is to survive long enough to go home," she said, closing her eyes and tilting her chin toward the sun.

The breeze blew tendrils of hair across her face and I reached out, tucking them behind her ear, before I could stop myself. Her cheek was cold beneath my fingers, the tips of her ears even cooler. The urge to cup her face between my hands, to warm her, drove me closer on the bench. Somewhere, deep down, I knew I should question what she'd said. What her words hinted at. But there was a growing mountain of desire burying reason.

One kiss.

It wouldn't be so bad, would it? While I wasn't allowed a true relationship, physical relations were another thing. A secret kiss wouldn't damage her reputation, even if someone did find out. All the ladies at court had small dalliances here and there. As long as a kiss was all it was, it wouldn't matter. My gaze fell to her lips. They parted as her breathing hitched, drawing me nearer. When my knee bumped the side of her thigh, I swallowed hard.

"Are you afraid now?" I asked quietly. If she was, I would leave. Leave and find somewhere new to spend my mornings to protect us both. *Hell.* Even if she wasn't afraid, I would need to leave this place behind.

"No," she whispered.

The way her lips formed a soft *o* around the word had my hand shaking where it still rested near her ear. *Fuck me.* This wasn't good. My mind was foggy, common sense lost. "You can tell me to stop," I said in a low voice. "If you don't want me to kiss you, that's all you have to say."

She remained silent, her chest rising and falling rapidly.

"I can't offer you anything." Maybe I was hoping she would push me away. Save me from myself. "Wings can never get married or keep a mistress. If I kiss you, that's all it can be, which is selfish and wrong. But I…" I swallowed hard. *Why isn't she pushing me away?* "I can't get you out of my head."

Her tongue slipped from between her lips, wetting them. "What are you waiting for?"

A pained groan built in my chest as I leaned in, inhaling her wildflower scent. Then my lips brushed hers. Despite the fact that they barely touched, I felt the sensation like a punch to the chest. Her hand covered mine where it rested against her cheek.

I winced, hating myself as I deepened the kiss, but was unable to stop. My tongue ran across the seam of her lips. That was all I allowed though. As hard as it was, I broke away before her tongue could answer mine.

"You taste like sunshine," I rasped. Then I stood, the motions sluggish. "Forgive me, my lady. I was out of line."

"No. It's—"

"Don't come again." The warning was forced from my mouth. I knew pushing her away was the right thing to do, even if it felt wrong. My whole life *felt* wrong, yet I continued to live it. This could be no different. "I won't be here."

She blinked up at me, eyes wide and glistening. Was it confusion or something more that I saw in her expression?

"I'm sorry," I said, and turned on my heel.

Fuck. Fuckfuckfuck.

One kiss, I had told myself. But one kiss wouldn't be enough. A single press of my lips to hers and my soul was doomed. If it hadn't been already. All I could do now was avoid her. Forget her. It wouldn't be difficult as I spent most of my time with Bastian, and he spent most of *his* time working.

Except tonight.

That would be spent sneaking out to see Faramond and receiving my *job*. What had seemed like an unnecessary risk before, now seemed like the perfect distraction.

Faramond was waiting when I slipped through the window of his office. Instead of sitting behind his desk, he stood in front of a small fireplace, nursing a glass of whiskey. "You took your time," he said in greeting.

"I got here as soon as I could," I told him through clenched teeth.

Faramond narrowed his eyes and gave a low *hm*. "Your prince is spending a lot of time in the archives."

Something I should have reported—along with why. "He's searching for an alternative to raising taxes." It would come out sooner or later so lying wasn't an option. "You should be pleased."

"Don't pretend to know what pleases me, Saer. The Governor of the People doesn't want to raise the taxes either, does she?" Before I could confirm or deny, Faramond set his glass on the mantel with a loud *clink*. "Coming to see me again so soon must've been difficult, so I'll get to the point."

The job. It wasn't a matter of *if* I would want to do it, but how *much* I wouldn't. "What do you want me to do?"

"Assassinate Governor Pevran." He held up a hand when I opened my mouth to reply. "Her job was to make sure the people of this country were pushed

to the brink. They need to fully embrace the Asters—
not that fucktwit of a governor or your pretender
prince."

Words stuck on my tongue. He wanted to destroy
Eradrist, let the people suffer, just so they could
rebuild it to look like saviors. All this time, I thought
the Asters wanted to replace the king because he was
a horrible person. That all of the awful things they'd
done were because they cared about the people. The
last bits of delusion I'd been clinging to crumbled
away.

"Am I to be your assassin now?" I asked through
gritted teeth.

"You—" He paused and glowered at me. "—Are
to be whatever I *say* you are."

No. He'd already decided enough for me. "I'm the
Prince's Wing."

Faramond slammed a fist on the edge of his desk.
"You're an Aster who was placed beside that shit stain
for the sake of the cause."

The cause… What were they fighting for, truly? To
topple the king and then what? There was no one of
the old royal bloodline to replace him with. Another
war would break out among the nobles over who had
the strongest claim to the throne. After using the
people of Eradrist, after grinding them into the dirt,
Faramond would do *what* for the country? If he were
willing to drown the people in debt now, holding any
real power would only make things worse.

"Wipe that look off your face," he growled.

I stood taller and lifted my chin. No longer was I
that scared four-year-old watching Lady Sol bleed out.
They'd trained me to be lethal.

"Growing a backbone all of a sudden?" Faramond scoffed. "I'll ask someone else to kill the governor then. And, when he's finished with her, I'll have him expose you."

Hot fear flashed through me. If the crown discovered I was working with the rebels, I would be tortured to the brink of death—*before* I stood trial. On the off chance I survived long enough to be judged, they would undoubtedly find me guilty. Sentence me to death. None of that scared me as much as the look of betrayal Bastian would wear. The fear cooled just as quickly as it came.

"If you do that, I'll tell them everything I know about you."

Faramond threw his head back and laughed. "You wouldn't live long enough to utter my name, let alone spin tales of my deeds."

Because he would kill me first, *then* present the evidence of my betrayal. Dead or alive, I didn't want Bastian to know. Didn't want to hurt him. If I had to kill the governor to continue protecting the prince, I would do it. "How do you want her killed?" I asked.

"Quietly." Faramond shrugged. "You have a week."

A week to plan a murder. To curse the people to higher taxes and emptier bellies. I clenched my hands at my sides and nodded. If I was dead, Bastian would have no one.

And Bastian was the only hope Eradrist had for a better future.

SIX

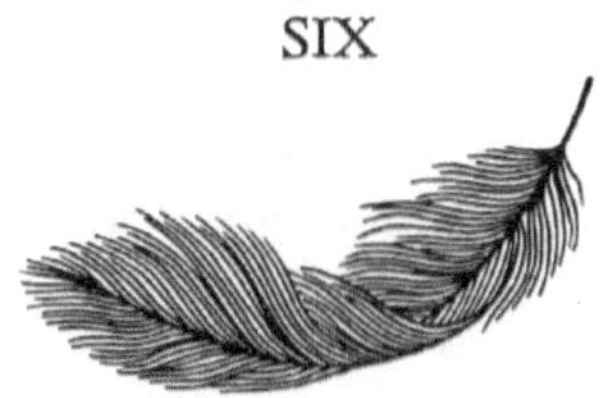

Poison. Hanging. Suffocation. Drowning. A knife to the throat. Faramond had given me license to choose how Governor Pevran would die as long as it happened in his time frame. I knew how to kill in defense, but this w as something else. It wasn't a natural reaction to preserve my own life or Bastian's. It was calculated. Cruel.

But if I didn't do it, someone else would. Then I would follow her to the grave. At least this way, I could ensure she had a kind death—as kind as a cold-blooded murder could be. I would inspect her residence, learn her routine, and sneak in while she slept. That would give me time to mull over the specifics. If there was a way to kill her quietly, painlessly, and appear natural, that would be for the best. No inquiries. No suspicion. Though, even if there *were* those who thought the death suspicious, it wouldn't lead back to the Asters after Pevran fought to keep the taxes low.

What a load of horse shit.

"You look upset." Karina's voice carried across the forgotten garden.

My head snapped up, eyes pinning her in place. She was already halfway to me and I couldn't decide if I wanted to flee or close the distance between us. Instead of an elaborate, beaded gown, she wore the white and blue dress of a lady's maid with her hair braided over one shoulder. She looked more at ease with herself than I'd ever seen her. And that was far too attractive.

"What the fuck?" I whispered to myself.

Her eyes flashed with uncertainty. "I know you said not to come back."

"Somehow I'm not surprised you didn't listen." She hadn't the last time I told her the same thing, and it was my mistake coming here again. It hadn't been intentional but, when I realized where my feet had taken me, I stayed. "I *am* surprised about the clothing."

She held out the paneled skirt and gave a half-twirl. "I've been assigned a teacher to help prepare me for life at court. This was the only way to get around her."

"You're staying, then? At the palace?" Her family likely had their eyes on a potential husband for her if they were taking on the expense of a court tutor. A suitor of high rank that needed to be impressed.

"That's not important," she said, brushing the question away with a flick of her hand. "What's bothering you?"

I inhaled slowly, rubbing my palms on my thighs as I sat up straighter. *Just plotting a murder.* "Nothing for a lady to be concerned with."

Karina scowled and came to perch on the bench. "I'll have you know that I've helped solve a great many problems."

But none quite so bloody. "I'm sure you have."

"Don't patronize me," she said quietly, casting her eyes to the ground.

"I'm not." I sighed. "I believe you, but there are things even I don't wish to be burdened with. There's no reason to share the misery."

She stretched her legs and leaned back, putting her weight on her palms. It called my attention to her chest, the way the fabric hugged each swell. And, lower, how her skirt gave the slightest hint of a *V* between her legs. I swallowed hard and forced myself to look away. Sitting that way was *definitely* not something her teacher would allow.

"It must be lonely," she said after a moment.

"What is?" I glanced at her but she was looking up at the sky. The same pattern of light that I enjoyed watching through the leaves now danced on her face.

"Not having someone to talk to." Her eyes shifted to watch me without turning her head. "It must be lonely."

I was a Wing and an Aster—I didn't have the luxury of a confidant. Not one I could speak my full truth too and, yes, it was fucking lonely. But I didn't want someone else to see it. To pity me. I ground my teeth together. "I'm fine."

"Because you have the prince?" It sounded like a genuine question, but after spending my entire life in the palace, I knew better than to believe sincerity from *anyone*.

"You're a curious one today," I said in a flat voice.

She gave me a coy smile. "If I don't ask questions, you won't say anything at all, and I need the distraction."

"From what? Learning which fork to use at dinner?" I stood, the frustration of her presence threatening my ever-constant control. "Go back to your tutor, Lady Karina. Make sure you pay special attention to the lessons about when it's appropriate to be alone with a man and when to watch your mouth."

Ignoring her sharp intake of breath, I strode from the garden. *Fuck her.* Fuck her keen eye and her willful innocence and how gods damn adorable she looked in that uniform. A low growl escaped my chest. *This isn't her fault.* It was mine. For letting myself be infatuated with someone I'd spent practically no time with. Even if we *had* spent more time together, feelings weren't allowed. Caring wasn't allowed. Nothing was *fucking* allowed.

I wasn't a man or a guard or a rebel—I was a prisoner.

The thought brought me to a halt. I returned to the garden just as she was about to exit, nearly colliding. Grasping her upper arms to steady her, I took a deep breath. "Meet me here tonight after night falls."

"I…" She bit her bottom lip. "I don't know if I can get away."

"Try."

A long moment stretched between us where I was convinced she would refuse, but then she nodded. "I'll try."

The corners of my lips turned up into a smile. I released her and left again, this time with a lightness in my chest.

Governor Pevran lived in a large building near the entrance to the Main Palace. It housed all six governors and their families, each with their own sprawling set of rooms. That would make it harder to infiltrate without being seen. Spouses or children could roam the communal halls at any time of day or night. Nannies. Multiple household servants. Why hadn't Faramond recruited one of them? Surely there was a mistreated maid or underpaid manservant willing to take on the task. Without a doubt, some of them were already working there under Aster orders.

If only I knew which.

Then I could pay them to slip a fast-acting poison into the governor's nightcap. Or, at the very least, get them to ensure my path was clear of locked doors and wandering residents.

I didn't hide my movements as I wandered around the outskirts of the sprawling red sandstone building. Floral bushes grew along the perimeter, lanterns hung at even intervals around the exterior, and a small fountain bubbled in the center of a private yard. *Private*, meaning exclusive to the residents, but anyone walking by could see the three women having morning tea in the gazebo and the young children running after each other.

Hopefully none of the youth lived with Pevran.

She wasn't married, but that meant little. Virtue was only important to nobility and the Governor of the People was always chosen *from* the people. There could be a brood of fatherless children living with her and no one would bat an eye.

Don't have children. Please.

If they existed, they would suffer the same fate as me without their mother—molded by Aster hands to do their bidding. Someone from the cause would take them in, fill their head with lies about the king personally making them orphans, and, when they were ready, set them loose as spies.

The guards at the entrance to the building shifted as I strolled by. *Checking perimeters*, I would've told them if they asked. Occasionally, I did that exact thing when I was too restless to go to the garden, or if there was a recent attempt to breach the palace walls. No one would question it.

But, unlike the other times, I was paying special attention to the windows and doors. The location of guards. The placement of trees to offer cover, and the trellis I could use to get onto the roof, if needed.

"My Lord Wing!" A young boy wearing deep red robes, marking him as a servant at the Main Palace, ran toward me, huffing and puffing. He stood a few feet away and kept his eyes downcast as he spoke. "Prince Bastian is ready to leave the palace."

A quick glance at the sun told me it hadn't been more than two hours since he joined the king. "Already?"

"Yes, my lord," he said without looking up from the ground.

"Did something happen?"

"No, my lord."

"Informative," I mumbled when he didn't elaborate and brushed past him. Based on past instances, the meeting most likely ended early with plans to reconvene later, but that didn't calm my sudden spark of alertness. The edge of nerves. I forced myself to walk at a brisk pace instead of running so I didn't accidentally cause a panic and rounded the corner to the Main Palace entrance.

As I approached, one of the guards swung the scrolling iron gate open. Bastian stormed out without preamble, his jaw clenched, auburn braids loose around his circlet, and the vein on his forehead throbbing. I fell in step beside him and matched his long, hurried strides.

"The servant said nothing happened," I hedged as he led the way toward his quarters.

Bastian released a hoarse laugh. "You won't fucking believe it."

Don't tell me. Not if it was something the Asters would want to know. If I didn't know, I wouldn't be pressured to reveal it or punished when someone else informed Faramond.

"We aren't to be disturbed," Bastian ordered the men standing outside his residence.

A command, not a request like usual. Whatever happened in the secrecy of this morning's meeting had to be bad. Faramond was *definitely* going to want me to pass this information along. If I were smart, I'd refuse to listen to Bastian—he wasn't meant to tell me anyway. There was a reason beyond my fighting skills that the king didn't want me in those meetings. *Paranoia.* Only, this time, he was right to be wary.

"She's here," Bastian blurted the moment we stepped into his private sitting area.

I froze, my hand still around the doorknob after shutting us in. It took a long moment before I realized he hadn't meant someone was in room with us. Then, slowly, I turned. "Who?"

"King Jonty's daughter." Bastian paced the room while gnawing on the pad of his thumb. "Lady Karina. She arrived secretly before I was even told of the engagement."

The blood drained from my face so fast I could practically hear the *whoosh*. It couldn't be *her*, could it? New to the palace. *Staying* at the palace. Gowns of a high-ranking noble. A tutor. Questions about the prince. *Fuck*.

"W—" I cleared my throat and turned toward the bookshelf, busying myself by pushing them all into a perfectly even row. "Why would they bring her here before you knew? You might've refused the marriage."

"We both know I couldn't," he snapped—not at me, but at the situation. "My father was worried that the news of the engagement would be leaked after he announced it to the governors, so he brought Karina here first to keep anyone from preemptively murdering her."

"Logical, actually," I murmured, though I hated siding with the king about anything. "Did you meet her, then?"

"No." He paced behind me, the thud of his boots increasing with his pace. "There's a formal dinner tomorrow night for the introduction."

My heart thumped heavy in my chest. The perfect opportunity for me to sneak into the governor's residence and wait for Pevran to return from the gathering.

"You're coming," Bastian said as an afterthought. "Father approved in case anyone acts against the match."

Whirling around, all thoughts of Karina gone, I held my breath. That was … unexpected. And unnecessary. No one would stand up to the king in a violent manner in his own palace, and I needed to use the distraction to accomplish Faramond's task. "You're not serious?" I asked.

"It's a special occasion," Bastian said, tugging at the buttons on his jacket sleeve. "He always allows you to attend those."

"But …"

Bastian stopped pacing and faced me. There was no denying him when he looked at me with such pleading eyes, but still, he said, "I need you there tonight."

"Of course." I swallowed hard. Killing the governor wouldn't be possible, but at least I could confirm that I hadn't kissed the future princess of Eradrist. *Saints be damned.* If it *was* her, what would I do? Tell Bastian that I kissed his soon-to-be wife? That would settle well—his best friend and his fiancée. My stomach twisted with guilt and I wasn't even sure I'd done anything wrong yet.

Bastian trudged to a cabinet with stained-glass doors and yanked it open, pulling out a nearly-full bottle of wine. "We're going to need this," he said, setting it down on the circular table with a *thunk.*

I took a deep, steadying breath. "I'll get the glasses."

"Do you remember the ambassador from ..." Bastian squeezed his eyes shut and waved his hand between us as if it would conjure the name of the country. "Fuck it—it doesn't matter. The one that always wore that long pearl earring. He was just caught with one of the princesses of ... Ah, shit. Her sister married that one duke."

"The second bottle of wine was a bad idea," I joked, then downed my third glass. Dinner was brought in an hour ago—baked fish, broiled potatoes, green beans, and cheesy rolls. The dishes were spread out between us on the small table, fish bones picked clean, with only crumbs and lemon wedges left. And, of course, the second, nearly empty bottle of wine.

Bastian chuckled. "I'm tired of *good* ideas. Where has that gotten me? Engaged to someone I've never met? I knew I would marry whoever my father told me to but I expected it to be someone from court. *Maybe* a foreign princess but I assumed that we could've gotten to know each other before the wedding. Through letters, at least. This is too fast."

I looked down into my empty glass and swirled the remnants. "Is there still time to steal the affections of that princess away from the ambassador with the earring?"

"Affection?" Bastian slumped in his seat and chuckled. "I doubt there was any between them. They were caught together at an orgy. He's awaiting trial right now for debauchery with a royal and she was sent off to a live with women from the Temple of Igeris. I have to wonder if she did it just to get away from her parents."

"Not everyone wants to get away from their family," I mumbled.

Bastian nodded, his body tilting with drunkenness. "You're right. I'm sorry, that was insensitive, wasn't it?"

"Why? Because mine are dead?" I asked in a flat voice. The grief I used to feel had dulled so much that it didn't truly hurt to think of them anymore. It almost felt like another life, as if it were a story someone told him about someone else's parents. Besides, he'd never once blamed the prince for any of it.

Bastian replied by filling his cup with more wine. "I wonder what my mother would've thought about my new fiancée."

The queen had died birthing Bastian so neither of us could possibly know the answer. If she would've been a good, supportive mother, or another harpy of the court. "I like to think she'd want you to be happy."

"It's a nice notion." He downed his wine in four gulps. When he set it down, his hand bumped one of the plates and knocked it off the table. It landed on the carpet with a dull thud but didn't break. "Fuck."

"All right, Your Highness." I stood slowly, feeling the effects of the wine myself, though I'd had less than him. But, unlike the prince, I wasn't finished with my day—I had Karina to meet. "I think you need to call it a night."

Bastian grumbled as he stood, swaying on his feet. I quickly stepped to his side and held him upright. Together, we made it to his bed and he flopped on top of the furs. "I'm not tired yet. We should keep drinking—*really* drown our sorrows," he pronounced, then promptly shut his eyes. His light snoring filled the room a moment later.

"Not tired, my ass." I grabbed the edge of the top fur and flung it over his body before heading to the door. The guards straightened when I stepped out of the Prince's Palace. "He's drunk. Make sure you check on him," I ordered, then returned to my small quarters behind Bastian's residence.

The door swung open silently and I stepped into the dark space. High windows usually let in the moonlight but it was a new moon tonight. No matter—it wasn't necessary. I could cross from my bed to the wardrobe and back to the door in my sleep. Unpinning the silver wing from my tunic, I tucked it safely beneath my pillow and grabbed a brown rough-spun cloak from a hook on the wall.

I paused for a moment as guilt weighed on me. Why had I thought this was a good idea? While I hadn't known Bastian's fiancée was at the palace when I asked Karina to return to the garden, it was still dangerous. If we were caught …

But she might not even come. It didn't hurt to see if she would, did it? If she was going to marry Bastian, I needed to know if she were the type to seek out affairs. I flung the cloak around my shoulders and snuck back to the forgotten garden undetected.

It was silent save for the gentle rustle of branches. Empty. It had been dark for at least an hour now so there was a chance Karina had come and gone. I shouldn't have stayed so long with the prince, but we both needed those drinks. To unwind. Forget for a moment.

And I *had* forgotten about meeting Karina a few times while we drained the first bottle. Now it could be too late. It would be for the better, of course, but I'd made the offer so I would wait.

Instead of sitting on the bench, I made myself comfortable on the ground with my back against the tree and released a long sigh. The wine made my heavy lids close. *Just for a moment.* It could take her hours to come, if she came at all, so five minutes of sleep wouldn't hurt.

I hovered somewhere between sleep and awareness for an unknown amount of time. Hours or minutes passed as my breathing evened out and my head drooped. Still, my brain registered the sounds around me, the boot steps of guards as they patrolled the gardens, the rustling of small animals in the hedges. And then … softer footfalls that moved quickly, nearly a run, and stopped a few feet away.

My eyes opened to see a petite figure approaching. Karina wore the maid's uniform again, this time with a black cloak over it, and her hair in a loose braid. "Hello," she whispered, casting a glance over her shoulder.

"You came." I shifted, leaning my elbows on my bent knees. What now? I'd never spent time with a woman like this before.

She smiled and lowered herself beside me in the grass. "I've made slipping away from my wardens an art form."

"Wardens?"

She shrugged and adjusted her cloak around her. "They might as well be. I wouldn't be surprised if a maid sneaks into my room at night to watch me sleep. She probably counts my breaths and reports it so I can be reprimanded."

"Let's hope you don't snore."

Karina laughed. "I do *not* snore."

"If you say so," I said with a chuckle, earning me a soft hit to the upper arm. Then, with a tense glance, I made certain no one had followed her. "If they're watching you so closely, it was too risky for you to meet me."

"No one will be surprised if they find out I'm gone. As long as I'm back within an hour or so, they won't raise the alarm or they'll be the ones in trouble."

That was true. Her staff would be responsible for keeping her in line and, depending on her family, it could mean anything from being fired to being caned.

Moments passed in silence and an awkwardness grew. I flexed my hands, questioning my sanity. He wanted to talk to her but about what? How did men speak to women they were interested in? Every topic that came to mind sounded worse than the last.

Karina shifted, lowering herself onto the ground so that she laid flat on her back, and I stared down at her. "What are you doing?"

"Looking at the stars." She patted the ground beside her, signaling me to join.

My gaze flickered between the grass and the sky before I hesitantly lowered myself down so we were shoulder-to-shoulder. Branches from the tree obscured half the view, but the other half was full of brightly shining specks painting the dark canvas.

"It feels like magic," she whispered.

With no clouds and the lack of moonlight, it was almost mesmerizing. Or perhaps it was *her* that held my mind captive.

"I used to do this all the time when I was young," she continued. "My friends and I would try to count them. We always got distracted and looked for pictures instead."

When my parents were ripping away from me, it was a night like this. The memories were hazy now with the exception of a few crystal clear moments. My mother's screams were loud in my ears, her begging to spare me as I clung to her skirts. My father screamed too—he told me to run. But I hadn't. I'd stayed until the soldiers ripped me away. Shoved into the mud and abandoned, I cried until I couldn't anymore… then I'd stared blanking up at the stars until I was almost trampled by a horse. I spent the next few days doing my best not to starve until I was found and brought to the Asters.

"Like that one." She pointed directly above our heads. "It looks like a rabbit."

I shoved the memories away and cleared my throat. "A rabbit?"

"The ears are right there," she explained, moving her finger to show me. "The fluffy tail is right there and the little nose."

She lowered her hand again, grazing against the back of mine. I turned my head to look at her instead and my breath caught at how close our faces were. I wanted to tell her that I didn't see a rabbit. That I saw a bird with its wings spread wide and talons poised to attack. Instead, I asked, "Why do you keep coming here?"

Her eyes widened slightly and she bit her lip. "To see you."

"Why?" Too many people had tried to use me to get close to Bastian in our youth and the royal engagement wasn't public knowledge yet. She could be trying to get me to put in a good word for her. *By kissing me?* Fuck. I didn't know what to think.

"There's a connection between us." Her breath was warm on my lips. "Don't you feel it?"

I swallowed hard, concentrating on the invisible pull between us. "I do."

"If I'm going to be forced into a marriage with someone I've never met, I want the chance to see what it feels like to ..."

When she didn't finish the statement, I urged, "To what?"

"To see what it could've been like if I had a different life." Her fingers laced with mine and a resigned sadness lit her eyes for a moment. "I know I shouldn't be here, Saer, but I can't seem to stop myself."

Ah, fuck. I knew exactly how she felt. Rolling onto my side, I slid a loose piece of hair behind her ear and let my fingertips linger. Her porcelain skin still had traces of shimmering powder. The gentle scent of wildflowers lured me closer, our lips a mere breath away.

I hovered there, relishing in the sweet torture of an anticipated touch. "I can't either," I admitted, my voice low and rough with want. My hand slid lower, fingertips resting on her neck, and I used my thumb to tilt her chin up slightly. I caught her bottom lip between my teeth in a gentle tug before backing away just enough to look her in the eyes. "Who are you, Karina?"

"I am … no one. A girl who doesn't belong here." There was a flash of panic, of pain, in her expression.

A woman who had arrived at the palace recently, was being prepared for marriage to a high ranking noble—or a prince? That hardly made her a no one. I wanted to ask her if she was *that* Karina, but I was scared to know the answer. If I didn't *know* then I could honestly say as much if it turned out to be true.

"Where do you belong then?" I questioned.

Her brow lowered a moment as if she were thinking about it for the first time. "Somewhere with fewer rules and fewer people."

"Does a place like that exist?" They did—he'd just never experienced them.

"I used to live in a place with fewer rules," she said, her tone hesitant, as if she were telling him something she shouldn't. "There were just as many people, but they were different. Everyone was loud and rough around the edges, and no one cared about which spoon you ate your soup with."

"The long one."

"What?"

My fingers slid down her neck, trailing along the top of the maid's uniform just above her collar bone. "The soup spoon."

She laughed. "No, the round one is for soup."

I narrowed my eyes, trying to visualize a table spread. It had been so long since I ate at a formal table and even then, I just worked my way through the utensils from the outside in. "It's possible you're correct."

"I *know* I am, but why don't *you* know? Didn't you grow up here?"

Her breath hitched as my touch slid just below the top of the bodice. Her breasts strained against the blue fabric, drawing my attention. "I came here when I was four." I forced my eyes back to her face, but couldn't meet her eyes, focusing instead on her lips. "I had a few lessons in propriety but my training focused more on harsher subjects."

"Sword fighting?"

A low *mmm* of agreement left my throat. "Sword fighting, archery, daggers, hand-to-hand combat. On my feet, on a horse, in a lake."

"A lake?"

I smirked. "I suppose if the prince and I were escaping a sinking ship, I might be forced to fight off ruffians in the shallows. They trained me in ice storms and under the hottest summer suns until I became the perfect Wing under any circumstance."

"So years of hard work have made you perfect except for cutlery."

My eyes snapped to hers. No amount of training could accomplish perfection, especially for me. "No one is without flaws, Karina. Even when everyone expects them to be, even when you *think* they are, it's all an act."

The air between us thickened. Her lips parted slightly as if the truth I'd spoken hit something deep inside. An understanding. Or perhaps hope that I was right. Her hand rose to my chest and hesitated before pressing her palm over my heart. I hoped she couldn't feel how fast the damn thing started beating against her touch.

Her fingers curled into the fabric of my tunic. "If it's an act and we're all actors, then does that mean what happens tonight isn't real?"

Was that what it meant? I was pretending there was no chance that she was Bastian's fiancée and that being here wasn't wrong. But it didn't *feel* wrong. She calmed me somehow while, at the same time, exciting me. No one had even made me feel like this before and I doubted they ever would again.

"I think this—here, tonight—is the only real thing I've experienced in a long time," I said quietly. His friendship with Bastian was real but tainted because of the lies he kept. The betrayal he continued to commit. Even if Karina wasn't being honest about who she was, he wasn't pretending with her.

Karina pressed closer and bumped her nose to his. "Will you kiss me again?"

There was no thinking as I sealed my lips to hers. This time was different. Slower. Kinder. A gentle exploration instead of an intense need. She tasted sweet, her lips soft as petals, and her tongue danced with mine.

My cock grew hard as I tugged her body more firmly against my own. She fit as if she were made for me. I explored the curve of her waist, her hip, lower, wishing the layers of her dress weren't between us.

A small moan escaped her and I swallowed it down. *More.* I needed more—I needed it all. Her body, her soul. My fingers dug into her thigh. *Fuck!* I couldn't have those things. Not even tonight. But I needed them like I needed air in my lungs.

"We have to stop," I groaned against her mouth.

She took a raspy breath and the desire in it went straight to my hard length. "Why?"

"I can't ruin your chances at a decent future." I winced, my grip loosening and shifting to her waist again. "I want to murder any man than even considers touching you like this, even if he'll be your husband one day, but that's selfish."

"I don't want another man—especially not one chosen for me," she claimed, leaning back in to kiss me again.

I obliged, but only for a bittersweet moment. "While I can't get married, I *can* ruin you. And I care too much to destroy your life."

Karina huffed and rolled onto her back. "As if being a spinster is the worst thing in life."

"Of course not." I leaned in and nuzzled her neck. "But it's rare that an unmarried woman doesn't find herself cast into poverty, as unfair as it is."

"I don't care about that," she insisted, her gaze on the stars again.

"You say that now, but I won't have the possibility on my conscience." With that, I forced myself to get up from the ground and hold a hand out to help her do the same. Our time had come to an end, as brief was it was, and I already mourned it. "Come on, my lady. You need to get back before they notice you're gone."

Karina slowly sat up and took my hand. Her delicate fingers rested so carefully in my palm as I helped her rise, and I closed mine around them, holding onto her a moment longer. My chest ached knowing that I wouldn't know her touch again, but tonight was enough. It *had* to be enough.

"Good night, Karina," I whispered and placed a final lingering kiss to her lips before rushing from the garden.

EIGHT

I couldn't remember the last time I wore the formal Wing uniform. Silver trim ran along the edges of the long jacket, following the bottom hem where it skimmed the floor in six separate panels. The black leather was cut into individual scalloped pieces, stitched together to look like scales running down my back and chest. The sleeves strained, my muscles having grown, as I twisted my hair into a low knot at the nape of my neck. A shorter piece escaped and dangled over my right eye.

"Saer, which jacket?" Bastian asked.

I blew the hair aside and leaned against the door frame leading from the prince's bedroom into the dressing chamber. An older manservant wearing gray robes held up a dark blue jacket with silver filagree and *another* dark blue jacket with silver filagree. "They're exactly the same."

"The design on this one goes all the way to His Highness' collar," the man said, holding one a bit higher. Then he switched, raising the opposite one. "This design branches out across the shoulders."

Was this a serious fucking conversation? *Jacket design.* The bastard daughter of King Jonty was inside the palace—*had been* inside for an unknown amount of time. Sneaking off to meet me in the garden, unsupervised. *Potentially.* But what were the odds it was another noble girl? We were both going to be strung up and tortured if anyone learned of those secret meetings—especially the kiss. That demise was a fear I lived with every day, but this time, I had to rely on another person to keep their mouth shut. Unlike Faramond, Karina didn't need me. My only saving grace was that she already knew who I was so there would be no surprise on her face tonight.

"It's just a dinner," Bastian said with one raised brow. "There's no need to look like you're marching to the gallows."

I forced a tight smile. *You have no idea.* "Wear the second one."

Bastian nodded to the servant and smoothed down the white silk shirt he already wore. The braids holding his coronet in place had been undone, the simple design replaced with a more formal one. A thin circle of silver now peaked all around his head with the braids woven between each sapphire tip, giving a fierce impression. The tightness of his expression and slightly-pinched eyes told another story.

"Try not to be nervous," I said.

"That's easy for you to say." He lifted his chin so the servant could fasten his jacket collar. "What if I hate her? What if *she* hates *me*?"

"Then I suppose you'll live like nearly every other royal couple." Miserably, with a mistress or two on the side. But Bastian took his vows seriously. When the prince married and promised fidelity, he would mean every word. "Besides," I continued. "You're the prince."

"I want a wife who loves the man, not the crown."

Plenty of men were ruined by their scheming wives, just as women were ruined by their husbands. A little sweet talking, a special move in the bedroom, and that was all it took. Fortunes could be lost to dressmakers or people ended up murdered. Either the spouse killed the lover or the lover killed the spouse. Once, a noblewoman convinced her husband to kill her own mother. It all depended on the game being played, but the game was best left untouched.

Bastian had something more important to lose than money though. He had power over a whole country and Countess Odelia undoubtedly taught her daughter how to get what she wanted.

"She will at least *try* to please you." I forced a touch of humor into my voice to calm Bastian's nerves. "A happy prince becomes a happy king, and a happy king will give her more power."

He tilted his neck, cracking it. "I don't want to be saddled with a harpy that only sees power when she looks at me."

I scowled, knowing exactly what he meant. When Karina saw me in the garden, she hadn't seen me as a Wing. She'd seen *me*. At least, it felt like she had.

Perhaps it was an act, but that didn't change the way it made my pulse race. Even if she was the same Karina we met tonight, I would never forget how that felt. The moment the raging anger and guilt in my soul had calmed. "I hope she's the wife you deserve," I said.

"We'll find out soon enough," Bastian said with a heavy sigh. "Let's go before we're late."

The Main Palace consisted of veined marble floors, curved doorways, and gold accents everywhere. Between the front door and the banquet hall, there were at least thirteen different portraits of the king in gilded frames. Statues of half-dressed women were covered in gold dust, and the curtain ties had strands of it woven in.

Inside the banquet hall, things only became more ostentatious. Three massive chandeliers hung over a long table adorned with floral arrangements low enough to see over while sitting, gleaming silver plates, and embroidered napkins. The chairs were gold and padded with crushed red velvet that matched the tablecloth. A fire roared in the massive fireplace behind the head of the table—King Edric's chair noticeably larger with tall spires rising from the back— and the walls had recently been painted white. A fact I knew only because I'd attended Bastian's birthday banquet a few months ago and the wood had been bare.

The back door to the room swung open and one of the King's Wings strode inside with heavy steps, chin held high. Volney was big-boned, his head completely shaved, and his face covered with a dark, bushy beard. He met my gaze from across the room and nodded once.

"Bastian." King Edric stormed around Volney, and headed straight for his son. His icy blue eyes spared me a cold glance before pulling Bastian toward the head of the table. The deepening lines at the corners of his eyes made me question his health. Mentally, if not physically. I hadn't seen him in a handful of weeks, but he'd already aged years.

A short, satin cape had been fastened around his shoulders, hiding what I knew to be a jagged, withering body. Any muscle he'd put on during his fight for the throne had melted away, leaving sharp elbows and sloping shoulders. The golden crown and brown braids that held it in place effectively hid his receding hairline.

"Are you ready to meet her?" the king asked, sounding *almost* fatherly.

Volney and the second Wing, Nen, flanked the king as he took his seat. Nen—the leaner of the two, with dark hair, a narrow face, and a crooked nose from too many breaks—slid the throne-like dining chair to the table.

"Yes, Father," Bastian said, slipping into his own seat to the king's right. He nodded slightly for me to take the seat beside him.

"Wings aren't meant to *sit*," the king admonished before I could make a decision.

"He's not here as a Wing." Bastian gave the chair a little shove, a silent order for me to sit. I winced as I obeyed, not because I thought it wise, but because

Bastian had just defied his father for me. I couldn't make him look like a fool by disobeying. "He's here as my guest, and I expect him to be treated as such," he added.

Red bloomed on the king's hollow cheeks. "I'll speak with you later," he hissed. Then, to the unseen servants outside, he called, "Let them in."

The main, double doors to the banquet hall swung open to reveal the waiting governors. They were all dressed in their finest—the men perfectly tailored and the women draped in silks. None of these women were nobility so their gowns were decorated with small glass beads instead of the real gemstones like Karina had.

"Sit," the king ordered the small crowd.

I scanned the governors and their spouses as they filed silently to their seats, but no one looked ready to pounce. Hesby, Governor of Coin, entered first, his white hair trimmed short, and his bird-like wife walked at his side. Then came Abaes, Governor of Agriculture, with her black hair braided over one shoulder and a dark-skinned man at her side. She wasn't married, so he could've been a close relative or a lover. The muscular Governor of Defense, Vetall, followed next. His wife was young enough to be his daughter, but the older governor had admittedly aged well. The Head Governor, Grosby, and his wife, strutted straight up to the table like they were the ones hosting the banquet, and took the seats directly across from Bastian and me. And, finally, the Governor of the People—the one I'd been dreading.

Governor Pevran entered alone which struck me as unusual, but somewhat expected as I hadn't heard any tales of exploits. She wore her blonde hair short, neatly curled and pinned, and only a hint of wrinkles lined the corners of her eyes. When she sat, it was beside the Governor of Defense's wife, and she offered the young girl a gentle, reassuring smile.

Of all the governors, Pevran appeared the kindest. And I had to kill her for it. For doing her job. Doing it the *right* way by looking out for the people of Eradrist and not the royal coffers. This could very well end up as one of my biggest regrets. Bastian could use someone like her when he inherited the crown, someone to do *real* good.

"Well," Governor Grosby boomed once everyone was settled into their seats. "Where's the girl?"

"She'll be here," the king assured him.

"Tardiness isn't acceptable for a future queen. This is why you should've chosen a foreign princess or even one of our noble—"

A figure stepped slowly into the doorway and hesitated while the head governor continued ranting about the king's choice of bride. I seemed to be the only one to have noticed the beautiful woman taking small steps toward the table. Beautiful and familiar.

"Enough, Grosby," the king barked.

My lips parted, my heart slamming painfully in my chest as the rest of my body stilled. It was her—the same Karina from the garden. My worst fear of the night. She wore a gown so white that it nearly glowed with a dozen strands of diamonds draped over each arm. Half of her honey-colored hair was twisted back with matching gemstone strings, the rest lightly curled. A soft shade of pink covered her lips and a dusting of white powder highlighted her eyelids. But the look in her eyes as she walked, alone, into a room with the most powerful men and women in the country had me balling my hands under the table.

She'd lied to me. Let me *kiss* her when she knew she was engaged to Bastian … Yet, I hated seeing how terrified she looked now. I knew from experience what she was feeling, only I'd been four years old. Newly orphaned, shoved into a room before King Edric—watched him murder a woman.

"Please forgive my tardiness," Karina said in a quiet voice and dropped into a low curtsy.

The room fell silent as every eye went to her. I heard Bastian's quick inhale and the delayed exhale, felt him tense beside me. *Fuck.* This was a disaster. A betrayal of our friendship. *Another betrayal.* How could I have kissed her? Even without knowing who she was, I knew I could never have her. *This* Karina wasn't supposed to have been at the palace yet though.

And now I had to weigh truths against lies to see which needed to be told to whom. Should I tell Bastian I kissed her? Should I keep her disloyalty a secret? While I hadn't known she was engaged, *she* was fully aware. The future relationship between her and Bastian would be shit if she didn't take her wedding vows as seriously as the prince. If he married her without learning of the kiss and it slipped out one day, what then? I could break his trust a little now or a lot later. Save him from hoping it would be a good marriage, or let him discover her true nature after she tore his heart out.

Then I had to wonder if the Asters told her to play mind games with me or if Faramond needed to know. Perhaps it was a test to see if I was loyal to the Asters or the Prince. Which would prove me innocent of treachery? If I told Faramond that Karina had sought me out in the garden and he *hadn't* instructed her to, I would be fucked for interfering with his plans. But if he *did* tell her to find me, to lure me in, and I kept it a secret, Faramond would know I kept things from him.

Fucking … FUCK!

I wanted to scream. To break something. To throttle the girl who appeared so innocent and lost while she stood at the far end of the banquet table. I focused on the table setting laid out in front of me. Was I not in a hard enough position? Could I not want something for a single moment? Everything good in my life was twisted and broken. My friendship with Bastian tainted. My mother's face long forgotten to me, but her screams when King Edric's men came for her were not. The sound of my father begging them to spare me. They had loved me, I believed, but that wasn't what I remembered. I only know there was fear.

Pressing my lips into a straight line, I pulled my mind away from self-pity to focus on the present.

Karina made her way toward my seat and I went rigid in my seat. The king or governors must've continued speaking while I was lost in thought, because now Bastian stood. He was beside his chair, bowing to Karina and, when she was finally directly in front of him, he lifted her hand to his mouth, kissing it.

The scent of wildflowers clung to Karina but was now mixed with a richer scent of perfume. Something I couldn't quite identify, but hated. Nearly as much as I hated her in that moment.

"The Prince's Wing was kind enough to warm your seat for you, Lady Karina," King Edric said with false joviality.

I clenched my jaw and stood, rounding the chair that Bastian had defied his father for. *One point for the king.* There was no denying him in a room full of governors, even if the prince demanded it.

Karina kept her gaze to the ground as she offered a gracious curtsy—one too grand for my station—and slipped into the chair. I tucked it beneath her as she lowered herself and caught the flash of annoyance on Bastian's face as he returned to his own seat. His father had bested him. As always.

I shifted to stand behind Bastian, slightly toward his right so I had an unobstructed view of the space between the prince and his fiancée. From where I stood, I couldn't see her expression, but her hands were folded tightly beneath the table. The diamonds in her hair shook slightly, giving away the tremble of her body. I wanted to rip the strands of gems from where they draped over her arms and wrap them around her neck until she confessed everything. Every motive, every person pulling her strings.

Servants filed into the room, carrying silver trays with bowls of streaming soup. One was set before each person at the table, starting with the king.

"It's lobster bisque," Bastian whispered to Karina. "Do you like seafood?"

"Yes, Your Highness." Her voice was soft, compliant. Nothing like the bold woman who had visited me in the garden.

With her head tilted to reply to Bastian, she cast a quick sidelong glance at me. Or, more specifically, my chest. Apparently, she didn't have the courage to meet my gaze after her lies. Who could blame her? And I wasn't complaining. While I'd learned long ago to keep my expression blank, I couldn't control what my eyes gave away, and I didn't know which secrets were visible there at the moment.

For two hours, I guarded the prince and his fiancée while the governors chatted about useless drivel. The king simply watched, his steely gaze shifting between faces as if he expected one of them to melt off. Occasionally, Bastian would lean closer to Karina and comment on the food—what it was, if she liked it— but otherwise, nothing eventful happened.

But, once the final course of miniature cakes drizzled with melted chocolate was served, the king pounded on the table. One loud, resounding *bang*.

"There you have it," he said in a stiff voice. "A formal introduction to Jonty's daughter, future princess of Eradrist. I expect you will accept the decision."

"My King," Governor Hesby said, pausing to wipe his mouth. "We have seen the girl, but are no closer to knowing if she is suitable."

"She will *become* suitable," the king yelled, spittle flying. His voice echoed throughout the banquet hall, leaving everyone frozen in shock. "I am king, Hesby. Not you. Bastian marries the girl and the rebels are appeased. If she has any defiant ideas—" the king swung his gaze to Karina and lifted his chin, "they will be dealt with accordingly."

The urge to tear Karina out of her chair and drag her from the room overwhelmed me. I had to dig my heels into the ground to keep myself still. What could

I do, really? The king was the king—free to threaten anyone he liked—and Karina was Bastian's to look after now. Princesses were assigned their own guards. Not Wings, but still highly trained.

With that, the king stood, his chair scraping across the floor, and strode from the banquet hall with both Wings close at his heel.

The governors erupted in harsh whispers. Bastian gripped the edge of the table and stood. He extended his hand to Karina. "Allow me to escort you safely back to your palace, my lady."

She removed the folded napkin from her lap, set it on the table, and placed her hand in his. Without thought, I pulled the chair away from the table so she could stand, and followed the couple from the room with every eye hot at our backs.

"You'll have to forgive my father," Bastian said as soon as we cleared the Main Palace. "The governors have been extra difficult lately."

"I understand," she said in a voice I wasn't used to. Too quiet. Too passive.

I narrowed my eyes at her back where swooping strands of gems hung against smooth pale skin. They seemed to dance along the curve of her spine, barely touching, only teasing. And I wanted to replace them with my fingers.

Fucking hell.

What was I doing? What was *she* doing, messing with my head? She *understood* Bastian's excuses for the king? She understood *nothing*. Not here in the palace. Even I was having trouble wrapping my mind around things at the moment. If the governors were so against the engagement, who presented the idea to the king?

Someone who was able to convince him that the rebels would back off if he agreed. A lie, of course, but someone close to the king made him believe it.

"I hope we'll get to know each other over the coming months," Bastian told Karina as we walked. "With so many meetings scheduled for me and all your lessons, it might be difficult. The governors are also insisting that we spend no time alone to protect both of us."

"I see." She glanced over her shoulder at me.

"Saer doesn't count," Bastian said, throwing me an unamused smile. "They don't trust him because he's too loyal to me, so next time we see each other, there will need to be someone else to chaperone."

My eyes darted to the side to avoid responding. *Too loyal to him.* Except for all the lies.

"My Lady!" Two maids rushed from the gates of the Women's Palace and stopped just long enough to curtsy to the prince. They were the same voices that called for her in the garden.

Karina turned to Bastian and gave a small curtsy. "Thank you for bringing me back, Your Highness."

"Of course." He lifted her hand and pressed a chaste kiss to the back of it. My eyes were glued to the movement, jealousy itching inside my chest. "Until next time."

"Yes." She blushed and gave another curtsy, this one seemingly directed at both of us. "Goodnight."

Then the ladies whisked her back into the Women's Palace. Before they closed the gate, I heard one of the ladies chide, "you were *supposed* to come back with the duchess."

As if Bastian and I weren't acceptable escorts? I scowled at the round-faced woman through the wrought iron scrollwork and, as if she felt my irritation, she peeked up. A small yelp followed before she sprinted to catch up with Karina and the other maid.

"Coming?" Bastian asked.

I jerked at the sound of his voice a few paces behind me. *Shit.* I'd been distracted. "Yes."

"Sorry about dinner," he said as we followed the path from the Women's Palace to the Crown Prince's. "I could only push him so far."

"You shouldn't have pushed him at all. He already hates me being in the Main Palace, but to have me sit at his table?"

Bastian sighed. "You're right. I know you are."

This wasn't right. Lying about Karina, keeping it from him like this. Faramond would kill me if I jeopardized his plan, but what about doing the right thing? King Edric distrusted Bastian, thinking he would steal the throne one day, and I was a spy. The prince deserved to have someone he could truly rely on, someone to love without conditions. I opened my mouth to tell him about what had happened in the gardens when we rounded a corner, meeting two lords.

"Your Highness," they said in unison, giving a quick bow before continuing on their way. I wanted to ask Bastian about the tension between the king and the governors, but not here. If anyone overheard, rumors would spread and the Red Asters would hear.

"She's quite pretty," Bastian said softly, chewing on his bottom lip. "Don't you think?"

I held my breath. "Who?"

"Lady Karina." He shot me a look as if it should've been obvious. It *was* obvious.

"Oh."

"I see," Bastian said with a smirk. "Still thinking about that noblewoman of yours, are you? Will you tell me who she is yet?"

My cheeks burned hot. Yes, I was still thinking about her. Because, despite how pissed off I was, despite the confusion raging through me, I still wanted to touch her. To taste her lips again. But I couldn't. Never again. With a silent sigh, I resigned myself to keeping another secret. Bastian could never know about the time I spent with Karina in the garden, no matter how much I wanted to tell him.

"No," I lied. "And I absolutely will not."

NINE

The warm scent of cloves filled my private quarters as I rubbed a thin coat of oil over my blades. I wasn't cleaning them to ensure I didn't run into Karina—at least, not *only* to avoid her. It was important to maintain my collection. So, I sat in front of the open window, soaking up the morning sun while Bastian met the king, with all my weapons laid out on a thin blanket. A long sword and a saber, a dozen different daggers, and several throwing knives. Propped against the wall beside me was a bow and quiver of arrows—there wouldn't be time to inspect them before lunch today.

Running the cloth down my favored blade—the falchion—I tilted it, inspecting the sheen along the curved tip, when my door flew open. I was on my feet and ready to attack until I recognized Bastian. Then my focus shifted to the door and windows, looking for the threat that sent him barging in here.

"What's going on?" I spun around and slammed the window shut, grabbing the first weapon I could reach. "How did you get here from the Main Palace? Where are the guards?"

"Relax," he breathed. "I snuck out of the meetings."

I turned slowly and glared at him, adrenaline still pumping. "You… what?"

Bastian shrugged. "I excused myself to take a piss and bolted."

"You walked all the way from the Main Palace? Alone? And no one stopped you?"

"I'm stealthier than you think." He moved around the room, taking in the array of blades, my small yet comfortable bed, and the lack of anything else. "I haven't been in here in ages. It hasn't changed."

Of course it hadn't changed. The room housed me for a handful of hours every night and a few mornings a month while I cleaned my collection—I didn't care if the walls were bare and the furniture sparse as long as there was somewhere to rest my head. Somewhere that was *mine*.

"Cleaning your blades?" Bastian asked.

I plopped back to the floor and crossed my arms. "This is the first place they're going to come when they realize you're gone, you know. I'll be expected to track you down."

Bastian lowered himself into a rickety chair in the corner of the room and waved his hand in the air. "Good thing you won't have far to look, eh?"

"Somehow this is going to be my fault," I grumbled. When we were barely ten, he'd run off, leaving his tutor lost in a hedge maze, and the king had blamed me despite the fact that I was training when it happened. They'd found Bastian napping in his own bed, and made me sleep outside his door for two weeks. In the middle of the rainy season. It was fucking miserable.

Bastian scooted down in the chair to rest his head on the back. "I couldn't do it today."

"Do what?"

"Listen to them bicker." He closed his eyes and let out a long breath. "You saw them last night."

Grabbing the oiled cloth, I resumed shining my falchion. "What *was* that about?"

"The governors have been getting a bit too vocal lately. They either can't agree with each other or they can't agree with my father, and forget finding a compromise. My father announced the engagement without consulting them which only made everything worse."

"He didn't consult the governors about your fiancée?" My eyes widened. That was news... News Faramond would need to know and I felt slightly inclined to give it to him. If the king and the governors were at odds, things could get extremely messy. Telling Faramond something he would eventually discover anyway could prove my worth to the cause. Save me from killing Pevran.

"Lady Karina was suggested by Governor Pevran but quickly dismissed by the rest. My father went ahead and secured the engagement without convincing everyone else to get behind the idea."

Pevran… Was that why I had to kill her? She'd brokered the engagement, then tried to lower taxes. Did she think Faramond would let it go since she'd gotten the Red Asters such a big win?

"Have you seen Lady Karina since last night?" Bastian asked quietly.

I flicked a quick look up from my knives to find him staring at the ceiling. "Why would I have seen her?"

Bastian shrugged. "She seemed genuine; don't you think?"

"If you think so." *She seemed like a good fucking actress.*

"The court will eat her alive."

It absolutely would. Unless she ate them first. It wasn't clear how devious Karina was yet. I spun a throwing knife around my finger and said nothing.

"They're putting her through intensive training before she makes a public debut."

I snorted. She'd said as much in the garden, but something told me that no amount of tutoring would be enough. Last night, she'd handled herself well, but she also barely spoke. A public debut meant every noble would be interrogating her without it seeming like an interrogation. I wasn't sure anyone could be taught to recognize the difference.

Bastian sat forward and cleared his throat, speaking in an uneven voice. "Can I ask for a favor?"

"Fuck no," I blurted. "The last time you asked me for a favor, I was caned."

"Sneaking into one of my father's private parties was ill-thought out, but how was I supposed to know he invited an entire whorehouse to the palace? I didn't even know what a prostitute was before that."

"Hence the caning," I deadpanned. "I was accused of corrupting you."

"We were young and stupid. Lessons learned." He winced, seemingly replaying the entire evening in his head.

Neither of us had seen a naked woman before that party, let alone what they did with naked men. Of course, a few years later, the royal brothel was open to us, but it was one hell of an anatomy lesson at the time. I could never get the image of King Edric's hairy ass out of my head though, no matter how hard I tried.

I exhaled. "What's this favor then?"

"Get to know her."

I raised an eyebrow. "What?"

"I want to know what I'm getting into. Lady Karina seemed kind enough last night, but what if it's an act? You can find out what she's really like better than I can—she'll be on guard around me and we have to be chaperoned. But you don't have that stipulation. Spend time with her, see what she's like and how she treats the servants."

Was he insane? He wanted someone else to spend quality time with his fiancée? Get to know her through someone else's eyes? And, of all people, *me*? Yes, I was his Wing. Trusted. Loyal. But I'd also fucking kissed her. A secret I'd need to take to my grave if I didn't want to lose my head.

"Wouldn't asking one of the ladies make more sense?"

"I don't trust anyone else," he said softly. "If they're secretly working for a governor or one of the nobles, they'll feed me lies."

The sound of heavy boots came from outside, saving me from answering. "Guards are here for you."

Bastian gave a weary sigh.

"Wing!" A guard called. "Come out quickly! The prince is missing!"

I pointed my dagger at Bastian. "See that? Unlike you, they're smart enough not to burst in here unannounced."

"You're so full of threats," he said with a smirk. Then he stood, stalked to the door, and swung it open to find six frantic guards approaching. "Missing, am I?"

"Your Highness." They bowed low, fist over their hearts.

I stood, tucked three daggers into my boot, slid a freshly-cleaned sword into an empty scabbard, and followed Bastian outside. "I'll escort him back to the Main Palace." Then, quieter so only Bastian could hear, I added, "And I'll see what I can learn."

Because apparently, I had no sense of self preservation. It was an opportunity though. One to discover what Karina's intentions were and how embroiled she was in Aster plots. No one could accuse me of anything if Bastian asked me to see her. To essentially *spy* on her.

"Thank you," he said with such relief that I almost felt guilty for wanting to refuse.

Almost.

Because either way, I was guilty of something.

TEN

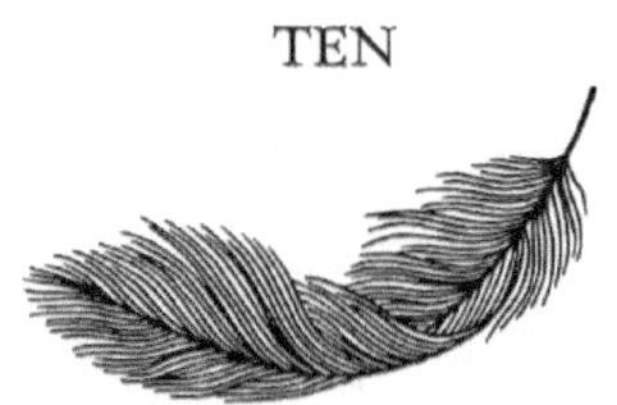

After safely returning Bastian to the Main Palace to be reprimanded by the king, I waltzed through the gates of the Women's Palace. The guards exchanged long looks as I passed, but said nothing. Did nothing. I wondered if they even knew who they were protecting.

Skipping silently up the handful of stone stairs, I made my way to the already-open doors of the palace. The main room was enormous with white decorative pillars, hand-painted gardens on the walls, and large vases full of lilies on every flat surface. All of the delicate furniture, draped with pastel fabrics and hanging beads, was shoved against the far wall. Karina shouldn't live here—she wasn't married to Bastian yet nor was she of *current* royal blood—but King Edric had moved her in anyway.

"Impossible!"

I winced at the old woman's voice as I stepped over the threshold. It belonged to one of the few adults I'd liked growing up. Respected, even. But Duchess Fransabelle was also terrifying if you were up to no good. More than once, she'd caught Bastian and I catching frogs in the garden fountain and dragged us out by our ears.

The duchess leaned heavily on an ivory cane, looking older than I remembered. She'd retired to her country estate when I was sixteen so it shouldn't have come as a surprise that her wrinkles had deepened. Or that she wore a simple gray wig, as many older nobles did to hide their thinning hair.

"Is she giving you a hard time, Your Grace?" I called out, hoping to break the tension.

The old woman spun, her dark red mourning gown brushing across the floor, and beamed. "Lord Tufaro. Is that you?"

Karina's stare burned the side of my face, and I wanted to meet it. To let her see me as a Wing instead of the man in the garden. But I ignored it and strode to the end of the room where they both stood. Taking the duchess's hand, I kissed her fingerless lace gloves. "You look well, Duchess Fransie."

She tutted. "I'm an old trout and we both know it. You, on the other hand." The old woman stepped back and scanned me up and down before tutting again. "A shame you're unable to marry. You would make beautiful babies."

Even if I were allowed—which I wasn't—I didn't particularly want children with things being as they were. Faramond would use the baby against me or, when I was inevitably caught one day, they would suffer for my choices. Perhaps if things were different…

"Now, now. I'd make a horrible parent with all the sharp objects I keep lying around," I chided. There were few people in the palace that I spoke with casually, but the duchess was different. She'd been something like a mother growing up. An absent mother, given how often she was actually at the palace, but when she did visit, she was warm and welcoming. And she snuck me snacks. "What brings you to Ora Et?"

She made a disgruntled sound and motioned at Karina where she stood a few feet away, hands in fists. "Look at her. They gave me *this* and asked me to make her a princess."

"Oh, I don't know," I said, casting a sideways glance at Karina. My chest tightened at the disheartened look on her face, but part of me also enjoyed her obvious discomfort. The way she refused to meet my eyes as I appraised her alongside Fransanbelle. How she shifted uncomfortably. I wondered what Fransabelle saw in her. Because, despite knowing she was deceitful, I also found her intriguing. Karina wasn't stupid, and she was clearly making an effort. Dinner with the governors wasn't a complete disaster. So, I added, "She might surprise you."

"Countess Odelia was always such a prim young woman. An utter bitch," she added in a mumble. "I don't know how she raised a girl who doesn't even understand how low to curtsy."

A valid thought. The countess was notoriously pretentious so it didn't make sense for her daughter not to possess certain skills. Noble children were trained to bow and curtsy from the moment they learned to walk. I filed the information away for later so I could study how Karina behaved.

"She's in good hands with you," I told Fransabelle.

"Lady Karina," the duchess crooned. "This is the Prince's Wing, Lord Saer Tufaro. I believe you met last night."

She jerked her chin up in a slight nod and spoke from between clenched teeth. "Yes, he was at dinner with Prince Bastian."

"Are you purposely testing my patience?" She banged her cane on the floor once. "Curtsy, appropriately, and greet him."

She hesitated before bending her knees slightly, the green skirts and emerald beads shifting. I smirked, knowing exactly what the duchess had done. As Bastian's future wife, she wasn't required to curtsy to me at all. It was a courtesy done by some at court to gain Bastian's favor, but in reality, *no one* needed to lower themselves to greet me, despite my being a lord. I was meant to be invisible—an extension of Bastian.

"A pleasure to meet you, my lord," Karina said in a voice entirely different than the one she used in the garden.

"The pleasure is mine," I replied with a stiff bow.

"I give up," the Duchess muttered, walking stiffly toward the doors to a rounded porch. "Warn your prince not to get his hopes up."

When Fransabelle lowered herself into one of the chairs facing a bubbling fountain, I turned my full attention to Karina. In the garden, she had seemed lighter. At the dinner, she had seemed terrified. But here, in the previously-unused Women's Palace, faced with a well-intentioned, grouchy duchess, she seemed… lost. Her rich green gown was covered in matching stones and sea glass that clinked as she moved, and her hair was partially tied back with a satin ribbon. They'd painted her face again, though less than they had for dinner. Only a touch of pink on her cheeks and red on her lips. Lips I very much wanted to kiss again. To slide my tongue against hers and taste how sweet she was. Because I was a selfish bastard. But it was her eyes—the overwhelming confusion with a hint of anger—that pulled at something in my chest.

All I should be feeling is rage.

Where had my anger gone? Why was I having so much trouble summoning it back to the surface? She was an Aster or being controlled by an Aster. It was my job to find out *why*, just like it was my job to stay the fuck out of this rebel scheme.

"You're not meant to curtsy to me," I said in a low voice.

She scowled. "You're a lord."

"Yes," I conceded, stepping closer. "But, before I'm Lord Tufaro, I'm the Prince's Wing. Something you knew from the first moment we met."

The color in her cheeks had nothing to do with the makeup now. Scarlet raced up from her neck, bringing small beads of sweat across her brow. "Not from the *first* moment."

"No?" I lowered my voice in case any servants were lurking nearby, unseen. "I think you did. And that's why you found me in the garden."

"I didn't know until you told me," she whispered almost in a panic. "The first time we met, yes, but not until just before I left."

"Liar," I hissed. *There it is.* The familiar scratch of suspicion and hostility. I wanted her to admit it. To confess that she had sought me out. Acted unafraid. Crawled under my skin on purpose. *Kissed me back* on purpose.

Her eyes *finally* rose to mine and I immediately wished they hadn't. Fear glistened behind tears as her chin quivered.

"I swear," she said, barely loud enough to hear. "I only wanted a moment alone that day."

My lips curled in distaste. Was she pretending even now? Fooling me with tears, hoping I'd take pity on her? I would not. Doing so would mean trusting her word and I'd long ago had the trust beaten out of me. "And the days that followed? The night you snuck out to meet with me?" I snarled. "What of those?"

"Bring tea," Duchess Fransabelle yelled, likely knowing a servant would hear. "A full set. We'll see how her table manners are."

"I know I shouldn't have," she whispered quickly.

"You must've had a reason," I prodded.

She drew two rapid breaths, seeming to search her mind. "I felt like I could finally relax next to you, even if it was only for a minute. What I said that night—that I felt a connection between us—I was telling the truth."

Her words were a blow, and I scrambled to remind myself that Karina was a good liar. The truth was that I understood the sentiment. After my suspicion waned, I had even felt the same around her. Like I didn't have to pretend. Not entirely anyway. It was the same around Bastian, but with Karina, there was no undercurrent of guilt… until now.

Karina took a single step closer. "Please don't tell anyone that—"

"That I kissed you? That you kissed me back? That I asked you to meet me alone, at night, and you did?" A small, derisive laugh left my mouth. "I don't particularly feel like losing my head, *Lady Karina.*"

"Saer, stop harassing the girl. That's my job," Fransabelle called. "Are you joining us for tea?"

I shook my head. "I have to meet the prince."

The duchess grunted as she stood and hobbled her way back to my side. She reached up and patted my cheek. "You've always been such a good boy."

I cut a sideways glare to Karina, then smiled down at the frail woman. "You'll damage my reputation with talk like that, Duchess."

She let out a short laugh. "You've spilled enough blood that no one would dare believe me."

Sobering words. Because I *was* a killer. A cold, distant shadow that followed the prince. "That I am."

With a tap of her cane on my ankle, she pointed at a round table. "Bring that away from the wall for us and you can be on your way."

"Anything for you," I assured her and lifted the table with ease. She pointed to a spot on the floor where she wanted it. I set it down and returned for two chairs, holding one out for her.

"Good boy," she repeated as I slid the chair under her and up to the table.

Standing behind her, I stared across the table at Karina. Her chest rose and fell with quick breaths as she twisted her hands in front of her stomach. My steps were light, my movements fluid, as if I were approaching an enemy. Because I was. She was a threat to Bastian and, thanks to my own foolishness, to me.

As Karina lowered herself onto the seat, I leaned down to whisper in her ear. "This conversation isn't over." Then I stepped away, allowing the serving girl to approach and set the tray of tea down. "The prince asked me to see how you were settling in," I said loud enough for the entire room to hear. "What would you like me to tell him?"

Karina licked her lips and the motion went right to my cock. *Fuck.* She was Bastian's fiancée and likely a spy. There wasn't *anyone* more off limits as Karina was.

"Tell him I'm settling in well and thank him for his concern," she said in a surprisingly steady voice.

I held back a snort at how well she hid the fear I knew she still carried. All it would take was a single word about what happened in the garden, and the entire Aster plot would unravel. But it was that portrayal of someone composed that told me everything I needed to know. It would be interesting, dragging the truth from her pretty lips.

"He wants me to keep him updated so I will see you again soon," I told the duchess.

"Wonderful news. Now—" she leaned her cane against the arm of her chair "—if you aren't staying, there's nothing I hate more than cold tea."

"Of course." I purposely ignored Karina as I gave the duchess a bow. "Enjoy your tea."

I left then. Strode back the way I came so I could wait outside the Main Palace for Bastian. Today Karina would drink her tea with the duchess, but tomorrow she would spill her secrets to me.

ELEVEN

When I reached Faramond's window, it was already cracked open. He wasn't expecting me, but he must've been expecting *someone* so I would have to make this quick. The last thing I needed was for someone to discover who I was and, if they were caught, use my name to save themself.

The soft sliding sound of the wooden frame alerted the Aster leader as I slipped inside without knocking. Faramond sat at his desk with paperwork again. He didn't bother looking up as I approached the desk and continued scratching his quill against a sheet of paper. "Report."

"King Jonty's daughter arrived at the palace and was introduced over a dinner with the governors." My tone told him that I suspected he already knew.

Faramond took a deep breath. "I didn't put you beside the prince to give me public information. What else?"

It wasn't exactly public information. It wasn't a secret, but nothing had been announced to the people of Eradrist yet. There would naturally be leaks, but rumors weren't the same as confirmed truths. "Edric is giving Bastian more responsibility, but he hasn't said what his new tasks are. He's fine with marrying the girl."

More than fine, in fact. He was cautiously excited, which made me feel like the biggest piece of shit in existence. I swallowed hard against the shame burning in my chest.

"As if he has a choice," he said with a snort.

Of course not—there was only the *illusion* of a choice. And that was sometimes worse than being forced into something.

"Is that what you risked coming all the way here for?" Faramond looked up at me without moving his head. "Don't you have a governor to kill?"

I forced myself not to lash out, slowly exhaling instead. "Pevran brokered the engagement for you."

"For me? No. She brokered the engagement for the good of Eradrist." His forehead wrinkled as he raised his brows. "If you have no relevant information, get out. I have other meetings tonight."

"If you could just tell—"

"You know what you need to know. Leave." He leaned back in the chair and glowered. "Now. And don't come back unless you're summoned or you have something real to report."

My hands balled in and out of fists as I met his stare. I couldn't go against him—not without bringing myself down. Unless I was willing to kill him. Which I wasn't. Just because I'd killed people before didn't mean that I *wanted* to. It was always to protect Bastian and myself—rebel assassins or servants seeking revenge against the crown—but never in cold blood. Though, I supposed murdering the Aster leader could be considered protecting the prince…

I bowed and left without another word. There was no arguing with Faramond, no compromise. He had pulled me from certain death, thanks to my parents' stance in the war, and convinced King Edric to take me in. So, in Faramond's eyes, I *owed* him.

After scaling the building to the cobbled street, I turned toward the palace amid flickering street lamps. It was a different city at night. Quieter, of course, but less hostile. Most of the people on the streets of Ora Et right now weren't trying to scrape out a living, but trying to *live*. A cheerful tune drifted from more than one tavern, some on fiddles, some from talented singers, as others clapped a beat or danced. I saw them through the windows, spinning around with carefree steps, smiling and laughing. Moans of pleasure drifted from more than one dark alley. A group of girls traveled down the center of the street, arms linked, giggling as they played some sort of game where they tried not to trip on each other's feet.

A handful of city blocks from Faramond's, all the merriment snapped something inside me and I ducked between an inn and a bakery. And punched the brick. "Fuck!" I screamed. And punched again.

I wanted this. All of it. I wanted… a life. One that was my own. But I would die long before that ever became a possibility. Either at the hands of an Aster or defending the prince—which would also be from an Aster. Faramond and the rebellion he'd forced me into had destroyed any trace of hope I ever had.

"Sir," a young voice called.

I spun around, ignoring the sting of my bleeding knuckles, to find a young boy wearing pants inches too short and a shirt that would fit someone twice his size. A worn, leather strap wrapped around the back of his neck to distribute some of the weight from the wire tray he carried. A handful of paper sacks still sat on its surface.

"Yes?" I asked.

"Maybe some roasted nuts will make you feel better," he ventured.

His innocent act wasn't fooling me, but the kid knew what he was doing. Bat his huge eyes at a noblewoman while pretending to be shy and it was almost a guaranteed sale. It *was* late though, and he had so many sacks left. Digging a gold coin from my pocket, I lifted the boy's hand and pressed it to his palm.

"Make sure you spend it on food," I instructed before grabbing one of the sacks. The boy's eyes went impossibly wide when he peered at how much I'd given him. "Off you go."

He ran off before I could change my mind, not that I would have. Flexing my sore fingers, I wiped some of the blood on my brown tunic—one I wore to blend in—and popped a few nuts in my mouth. The hint of cinnamon came as a surprise, but it wasn't what I needed.

I needed ale.

A lot of ale.

So I slunk from the shadows and went straight for a questionable tavern near the edge of the capital. One nowhere near Faramond's office. One where the only music was that of masculine shouts as two patrons pounded on each other. Their cheers were for blood, not singing. The dancing done with fists, not feet. Here, there was nothing to *want* except a drink… or several.

Hours later, I was far too drunk to sneak back into the palace, so I stumbled through the lesser used pathways, only losing balance a few times. The walls caught me before I could hit the ground, but by the time I made it to the Prince's Palace, I was never happier to have my small, personal building behind Bastian's. Somewhere I could crash without being seen.

But candlelight flickered in the prince's rooms. I stopped, leaning on the now-open gate for support and glared at the guard who'd opened it. If he told anyone I was this drunk, I'd find a way to make him pay.

"Who's visiting the prince?" I asked in a surprisingly steady voice. At least, it sounded fine to me.

The guard kept his eyes averted. "No one, my Lord Wing."

I grunted and brushed past him to see what the prince was doing up so late. Slipping inside, I followed the light to Bastian's sleeping chamber where the prince sat behind his desk, reading letters. "You should be asleep," I mumbled.

"Should I?" he asked without glancing up. "Tell that to my father."

I stepped into the room and my boot caught on the corner of a large fur rug, pitching me sideways into a chest of drawers. "No one can do *that*."

Bastian snorted. "I'm being punished for disappearing earlier. This entire stack of correspondence must be ready to dispatch before the morning meeting."

"I can help."

"Absolutely not."

"Why not?" The room spun and I eased myself down onto the thick rug before I fell. There was a very comfortable-looking lounge a yard away, but I wasn't sure I'd make it. "I have wonderful penmanship."

Bastian held up a letter. "If you were to answer Duke Stoll's letter about grain prices, what would you say?"

"Dearest, Most *Benevolent* Duke," I began. "The prices would not be so high if you hadn't supported that idiotic law in the first place. Also, stop fucking your wife's cousin, you disgusting prick."

A loud laugh filled the room as Bastian set the letter down. "Exactly my point, though someone really should call him out on the cousin-in-law bit." He turned in his chair and paused. "Are you... *drunk?*"

I bristled. "What makes you ask that?"

"To begin with, you're lying in the middle of my floor in peasant clothes."

Ah. The clothes. I should've changed first. Become a Wing again so Bastian didn't think I snuck out. Not that he would care. *I think.* What *did* he think about it? It was too late to worry about that now. I *should* worry about those guards outside seeing me like this though. And I would. Tomorrow. Or maybe toss them a coin tonight on my way to bed. I patted my pockets. *Oh.* I almost forgot I tipped the bar maiden the last of my coin. She had been very pretty, but not as pretty as Karina…

"You went into town, didn't you?" he continued, brows raised.

"Maybe I had an ale or two at a tavern," I admitted.

Bastian smirked. "One or two?"

"*Shhh.* Don't worry." I placed a finger to my lips, then reached into my cloak pocket and tossed him the half-eaten sack of nuts. "I brought you these."

Bastian caught them midair and peeked inside. "Roasted nuts?"

"For the royalist of squirrels." I chewed on my bottom lip and made a quick rodent sound. "Next time we are ambushed on an ill-prepared journey, you'll have a snack."

"You're a fucking mess." Bastian slowly put one of the nuts in his mouth and chewed. A moment later, his brows raised in surprise and he ate two more. "You better not vomit on my floor."

I wasn't entirely sure I could promise that. I flung an arm over my eyes and took shallow breaths to try easing my rolling stomach.

"Are you going to tell me why you snuck out to a tavern?" Bastian asked curiously.

"It sounded like a good idea at the time," I grumbled. "I'll stay here until you're finished working."

The creak of Bastian's chair and the rustle of papers followed along with a mumble. Much to my relief, the prince didn't push the issue so I closed my eyes. I was quite possibly drunk enough to say more than I should. To divulge my suspicions about Karina or reveal what happened in the garden. But I slowly drifted to sleep, secrets intact, because Bastian wasn't one to take advantage of anyone. Unlike both his father and the rebels.

TWELVE

Sharp pain sliced down the center of my head. I flew up, instantly awake, and clutched my forehead. It took a few long seconds before I could crack my eyes open, and when I did, Bastian's room slowly took focus. The events of last night came back in a rush.

Sneaking out to see Faramond. The boy with the roasted nuts. All the drinks at the tavern. Finding my way back to the palace, to Bastian's room, and how I needed to threaten a couple of guards. *Motherfucker.* I was never drinking again.

I rolled and shifted to my knees on the fur rug. Bastian was slumped over at his table, head on his folded arms, snoring. "Bast," I croaked, climbing unsteadily to my feet. "Wake up."

Bastian jumped, scattering papers to the ground. "What time is it?"

"Damned if I know." I rubbed my forehead. No one had come knocking to get Bastian dressed yet, so it wasn't late. Unless someone *had* come knocking and I was sleeping too deeply. Bastian would've heard though, or the guards would've burst in thinking the worst.

Bastian groaned and scooped the fallen letters from the floor. "It's going to be a long day."

I grunted in agreement and caught a whiff of myself, cringing. "I need a bath."

"That stench is coming from you then?"

"Ha. Ha." Though, yes. Yes, it was. The scent of yeast seemed to ooze from my pores and something else—a musty smell with a hint of rot—clung to my clothes. Had I sat in something dead at the tavern? I would need to obtain new clothes for sneaking into the city now that people had seen me in them so I might as well burn these. There was no getting this rancid odor out.

A knock on the door pulled both our attention.

"If my father asks, I'll tell him I gave you the night off," Bastian said quickly. "But even then, if anyone tells him you were drunk, he might demand you be whipped."

Wouldn't be the first time. I nodded once, well aware of the potential repercussions. "What's a few more scars?"

Bastian cast me a guilty look. It wasn't his fault I had lash marks covering my back. There had simply been a learning curve to becoming the perfect guard— or appearing to be. I moved to open the door but Bastian spoke first.

"I… know it must be hard," he said. "To have this be your whole life."

I lifted a brow. "You're apologizing a lot lately. Where's this all coming from?"

"I don't know." He ran a hand through his mussed hair, the strands reaching past his shoulders in harsh waves due to the near-constant braids. "The engagement, maybe. My life is changing and yours never will."

The words were a slap, though I'd accepted the truth long ago. "My life changes the same as yours."

"Exactly. The same as mine, but never as your own."

I scowled. "Can we not do this?"

Another pound came on the door, louder, followed by the head servant calling, "Your Highness. Are you well?"

"Enter," he replied.

The elderly man shuffled in with three younger servants behind him. They all wore deep blue robes, their hair sheered close to the scalp, and each carried a different piece of the prince's clothing. They bowed before descending on him with their embroidered fabric.

"I'll meet you outside," I mumbled. It took at least an hour to get him ready every morning which was more than enough time for me to bathe and put on a clean uniform.

"Wait," he said, sounding more official than he had before. "The thing I asked of you yesterday…"

Karina. But I'd already relayed her message about settling in. "What of it?"

He looked past me, through the sitting room to the still-open door, and took a deep breath. "It's an ongoing request."

"I understand," I assured him. And I did. It was necessary for a lot of reasons, but that didn't mean I *liked* needing to see Karina again.

He nodded once before holding his arms out for the servants to start the tedious process of dressing him.

Two lady's maids sat on the side porch of the Women's Palace—the same one where Duchess Fransabelle had rested the day before—whispering as they stitched strands of emeralds onto a shimmering black gown. I shouldn't have paused to listen, but they should've noticed my approach from the side gate. It was their job to know who entered the palace and to welcome the visitor while the residing Lady was told that she had guests.

There hadn't been a queen or princess since King Jonty's days. Bastian's mother died giving birth to him while the war for the throne still waged, and the king hadn't trusted any woman enough to remarry after. The brothel took care of his carnal desires so there was no real need to share the crown. But whoever was training these lady's maids was lacking.

"I've met smarter girls in the streets," the blonde whispered. "How does the daughter of a countess not know how to sit properly?"

The older of the two pursed her lips. "I caught her kneeling on the lawn early yesterday morning to look at a toad, and in her nightdress no less."

"No!"

She nodded. "Not even a shawl."

"Well, she *was* raised in Port Black," the blonde said, sounding disgusted. "You know what the women there are like."

The massive port city was known for three things: exotic imports, numerous brothels, and luxury apartments noblemen rented to keep their mistresses. She was implying *Karina*, the future princess—and, one day, queen—was a whore. My pulse thrummed loudly in my ears as I fought the urge to storm through the main room and out onto the patio. I wasn't here to cause a scene. Duchess Fransabelle would do that for me.

I stomped up the steps, purposely making enough noise for them to hear my approach. By the time I entered the main doors, both women were there to greet me.

"My Lord Wing," the older one said, the blonde cowering slightly behind her.

"Where is Lady Karina?" I snapped.

"In the library with Duchess Fransabelle," she replied.

I brushed past them without another word. While I wasn't familiar with the layout of the Women's Palace, I was sure to find it eventually. I walked quietly, listening for the duchess's frustrated instructions, but it seemed Karina was doing better today. Either that or I was nowhere near the library. I peeked into rooms with furniture still hidden beneath dusty sheets and shuttered windows. Sitting rooms, bathing chambers, a sun room, closets. None of them were locked, and only the dining area appeared lived in. T

he rectangular table sat six with a lace cloth covering its surface. Blue and white floral wallpaper covered the walls and large portraits of men and women unknown to me hung every few feet. Tall planters were arranged in every corner with bushy plants.

But I wasn't interested in the dining area. I needed the library, so I continued on until, finally, I came upon an opulent door at the end of a hallway.

On the other side was a large sitting room, almost exactly the same as the one in Bastian's residence. Only, instead of deep, rich colors, the decor consisted of white, gold, and mauve. I zeroed in on the far door, knowing it would lead to Karina's private chambers, and quickly went through it. Would I get in trouble for this if someone caught me? Karina was a bastard but a *king's* bastard who was also Bastian's fiancée. Society, in general, owed her some respect. I rubbed my chin, considering. If Karina herself caught me, I could remind her how I didn't tell anyone about the garden or the kiss. Her ladies could be silenced if I told them Bastian asked me to be there, but I really didn't want to drag Bastian into this.

Fuck.

I was wasting time. This was the palace—no one had the luxury of privacy. In all likelihood, I wasn't even the first to go through her things since she arrived. Before I could think any more of it, I slipped inside. The scent of wildflowers instantly struck me. I took a shallower breath and did my best to ignore the memories it conjured of the garden.

Brocade curtains were drawn, casting the room in cool morning light. The bed had already been made, the down-filled comforter pulled tight, and at least a dozen pillows were piled near the white headboard. Gauzy material hung from the ceiling around the entire bed, also drawn back now with golden rope. There was nothing that stuck out to me as strange. A lounge chair near the fireplace, a ridiculously large wardrobe that took up an entire wall, and a small dressing table with a mirror.

But no Aster would leave incriminating evidence where it could be seen, so I began my search. There would be nothing beneath the mattress or hidden between gowns as any maid could find them, but still I looked, fruitlessly. The hiding places for secret notes or other contraband would have to be much more creative. Loose floorboards. Hidden compartments inside the wardrobe. Tucked inside a ripped curtain or fastened beneath a drawer. In the heels of her *numerous* shoes or sewn into the lining of a cloak.

After checking behind the paintings on the wall and examining each piece of jewelry for hidden compartments that may hide poison, I was nearly at a loss. Had I been wrong about her? Perhaps Karina was an innocent pawn in all of this. But then I bent down to look beneath a padded stool in the corner of the room. A frayed piece of ribbon dangled from a rip near one of the legs. I carefully pulled it free and ran the pink ribbon between my fingers. It was old and faded with creases worn into it, and bits of dirt embedded into the weave. The countess would never have allowed her daughter such a filthy thing.

There was no definitive way of knowing if it belonged to Karina, however. For all I knew, it was from another time, a different lady.

I swept my eyes over the room once more before stuffing the ribbon back where I'd found it. Nothing incriminating was to be found, save the ribbon, but that didn't mean I was finished looking. The Red Asters were smart enough not to allow Karina to bring anything with her that could give their plan away, but from what I'd seen, she was good at sneaking. If not, she never would've lost her lady's maids and made it to the garden.

With a sigh, I snuck from Karina's private rooms and continued searching for the library.

Luckily it wasn't far.

"Hello, Saer," Duchess Fransabelle greeted warmly as I stepped into the sprawling room full of old books. From the corner of my eyes, I saw Karina sitting in a cream-colored wingback chair, a crease between her brows.

"Duchess," I said, kissing her hand, and led her toward the library doors. "I need to speak with you."

"Oh?"

I nodded solemnly and relayed every word I'd heard from the maids. Her face grew grim, her frail shoulders squaring. "I will have none of it," she vowed. "Stay with her, won't you? She has a tendency to disappear if left unsupervised."

A smirk tugged at my lips. Two problems, solved. "She'll be right where you left her."

"Good boy," she said, and left the library faster than I thought she could move.

I whirled on Karina the moment the door shut and my traitorous heart slammed into my chest. Her honey brown hair looked golden where it curled against the rich purple dress. Shimmering ribbons crisscrossed down her arms, forming sleeves. Strands of gems stretched across her upper chest, the lowest grazing the top of her cleavage, and gold dust shimmered on her eyelids.

"Lord Tufaro." Her grip tightened on the book she held. "You're back again today."

My eyes swept the small library, ensuring we were alone among the white shelves and potted wisteria. "I told you our conversation wasn't over."

Her breathing increased, chest heaving, eyes wide. "I don't think there's anything left to say."

"Isn't there?" I prowled toward her and Karina shrank back into the chair. She held her book against her chest as if it were a shield. *Treaties of the North.* "Interesting choice in reading material."

Karina sucked her bottom lip between her teeth and flicked a glance at the tome. "Before I got here, I was told I wouldn't have a role in politics."

"Oh?" I perched on the table in front of her and leaned forward. The scent of wildflowers hit my nose. I swallowed hard, ignoring how it made my chest tighten with want. "What did you think you would do as a future queen?"

"The countess—my mother—she said…" Her cheeks flamed. "Well, she never taught me politics because she said the prince wouldn't want my opinion. And all I had to do was…"

Kill him as he slept? "Was what?"

Karina looked down at the book in her lap. "To give the prince heirs."

I blinked in surprise, then let out a sharp laugh without meaning to. "If producing living children was all it took to be queen, anyone could be plucked from the street."

Her blush deepened. "Please don't make fun of me."

I sobered at the sight of her trembling fingers. If she wasn't lying, if she really expected to give Bastian children, she wasn't planning to kill him. At least not right away. "Forgive me," I said. "That wasn't my intent."

She nodded once, lowering the book to her thighs, and traced the embossed title. My skin tingled, wishing it was me she touched like that.

Fuck. No. Control yourself.

"Your mother was wrong. Prince Bastian will want your opinions on many things so it's good the duchess is giving you lessons." I sucked in a breath. Fransabelle wouldn't be gone forever—I had to spend more time getting answers and less time needlessly comforting a liar. "I need you to be honest with me now, while we're alone. Why are you here?"

Karina's breath hitched. "To marry Prince Bastian."

"Yes." My eyes narrowed. "But why? Who sent you? What's your *real* goal?"

"I don't know what you want me to say," she whispered, eyes downcast. "I'm here because my marriage was brokered."

"And you jumped at the chance to become a princess?" As anyone would. Unless they belonged to the Red Asters—or *especially* if they did.

"I was given a choice," she said carefully. "But in reality, it wasn't a choice at all."

My top lip curled into a sneer. "It *was* a choice to kiss me in the garden."

"You kissed me too," she said in a rush.

I leaned in closer, eyeing her lips. "Yes, but I didn't know who you were. You did know who I was and who what it would mean."

A harsh breath left her then, her gaze snapping to me. "I did. Is that what you want to hear? I let you kiss me and I kissed you back. Because I wanted to."

"That's it then." I tilted my head, studying her. "You're here to drive Bastian and I apart. To make him vulnerable."

Of course. Why hadn't I thought of that before? It made sense. Faramond doubted me, thought I was useless or compromised. Sending in Karina would not only get me away from the prince, making him open to attack, but also put an Aster in line for the throne. I believed she wasn't privy to the entire plot—I was beginning to think *no* Aster was—but she had to know this wasn't a simple marriage to bridge two families.

"No." Karina's voice became sharp as she inched to the edge of her chair, invading my space. "I wanted to know what it felt like to kiss someone because it was *my* choice. Someone I *wanted* to kiss. Just once before I promised myself to someone else."

My chest tightened. *She wanted to kiss me.* I leaned in until there was only an inch between our lips. It was torture being this close. Her scent. The invisible pull demanding I close the gap. Taste her. Touch her. "Why me? You could've kissed any number of guards when you were traipsing through the palace."

"I didn't plan any of it." Her breath skated over my skin and I shivered. "Meeting you, talking to you, kissing you. All of it just *happened.*"

My hand came up to her cheek, thumb sliding over her cheekbone. Her warmth sent a rush through my body and my breath hitched. "It can't happen again." Was I telling myself? Or her? Both of us? "Bastian is all I have. I won't betray him. He can never know."

Her chin tilted toward me, lips parting. I inched closer. *Fuck.* I wanted to dig my fingers into her hair, pull her close, kiss her until our lips were swollen. The way her breath hitched told me she wanted that too. Instead, I ripped myself away before I could lose control.

"I'm sorry," she breathed.

I ran a hand through my hair, accidentally loosening pieces from the knot that fell into my eyes. "So am I."

What the hell just happened? I'd meant to get the truth out of her... and maybe I had. Maybe she knew nothing. But I *wouldn't* betray Bastian now that I knew who she was. I couldn't even be angry with her that she'd nearly betrayed him too. It took two. We were both walking a fine line.

It had to end here.

There was nothing hidden in her room to hint at a grander plan, and deep down, I believed she wasn't aware of one. That made us both pawns at the mercy of higher powers, but there were still lines we couldn't cross. And, just because she wasn't planning to murder

Bastian herself, that didn't mean *no one* was. I had to keep searching. Keep digging. And, more than anything, I had to stay far away from Karina. Even if Bastian begged me to keep visiting.

"That takes care of that," Duchess Fransabelle said in a stern voice as she hobbled back into the library. "You'll have new maids by dinner."

"Why?" Karina asked.

The duchess shot me a look that would silence even the biggest gossip. "Because I said so. Are you still reading or shall I test you on Eradrist's history?"

"I'm still reading," she grumbled, the spine of her book cracking open.

"Enjoy the rest of your day, Lady Karina." I gave her a stiff bow, then bent again to Fransabelle. "Duchess."

I'd never been happier to flee a room than I was today. But every step that took me farther away from Karina was also a step closer to Bastian. Fresh waves of guilt washed over me, icy cold then blisteringly hot. How would I face him when he left his morning meeting with the governors? How would I face him ever again?

THIRTEEN

"Remind me where your father thinks you are right now?" I whispered.

Bastian wandered slightly in front of me through the capital. The entire city center of Ora Et was full of stalls selling different wares—if you wanted it, you'd find it at the weekly bazaar. And if you *couldn't* find it, someone would know where it was attainable. People came from far and wide to buy or sell here, which made my job nearly impossible today. Both me and the prince wore civilian clothing—a rough-spun tunic and pants, complete with stains, rips, and a few dirt smudges for good measure. Bastian's long hair was tied into a messy knot at the nape of his neck while mine hung, limp, to my shoulders.

I blew a stray piece from where it caught my eyelash and regretted my choice to slick it back with grease. While I usually kept it tied back, I never used anything to keep it there, but I had to replicate an unwashed look while maintaining full visual range.

"I'm going over ledgers," Bastian replied.

I casually scanned the crowd. "Isn't that what the Governor of Finance is for?"

Bastian shrugged. "That doesn't mean I shouldn't also go over them. Maybe someone is brave enough to swindle the crown."

Someone definitely is. Someone always was, especially with this particular monarch.

"What do you think of these?"

I turned my attention to a long, crooked table. Jewels of every color were spread out across its length, glittering under the sun. They were set in rings, bracelets, necklaces, and hair pieces, while others sat on their own, waiting for the buyer to choose how the stone would be used. None of them were as well-made as what Karina already wore, but these had more character. Still…

"I think if you add another gem to her, she'll blind you the moment she steps outside," I mumbled, keeping my voice low so the merchant couldn't hear. Besides, we were trying to keep a low profile and I was sure the merchant was already growing suspicious, thinking that we either weren't low-born or were about to swipe a precious gemstone.

Bastian snorted. "What do you suggest then?"

I had no idea what Karina liked but I *wished* I did. Even if it was something small, a little piece of knowledge not involving treason, that I alone knew, even after she married Bastian. Who was I kidding? I already knew something about her that no one else

did. *Betrayal.* I was a shit friend. A shit guard. Just…
shit.

"A book?" Bastian suggested.

"Definitely not." Not when the duchess was likely forcing her to read through every history book in the library.

"Shoes? Women like shoes."

I shook my head. She had plenty of those in her room, not that I could tell Bastian without raising questions.

Bastian rubbed at the back of his neck. "I didn't think it would be this difficult."

"It's hard because you don't know her. Maybe instead of a gift, you should visit her." Also, if Karina suddenly took a liking to Bastian, it would make things a lot easier for me. Maybe not to watch as they held hands, exchanged knowing glances, shared intimate moments—a spike of jealousy struck me. I wanted to be the one to slip my tongue between her lips again. *Me.* Not anyone else. I clenched my jaw. No, it wouldn't be pleasant to watch her fall for Bastian, but it would definitely help keep me in check.

"You know I can't." He ran his hand over a rolled carpet with a tasseled edge as we walked past a robust man selling them. Different designs hung behind his stall and smaller ones were piled on a table.

"You can if you have a chaperone and what do you know? A perfectly good one happens to be tutoring her from sun up until sun down."

"I'm… busy."

I took a deep breath and shot him a withering look. "You're avoiding her, aren't you?"

"No." He winced. "Maybe."

"Why?" Why send me when *he* was the one marrying her?

"What if she doesn't like me?" he blurted, followed quickly by a wince.

I nearly tripped over my own feet. "What?"

"*Me*. What if she doesn't like who I am as a person? My"—he cast a glance over his shoulder—"*profession* draws a lot of attention but she'll be trapped with me, as a man, for the rest of her life."

"As opposed to her being trapped with you as a dog?" I asked, leading the way around a tin-smith selling decorative baubles.

"You know what I mean, Saer," he whispered. "We should have more than general respect for each other, shouldn't we?"

"I do know," I agreed. Karina was marrying a prince, but she would be living beside a person—not a crown. Bastian wanted her to like *him*. And, though I doubted he would admit it, I believed he wanted to fall in love with her. Could anyone blame him?

"This?" Bastian asked, hopeful.

Catching a whiff of something rich and sweet, I glanced at a stand a few places down. It was overflowing with chocolates—a luxury item that would've melted if winter wasn't approaching.

A female customer with delicate features picked a small square up and placed it between her lips, but in that moment, all I could see was Karina's face, her hands. The fact that I wanted to give such a delicacy to her ripped at my insides. What was wrong with me?

"Perfect," Bastian said, following my gaze. A boyish grin spread across his face. When was the last time I'd seen him like this? He breezed toward the chocolatier as if he hadn't a care in the world.

"An assortment," I told the merchant. Bastian had never been able to nail the casual way of speaking that they used in Ora Et, and I didn't want to blow our cover just as we finished our task. "A large box." The merchant scowled, looking us up and down. "Our lord sent us for them," I tacked on with a tight smile.

Bastian tossed a small bag of coins at the man and I winced. He didn't even count it. Didn't wait for the man to tell us how much we owed.

"Whatever that will get us," I said to cover our tracks.

The man's eyes widened as he looked inside the bag. *How much did Bastian bring?* When the merchant pulled a large box from behind the stand and began carefully arranging *dozens* of chocolates into small papers, I fought a groan. Now we had to carry a box that screamed *made of money* back through the market without an assault attempt. Which I would need to thwart. Without scattering chocolate all over the street. And, inevitably, making a huge scene that would end with King Edric finding out we snuck out of the palace.

"You're lucky I like you," I said so only Bastian could hear.

The prince side-eyed me and laughed.

While Bastian waited for the chocolates to be boxed up, I turned to watch for threats. Bastard thieves were probably already watching us. Waiting. Though what they hoped to steal now was a mystery. The chocolate? Good luck selling that second-hand. My hidden weapons? I dared them.

But I wasn't expecting *this* type of danger to appear.

Countess Odelia strolled between stalls in a gold gown, the fabric nearly invisible beneath the strands of beading, her hair braided and worn like an imitation crown. She looked exactly like her portrait—the one stuffed into storage with other forgotten things from King Jonty's time—only older. Two male bodyguards followed her with grim looks. A scar ran across one's throat as if someone had sliced it open, while the other appeared unblemished. The crowd hushed and moved aside at her arrival. Not even a whisper rose through the market. With how cruel the countess was said to be, I wouldn't have risked her overhearing a snide remark either.

But it felt heavier than that. Like the countess was dragging the old monarchy back to Eradrist on the train of her dress. I scowled at the tall woman. Her features were sharp and almost birdlike, her dark hair run through with gray. How did someone as light as honey call the countess *mother?*

At Odelia's loud cackle, Bastian shifted beside me and froze. "Is that…"

"Yes," I said quickly.

"She was ordered to stay in Port Black with her brother."

And yet, there she was. Bastian couldn't tell the king without giving away our secret outing, but it wouldn't be long before *someone* did. The countess was clearly not trying to hide her arrival. I swiped the half-filled box of chocolate from the stunned seller. "Move," I told Bastian. "Don't look back. All we need is for her to recognize you."

"How would she do that? She was banished before I could even walk."

"The same way we recognize her. Portraits," I grumbled, urging him away from the shrewd woman.

"How long has she been here?" Bastian asked, though I could tell from his tone that he didn't actually expect me to know.

"I'll find out." First, I'd visit Karina and see what she knew. Then, I'd return to the capital and track the countess down myself. If Karina was smart, her story would line up with the truth. I flicked a glance down the street at Faramond's office and aimed our path directly toward the palace. The Red Aster leader was aware of this… He must have known. *Fuck.* I was tired of these games.

Bastian had agreed to give me as much time as possible to learn what I could about Countess Odelia's arrival. Which meant he would likely be dining with his father tonight. I was sure they had royal wedding plans to sort out or an argument with the governors to have— perhaps an argument about the wedding. It was too much to hope that it would be called off… Not that I could pursue Karina anyway.

I shook the thoughts from my head as I followed the directions given by a silk merchant. He'd delivered a shipment of his finest a week ago to the largest brick house on the wealthiest street in Ora Et. Which meant Odelia had been there at least that long. Slipping between the red brick of Odelia's rental house and a spiked, black iron fence, I eased up to an open window. Sheer curtains billowed from inside. It was too high to see inside and discover if the room was occupied. But standing out here wasn't going to get me answers.

I adjusted my spine between two of the iron poles and leaned back, placing my feet on the brick to brace myself, and began inching upward. When I was nearly at the ledge of the window, an interior door opened and shut.

"I can't *believe* her," Countess Odelia seethed. "Did you read this?"

Paper crinkled before a male voice replied, "I don't need to. You've told me what it says six different ways."

The countess let out a small, wordless shriek. "This is the thanks I get? I plucked that little bitch out of the gutters of Port Black and made her a *princess*. She'd be selling herself on the docks by now if it weren't for me."

Wait. What?

"You'll be invited back to the palace soon enough, dearest. People will expect you at the wedding."

"The wedding?" she said, words dripping with condescension. "If there is one! Without me there to make sure she isn't dismantling my plan one snide remark at a time. The false prince probably won't even agree to marry that useless cunt."

Gutters of Port Black.

Selling herself if not for the Countess.

"You chose her," the man said, sounding resigned.

"I know I chose her," she snapped. "She has Jonty's coloring and looks enough like him to make it believable."

Chose her.

My pulse thundered in my ears. I couldn't be hearing this right. Because this… It sounded like Karina wasn't King Jonty's bastard.

"Faramond shouldn't have pushed us," she added.

The man crossed the room and I caught a hint of black hair. "The boy has been old enough to marry for a few years now. You know it was foolish to wait any longer and risk a royal marriage with another country."

"If I was *with her*, things wouldn't be so worrisome. You know how she is! These last few years have tested me like nothing ever has before."

Faramond.

The boy.

The chosen *girl.*

Risk of a royal wedding.

What the fuck?

Karina wasn't Odelia's daughter. She was someone else entirely. I scaled back down the wall, my back aching from how hard I had braced against the fence. Shaking my numb hands out, I attempted to process what I'd learned. Tried to make sense of it as my body stilled in preparation for an attack that wouldn't come. Not here, where I'd already checked for guards. Checked and found none because this wasn't the palace.

There were no royals here. No *parents* of royals. Only lies. Layers of them, each rottener than the last. And if I wasn't careful with the information I'd just learned, I wouldn't only be a liar but a *very dead* liar.

FOURTEEN

A new lady's maid greeted me—*attempted to greet me*—as I stormed into the Women's Palace. I brushed past the young, dark-skinned woman without a word and headed deeper into the palace, through several brightly lit hallways, without knowing where Karina was.

"My Lord Wing," the lady's maid called after me. "Please, wait."

"Where is she?" I demanded, voice low.

"Eating dinner in her private rooms," the maid answered as she rushed to keep up. "She requested not to be disturbed. Even Duchess Fra—"

I whirled on her and held up the box of chocolates that Bastian had bought earlier. "I'm here with a gift from the prince."

She hesitated, opened her mouth, then shut it again. *That's right*, I thought as fear flickered over her face. I was death itself. Stand in my way and feel my blade. Or whatever it was the people at court told themselves. As long as it got me into Karina's room so I could rip the truth from her lying mouth, it didn't matter.

Nothing was said as I turned toward Karina's rooms again. Nor did she say anything about how sure my stride was as I navigated the halls like I knew the exact path to Karina's room. The maid was too smart to imply anything to my face. For her own sake, I hoped she was smart enough not to say it behind my back either.

Without knocking, I swung open the ornate doors to Karina's private rooms and slipped inside. The maid paused, mouth open, as I turned to meet her gaze. I lifted a brow and swung the door in her face before she could attempt to follow.

The clatter of a chair drew my attention. I whipped around to find Karina clutching her throat. Choking.

"Fuck!" I dropped the chocolates and raced up beside her. Quickly leaning her forward, I pounded a flat palm against her upper back. Once. Twice. Three times. And a rattling gasp filled the air. "Can you breathe?"

Karina slumped against my arm where I held her around the waist, one hand gripping the edge of a small table. A half-chewed bite of lamb sat on a plate beside three small potatoes and a pile of green beans. "Yes," she rasped after a moment.

I eased away from her slowly to be sure she wouldn't collapse. Picking up her fallen chair, I arranged it behind her so she could sit. "Do you want something to drink?"

The beads hanging around Karina's arms clicked together as she plopped into the chair and nodded. I grabbed the glass of wine beside her plate and held it out. She winced a little as she took it and drank. My eyes trailed down from her lips to where her throat worked with each swallow. I should hate her, want to rip her from that chair and throw her out of this kingdom. And yet, the urge to trail my fingers along her neck burned with need. I pushed the red-hot lust aside focusing on why I was here.

All the lies that had flowed from her pretty little mouth.

"Thank you," she said once the glass was empty. "You scared me coming in here like that and I swallowed when I shouldn't have."

I studied her. "I noticed."

"Do you need something?" Karina glanced around me at the door.

"In a hurry to get rid of me?" If I were gone, her secrets would be so much safer.

"No." She shifted uncomfortably. "But you nearly ripped my door off the hinges. Without knocking first, I might add. Did my new lady's maid not tell you I wished to dine alone?"

"She told me." I yanked the second chair away from the table, spun it around, and straddled it. Folding my arms on the curved back of the seat, I glared at her. "I went to the market today."

Her brow creased. "Oh? I've heard it's the largest in Eradrist."

I studied her face, finding it calm. *She's good.* "It *is* the capital."

Karina chewed her lip as she lifted her fork to poke at the potatoes. "Port Black has one once a month."

"With stolen goods, no doubt," I mumbled.

"Port Black is more than pirates and convicts." She stabbed one of the potatoes a little harder. "There are master craftsman and food from all over the world. Duke Milo"—she paused—"my uncle, has a very profitable and *legal* transportation company. The men and women who live there are mostly honest. The most readily available jobs may not be desirable, but people are happy to put in the labor instead of thieving."

I leaned closer and scowled. "You're taking my comment rather personally. Didn't the Countess keep you at the family estate? I have a hard time imagining you were allowed to interact with the commoners, considering how valuable you are."

"My mother hasn't liked me from the moment she laid eyes on me." Her mouth opened as if she wanted to say more, but nothing followed. No grand confession—not that it was expected to come so easily. But, just as I was sure she wouldn't elaborate, she added, "You're right, though. I haven't gone into the city in years."

The sadness in her voice, the longing, hit a nerve. I could see it hadn't been her choice. That she longed for it. Or perhaps there was some*one* she yearned for. If she wasn't the bastard daughter of King Jonty, then she was the daughter of someone else. With the countess and the Asters snapping at her heels, I would have to coax her into telling me. Demanding the truth would seal her lips tighter than the royal vault.

"Perhaps Bastian will take you to the market one day," I said.

Her eyes widened. "Would he do that?"

I smirked. "As much as I would want to throttle him for it, yes."

"Is that something you should say about the prince?" It wasn't accusatory, but genuine curiosity.

"We grew up together." We'd been forced to act properly in public, but everyone knew we considered each other friends. "He's the prince. I'm his Wing. But we're more like brothers behind closed doors."

Karina halted her assault on the potato and stared at the steaming vegetable. "I wish I had someone like that."

"You have the Countess, don't you? Rumors are that you two are very close." *A lie.* I hadn't heard anything about her relationship with the old king's mistress. Which, now that I thought about it, seemed strange.

Karina rolled her eyes. *Most unprincess-ly.*

"She's followed you all the way to Ora Et despite the royal decree she stay in Port Black." I tried to sound comforting. Like I was offering her precious, happy news.

The color drained from Karina's face. "N-no. She stayed. She did! My uncle brought me here and returned straight away. Neither of them are here."

"I didn't say *they* were here." Although, now that I thought about it, it was most likely Duke Milo inside the house with his sister. There had never been restrictions to prevent the duke from visiting the capital, but I couldn't remember him ever coming to court. "I only saw your mother at the market."

Karina set down the fork and tucked her shaking hands under the table. "It must've been someone who looked like her."

"She was making a show of herself, *Lady Karina*. The prince saw her as well."

Her chin quivered for a moment. "I'm doing everything right." She sucked in a breath. "I'm *trying* to do everything right. Has Duchess Fransabelle complained? Which of her lessons am I not doing well enough in?" she asked earnestly. "Or was it the prince? Or the king? I know I was late to dinner, but I was nervous and… I'll try harder, I swear. And I'll stop sneaking out too."

I forced myself not to look as surprised as I felt. This was not the reaction I expected. The look on her face was one I knew well. I'd seen it on her maid's face on the way here and from nearly everyone who crossed my path. Gripping tight to the knowledge I'd gained outside the Countess' window, I beat back the need to protect her.

"I'm not sure what your behavior has to do with your mother breaking a royal edict."

"She said if she received a negative report, or if there was any sign the prince wouldn't marry me, that she would drag me home herself." She closed her eyes for a moment before staring at her plate. "I don't want to go back with her."

My lips twitched into a sneer. "No one this close to the crown would want to leave."

"It isn't the crown." She slammed her mouth shut and took a deep, shaky breath. "I forget myself, Lord Tufaro. Forgive me. I wasn't aware the countess was in Ora Et nor do I know why she would come."

I raised a brow. "Unless she came to bring you home."

"Unless that," she whispered.

I wanted to comfort her with the knowledge the wedding was still very much moving forward, but her reaction left me unable to. As much as I hated the idea, I wanted her scared. It would keep her on her toes—keep her safe. Besides, this could be a chance to get her to take me into her confidence. I believed she didn't know about her mother's arrival, but it didn't change the fact that Countess Odelia *wasn't* her mother at all.

"Where would home be, exactly?" I asked.

"Port Black, of course."

"But not the family estate."

Her eyes snapped to mine. "What do you mean?"

"I mean, where did you come from?" I leaned forward until my chest hit the back of the chair, hands gripping the wood tightly. "Because you aren't the daughter of King Jonty and Countess Odelia."

"What are you talking about?" she said, tripping over the words, pupils blown wide. Her breathing quickened as she gripped the arms of her chair.

I smirked. "The countess found you. She trained you. And now she expects to be welcomed back at court."

Not a single drop of color remained in her face. "How…"

"Always assume I know everything." *Even though I'm rarely privy to a lot of things.* "So, tell me. Who are you and where do you come from?"

Karina simply stared at me with wide eyes.

"I'll find out what your name is, even if you don't tell me. The only difference is whether I alert the wrong person while asking around."

"Please." It was the barest of whispers.

"Please what?" I snarled. "Let the countess slip a stranger into the prince's marital bed? Do the Asters know about you or has she lied to them too?"

She lunged forward, slapping her palms over my mouth. My hands went instinctively out to stop her, but only ended up gripping her hips. We stared at each other, neither of us moving. Even now, her touch sent blood racing straight to my cock. The light blue material of her dress was so thin I could feel her heat. My thumbs slid in a circular motion over her lower abdomen before I could stop myself. I looked up at her, waiting to see what she would do next.

"Don't talk about… *them*. The countess might be using me to get back into court but the rebels have nothing to do with it. If anyone hears you say that—"

I moved my hands from her hips to her wrists and pried her hands away so I could speak. "What if someone does hear me? Are you afraid they'll learn the truth? That the rebels forced you to marry the prince so you could destroy the royal family from the inside."

"What? No," she hissed. "You don't understand."

"You better *make* me understand. Otherwise, I'll have no choice but to tell the prince." And, damn me—I didn't *want* to tell Bastian. What I wanted was for her to have a flawless excuse. Any excuse, really. A reason to keep her secret so she would be safe. And a magical solution to make this whole situation disappear.

Karina slumped, falling to the carpet in a heap, and I released her hands. The light from the fireplace danced over her hair as she bowed her head. "What you said is true," she admitted in a hoarse whisper. "I'm not Lady Karina. My mother isn't Countess Odelia and my father isn't King Jonty. Their real daughter caught a fever and died when she was three. No one in Port Black knew about it—we all thought she was kept inside because she was sickly, or ugly, or because the countess was so hateful. The servants weren't allowed out of the residence to spread rumors of the child's death so no one knew any better."

I folded my arms and glared down at her. "And?"

"And." She let out a shaking breath. "And, four years ago, the countess bought me from my parents to pretend. I know what you're thinking, but they're good people. It's just that my brother was born with health issues and we couldn't afford all the medical care he needed. My mother and father took the deal because my brother would get his treatments and I would become a lady. Everyone benefits, right?"

"And yet, here you are. Served up to the crown by the Red Asters."

She looked up at me then, eyes glistening with fear and defeat. "The rebels didn't plan any of this. Countess Odelia is only using me to return to court."

"Is that what she told you?" I asked. There was no way she believed that. So much effort must've gone into teaching Karina how to be a lady—even one that still lacked so many skills. She nodded. "And you believed her?"

"What other reason could there be?" she whispered.

I squeezed my eyes shut and let out a harsh sigh. "You're a bigger fool than I thought."

She laughed then, a broken, crumbling sound. "Yes. I'm thoughtless and uncultured and not fit to be a princess. But I never wanted to be one, never wanted any of this. I was seventeen when the countess took me home with her. I had a life. Friends, goals, and a future of my own choosing."

An irrational spike of jealousy ran through me. "A lover?"

"He was a friend, but things between us were changing. I don't think it was love but..." Karina turned her head away, toward the window. "It doesn't matter anymore, does it?"

My next breath was a little lighter, though I had no right to feel that way. "I'm sorry you missed out on that life." A quiet life. A *safe* life.

She scowled. "Are you?"

I crouched down so I could meet her gaze. She kept her eyes lowered so I reached out and tilted her chin up until she was looking at me. "Yes. I am."

"What will they do to me now?" Her voice quivered.

"Who?"

"Prince Bastian. King Edric. Lying to them is treason." Tears slipped from each eye, racing down her reddened cheeks. "Will they torture me before they kill me?"

I snatched my hand back as if her words burned. Lying *was* treason. Being as paranoid as the king was, he would most definitely order her *questioned* before having her publicly hanged. He would do the same to me if he discovered my deceit—only instead of a simple hanging, my stomach would be cut open first so my intestines could spill out as I swung from the noose. A shiver ran up my spine.

"Say nothing. *Do* nothing," I told her in a low voice.

She blinked in surprise. "You're not going to tell the prince?"

"I don't know yet." I winced. Enough things were kept hidden from Bastian—what was one more? But it also meant everything. Somehow, having her killed for lies similar to my own felt like the worse sin. Karina—*no*. She wasn't Lady Karina. She was someone else entirely. "What's your real name?" I asked before I could stop myself.

Her lips parted on an inhale as she studied my face through glassy eyes. Finally, she said, "Anais."

Anais. My pulse thudded with the forbidden knowledge. I wanted to speak it, to give it life, but saying it even once seemed like a bad omen. This was a secret—our secret—like the kisses in the garden.

"This conversation never happened." I stood and crossed the room to scoop up the box of chocolates. "Stand up. Fix yourself."

If I left her with wrinkled skirts and a tear-stained face, her ladies would know something happened. They would undoubtedly descend upon her the moment I left too. Demanding to know why I'd visited, though it wasn't their place to ask.

Karina climbed back onto unsteady feet and shook out her skirts. "What do I tell them?" she asked, apparently realizing she still looked a bit ruffled.

"Tell them to remember their place and not to question you." I walked toward her and held out the box. "Bastian was the reason I went to the market today. He bought you these."

Karina scowled at the blue box and took it gingerly from me. "Thank you."

Before I could stop myself, my hands cupped her face, wiping away the tears. "Please," I said in a raw voice. "Please don't be lying about this."

"About what?" Her breath was warm on my hands.

"Who you are. What you're doing here." My fingers dug in slightly where they rested at the nape of her neck. "Any of it."

"I'm not—"

"Because I can't protect you if you are," I said, cutting off her denial. "I shouldn't protect you now. I should leave here and tell the prince, but you make me lose common sense. Every time I come to you furious, I leave feeling something else entirely. Something that isn't guilt or hatred, even though I *should* hate you for lying to Bastian." *Just like I had lied.* He deserved someone who wouldn't do the same.

She stepped closer to me. "So why are you protecting me then?"

"Because I don't want them to hurt you." I tilted her head up more and lowered mine so there was only an inch between us. "Because every time I see you, I want to kiss you again."

"Why don't you?" she asked—*dared*—and her lids lowered in anticipation.

Fuck. I wanted to. I wanted to do *more* than kiss her. But I couldn't. Not now that there was no denying she was engaged to Bastian, secret identity or not.

Instead, I took one hand from her face and pried a corner of the box open, pulling out a single piece of chocolate. I brought it to her mouth and rested it on her lips until she opened for me. Her breath shook as it skated over my fingers. Pushing the treat into her mouth, I dragged my thumb across the inside of her lower lip and a small groan came from my chest.

I dipped my hand back into the box for a second piece. This time I put it into my own mouth. The semi-bitter flavor of dark chocolate exploded on my tongue and, with a single bite, sweet raspberry cream mixed with it, flooding my senses with rich ecstasy. My eyes caught on the tip of her tongue as it darted from between her lips, licking away any trace of chocolate. I forced myself to swallow.

"Now I know exactly what you would taste like if I did," I said in a husky voice.

Her breath hitched. My cock swelled.

Go. I urged myself. I'd already been alone with her for too long and the lady's maid was likely waiting in the hallway where I left her.

"I have to go," I told her and stepped back. A flush colored my face as she clutched the chocolate box with both hands. I turned my head toward the door before the sight of her, breathless and clearly wanting, made me change my mind about staying. "Remember. Say and do nothing."

"I won't," she promised.

Then fled the room faster than I'd entered it.

FIFTEEN

Whenever Bastian's stress threatened to overwhelm him, he would eat himself sick on meringues. It was his comfort food, he claimed, but I wasn't sure how comforting it was when his stomach turned on him. Four empty platters were now stacked on his small dining table while he laid in the middle of the floor. His crown sat on his bedside table where the servants had placed it, and he wore nothing but a loose pair of sleeping pants.

"I don't feel well," he groaned for a third time.

"Shocking," I mumbled.

"Why didn't you stop me from eating *all* of them?"

I snorted from my seat. "I told you that you'd regret it." *Just like I regretted nearly kissing Karina*—no, *Anais—earlier.* It had been a lie when I said I knew what she tasted like after eating a chocolate. She would taste *better* than that.

There had to be something wrong with me. She was a liar and an Aster pawn. But so was I. The only difference was that she didn't seem to know it while I was fully aware. Maybe that was why I felt a connection to her, though. Our pasts were different but, right now, we were both walking the same fine line. And I... I wanted her. Her beautiful smile, her laugh, the way she made my chest lighter. For the first time in my life, I wanted something specific. Not some vague sense of a life outside of protecting someone else. I wanted *her*. But I would have to settle for keeping her safe. Which meant not telling Bastian the truth even though it hurt like hell, and I definitely couldn't tell Faramond.

"You could simply *not* tell your father," I said. The meringue eating all started when I informed Bastian that the countess had been in Ora Et for at least a week, undetected. "There's no reason you and I should know Countess Odelia is here."

"You're not wrong."

I leaned my head back to stare at the tiled ceiling. "But you'll tell him anyway."

"Don't say it like that," he said on a moan.

"Like what?"

"Like I tell him everything." He scowled. "If something happens that will affect the country, I don't see how I can keep it to myself."

I nodded. What else could I do? Bastian and I were the closest of friends, but the king was the king. Even if Bastian would rule the country one day, he didn't rule it yet.

"Tomorrow though," he rolled onto his stomach and pushed onto his feet. "I'm going to bed now. You should too."

I should. But I had business left to take care of first. "Night."

The Governors' building was easier to sneak into than I originally thought. After keeping to the shadows and cutting through the garden, I slipped in the open servants' door, leaving the chilled air behind. I wore a gray robe over my uniform to masquerade as a manservant. No one noticed as I stepped past the entrance to the kitchens and crept through the passages meant for the workers to use, unseen by the residents.

Governor Pevran lived on the lowest level overlooking the front of the building which meant I didn't have to navigate any stairs. It took practically no time to slip through her door and find a place to hide. Her wardrobe was long, tall, and deep and contained multiple plain robes. There were other clothes too, though. Heavy wool dresses, perfect for winter, two cloaks, and lighter clothes for summer months. There was even a pair of loose men's slacks hanging beside the long sleeping gowns. I made sure to hide at the opposite end from those as she would likely change when she returned from her nightly trip to the bath house in about—

The bedroom door opened, my timing apparently off.

"No tea tonight," Governor Pevran said. A maid mumbled something in return. "No, no. Go on. I'm rather tired."

The door shut with a soft thud and my heart thumped. There was no going back now—it had to be done. She had to die. And I had to kill her. Still, my palms sweated when I pulled the dagger from my belt.

When the wardrobe opened, the governor reached inside and removed a lightweight violet dress. "If I'm to haunt this place, I will do it in style."

My blood ran cold at her words. Did she know? No one had seen me… Had they?

"Wherever you're hiding," she continued as clothing rustled, "you must be wondering how I know. I arranged the rug so the corner would flip up if the door was opened in my absence."

My chest tightened. Would she call the guards next? Had she already?

"I've been expecting you." The other wardrobe door swung open, exposing my hiding place. "Come now, assassin. Don't play me for a fool at the end."

Fuck.

I was caught, but she still didn't know who I was. There had to be a way out of this without exposing my identity.

Robes were pushed aside with a scrape of clothes hangers against a metal bar. Suddenly I was face-to-face with Pevran. Her hair was still wet, the violet dress hanging neatly over her frame. Fine wrinkles fanned out from the corners of her eyes. Her sharp inhale echoed.

"This is unexpected," she said softly, her gaze catching on the knife in my hand. "How long have you been working for the Asters?"

As if I would tell her anything. I leaned forward, my feet following the movement as she stepped back. I stood at my full height before her and regretted so many things. Everything that had been forced upon me. The things I'd done and would still do.

"I'm sorry," I croaked. "I don't want to do this."

"But if you don't, they'll kill you. Or expose you. Though, if you ask me, exposure is an empty threat. Why wouldn't a rebel sing like a bird if their own cause betrayed them? I suppose they know that though, and that's why you're here."

An empty threat. She was right. My stomach bottomed out. Faramond would never turn me in—I knew little about the Red Asters' plans, but I knew *enough*. They would simply kill me instead of risking a leak.

"Well, I knew this was coming after the tax ordeal, so let's make it quick, shall we?" She eyed the knife. "And perhaps less bloody."

"You're not going to call for help?" I asked before I could stop myself. Even if I knew I would die, I would *try* to save myself. Anyone would.

She laughed mirthlessly and moved to a jeweled box on her vanity. After pulling a key from a chain around her neck, she unlocked it. "I accepted this would be my fate long ago." She turned and met my eyes before downing the contents of a blue glass vial. "It took longer than expected for the day to come, but I'm more than ready to end this game. I thought I could do some good for the people but that wasn't what the Asters really wanted from me. Not from you either, I suspect."

Definitely not. I swallowed hard. "What did you drink?"

"A fast-acting poison that will make me sleep before stopping my heart." She sighed and retrieved another object from the box. An envelope. "A suicide note. Technically that's what just happened, so don't think of this as blood on your hands, Wing."

I replaced the knife on my belt with unsteady hands. "You could be lying. It could simply slow your pulse so I believe you're dead."

"It could do that." Her knees gave out but she caught herself on the vanity. "But you're welcome to stay and make sure."

I stood there, numb, and watched as she struggled to cross the room to her bed. The longer it took, the worse I felt. She'd taken away the burden of killing her, but I was still responsible in a way. *Faramond was responsible.* Not me. Pevran had expected her death long enough to have poison and a letter ready. She didn't even seem upset.

How could she be so… so…

"You should close the wardrobe," she mumbled as she settled on the mattress.

My body moved to the doors on its own, shutting them silently, feeling numb. "Do you need anything?"

"What could I possibly need now?" Pevran blinked heavy lids and motioned me forward with a wave of her hand. I inched closer and knelt at the side of her bed. "I spent too long living for other people. Don't make the same mistake."

"There's no way out of the Asters," I whispered.

"Run," she said on a labored exhale.

Then her eyes closed. Her chest slowed. A wheeze escaped her throat. Within a few minutes, she was gone.

I sat beside her for as long as I dared and contemplated her life. What had she done for the Asters? Why had she joined the cause? If she even had the choice. How had she come to change her mind? To expect betrayal?

But no answers would come now, so I stood. The lines in Pevran's face appeared to have eased with death, the worry carried away with her soul. I released a shallow breath and pulled a blanket up around her shoulders. Faramond had always been an asshole, but this only brought the realization to the front of my mind. I'd become too compliant, too afraid. Rightfully so. My next exhale shook with sorrow for Pevran, for all Asters forced into a similar position. Myself included.

SIXTEEN

"You're as graceful as a bull," the duchess lamented from inside the Women's Palace. "Again."

I paused outside the door as the old woman hummed a song. Dance lessons, if I had to guess, which wouldn't afford Anais and I a moment to talk. I'd thought about my last interaction with her—thought about it all night, even when Bastian was telling me about a newly proposed law. Faramond would've wanted me to pay attention to that conversation and pass the information along, but no matter how hard I tried, my mind wandered between Anais and Pevran instead.

Run.

Pevran's final warning tore through me like wildfire. Could I run? Where would I go? Bastian would be left vulnerable so I couldn't leave… But *she* could. Anais hadn't yet been introduced to the general nobility, and I doubted that the governors would recognize her after one dinner. Not if she wore common clothes. She would easily blend into any city after growing up in a city like Port Black. There would be no delicate noble mannerisms for her to overcome.

If Anais ran—if I *helped* her run—this nightmare would be over. She would be safe, Bastian wouldn't be engaged to a potential threat, and I would no longer need to fight wanting her with every breath.

Stepping into the doorway, I leaned on the frame. Anais took the steps of a popular Eradristian dance while the duchess circled her like a vulture, eyeing every movement. She made each step at the right time, kept her shoulders straight, head up, but there was no life to her dance. Instead of it being the lively, flirtatious dance it was meant to be, it was flat and mechanical. The distress it put on the duchess' face made me chuckle.

Somehow, the older woman heard it and rounded on me. The surprise on her face quickly gave way to pursed lips. "You find this funny, Lord Tufaro? Need I remind you how well *you* danced?"

"Ah," I said, forcing back another laugh. She'd made me learn how to dance even though I would never have the opportunity to use the skill. The prince would dance—the Wing would watch and protect. "I improved due to your careful instruction, duchess."

"A lot of good my teachings are doing *her*."

My gaze flicked to Anais. She stood in the middle of the room, arms crossed self-consciously. "In her defense, it *is* difficult without a partner."

The duchess stood straighter and clapped once. "Wonderful!"

I pushed off the doorframe. "That wasn't an offer."

"It sounded like one to me." She motioned me forward with a sweep of her arm.

"I'm not sure that's appropriate." A hand on her hip. Our bodies pressed together. The way I knew she would follow me across the dance floor, giving me far too much trust. I hated the idea. And I wanted it desperately.

"Appropriate," she scoffed. "The prince asking you to sneak over here and check on her isn't appropriate either. Why doesn't he come himself— and don't give me any nonsense about the king wanting him to avoid attention. You pull the same amount that he does."

I'd asked myself the same thing multiple times. King Edric didn't want to call attention to Lady Karina's presence before she was ready to be seen by the court, but Bastian could see Anais in the Women's Palace with a chaperone. He was busy, but not so busy that he couldn't take breakfast with her. Not that I could complain. Watching Bastian court her wasn't high on my list of things to do.

"As I'm sure you've heard, Governor Pevran passed away last night," I said as emotionlessly as possible. Bastian had been pulled from his bed hours earlier for an emergency meeting about the situation and I hadn't seen him since. The rumors had spread, however, claiming everything from a bloodbath to natural causes. "Besides, unlike His Highness, I am able to get here unseen."

"Yes, yes. A shadow, you are," the duchess mumbled. "Now, dance with the lady before I'm forced to present *this* to your prince at the engagement ball."

Engagement ball? I hadn't realized they were having one. It was a royal tradition though, so I should've expected it. A ball to celebrate the bride or groom with the nobility before the official announcement to the kingdom. Anais was going to need to master harder dances than this.

"Perhaps," Anais spoke up, "we could ask one of the servants to dance with me instead."

The duchess grabbed my elbow and practically dragged me inside. "You think any of them know how to dance? Are you trying to make yourself *worse*?"

Logically, the suggestion of dancing with a servant instead of me should've been a relief. A way out of tempting myself unnecessarily. But it wasn't. I wasn't a jealous man—I'd accepted that I wouldn't have what normal people did—but the idea of her so close to someone else had me pursing my lips. *She'll be close to Bastian one day, closer than dancing*, I reminded myself. A mistake. All it did was send me striding up to her.

I took Anais' hand and her small gasp went straight through me. She looked toward the duchess with wide eyes, almost as if she were hoping for a reprieve. When we'd last seen each other, things had ended with a tense truce, but with the duchess here, I couldn't ask what happened to make her so nervous. Though, perhaps it was the same thing that happened to me; common sense returned.

"Relax," I whispered, looking down at our hands. Hers was small in mine, flawless where mine was scarred and calloused. "It's just a dance."

She let out a quick breath as she situated her other hand on my shoulder. "That's impossible around you."

"Do I scare you now?" I asked, one brow lifted. In the garden, she'd denied being afraid and, more than anything, I didn't want that to change.

She looked down to study her feet. "You told me you scare everyone."

But not her. I placed my free hand on her hip, fingers wrapping around to her lower back, and tugged her closer. "Do I scare *you* though?"

She chewed her bottom lip instead of answering. I'd had stab wounds feel better than her response.

"Don't look at your feet," the duchess scolded. "You know the steps. Let him lead."

"Easy for you to say," Anais mumbled.

Duchess Fransabelle began her off-tune humming again and I moved, pulling Anais with me. It had been years since I'd danced. My last opportunity had been just before the duchess left court, when she made me participate in one of Bastian's final lessons, but it came back naturally as I spun through the room. She missed steps and stumbled along, but I kept her up, kept her moving. I wouldn't let her fall. Not here, dancing, and not to the Asters' scheming.

Because she would eventually. Faramond was playing a song Anais couldn't hear with steps she hadn't learned, but one day, she would be expected to perform the rebel's dance with precision.

On our second lap around the room, Anais' muscles relaxed slightly. I felt her give over control of our steps. Felt her decide to follow. But the small sliver of trust was overshadowed by her reaction to my previous question.

"What have I done to change your mind?" I asked quietly enough so Fransabelle couldn't hear. I'd discovered her secret, but no one had stormed into the Women's Palace to arrest her. No one else knew—not even Bastian—as I had promised. At least, until I sorted through what was going on.

She glanced down at our feet, earning a tap of the duchess' cane on the marble floor. "I'm not… scared of you," she said, leveling her gaze at the silver wing pinned to my chest.

She was. I could see it in the way she blushed, hear it in the hesitation of her reply. Maybe she wasn't *as* afraid of me as everyone else, but it was there. Lingering.

"I don't blame you for it," I said. "But, you should know, I haven't said anything."

"Not yet."

My grip on her hip tightened slightly. "I don't want to see you die, Anais."

"Don't call me that," she hissed, body tensing beneath my hands. "Weren't you the one to tell me someone was always listening?"

"Less talking, more dancing," the duchess snapped.

I gave *Karina* a stiff smile and spoke without moving my lips. "We need to talk privately."

"Again?"

Always. "I'll find you."

The duchess slapped my arm with the end of her cane, but through the bracer, it barely registered. "Stop distracting her."

"I'm giving her suggestions, duchess," I lied.

"Leave the teaching to me and dance. From the beginning." She began humming again.

We moved in silence then, running through the steps three times. My eyes were glued to Anais' face. Each time she did something wrong, she pursed her lips, and when she didn't stumble over the more complicated steps, the corners of her lips twitched in the threat of a smile. I was hyperaware of where our skin met, of the heat of her hip through her gown. It took constant conscious thought not to pull her flush against me. If I slid my hand from her hip to her lower back, I knew I would find bare skin where the dark red fabric swooped down to showcase the rows of beads. It was fucking torture being this close to her, her scent of wildflowers beckoning. And, if the redness of her cheeks was any indication, she felt the same way.

"Enough," Fransabelle said when the song ended. "All this humming has dried my throat."

"I'll order tea," Anais said, quickly pulling away from me and hurrying toward one of the side doors.

I turned to face Fransabelle. "She isn't so bad."

"*Hmm.*" The duchess narrowed her eyes. "I'm an old woman, Saer, but I'm not senile."

I lowered my brows. "I don't know what you mean."

"You know *exactly* what I mean," she said, and turned her back to me. "Have the tea brought to the terrace. This might be one of our last decent days before winter settles in."

My heart thumped heavily as I realized she saw the connection between Anais and me. "I should go."

"Indeed."

I watched her shuffle from the room, through the doors to the small porch. Did she know we'd kissed? No, that was impossible. My visiting Anais in her rooms was another story. Anais returned from ordering tea and glanced between me and the terrace.

Without thinking, I closed the distance between us before she ran straight to the duchess' side. Lifting her hand, it appeared to anyone watching that I was telling her to have a pleasant afternoon. "Make an excuse to return to your rooms."

"Wh—"

I spun on my heel and left. Or appeared to leave. Instead of heading for the gate, I circled back around and slipped through the servants' door. Unlike the governors building, it wasn't the middle of the night so the chances of being caught were so much higher. As soon as I saw a door into a main hall, I took it and navigated the same halls I'd found while searching for the library. A maid hummed somewhere nearby. *Fuck.* I ducked into the first room I came upon.

Blue tiles covered the floor and walls of a bathing chamber. In the middle of the room hung a delicate chandelier with two dozen unlit candles, and below it, a large bath set into the floor. A lounge sat on the other side of it with a bushy plant placed at each end.

Footsteps moved at a brisk pace in the hallway and I plastered myself to the wall, waiting to hear the click of gemstones that would tell me it was Anais and not a servant. When I heard the soft sound, I opened the door and grabbed Anais' arm, tugging her into the bathing room with me.

"Shh," I warned quietly in her ear as I pushed the door shut. "Your lady's maid must've told Fransabelle that I was here the other night."

Anais pulled her arm free. "Don't do that."

"What?"

"You can't just go around pulling people into rooms." She placed her hands on my chest and pushed me back a step. Only, once there was space between us, she didn't remove them. "It's not polite to sneak up on a lady."

I smirked and curled my hands around her wrists, holding her against me. "It isn't polite to invade a man's private sanctuary either, yet you continued to visit the garden despite my warnings."

"That's different." Her chest rose and fell with quickened breaths, drawing my attention.

"Is it?" I leaned forward, reaching behind her to click the lock into place, and inhaled her intoxicating scent. A quivering breath left her, breaking my thin strand of control. My tongue flicked out, tracing the curve of her ear.

Her fingers curled into my shirt. "Saer."

It wasn't a warning, but a plea. I backed her against the door and lifted her chin with my finger. "I didn't ask you here for this," I said in a hoarse voice.

"I know." Back arched, her breasts skimming my chest. "If you aren't planning to turn me in and you don't want to kiss me—"

A low growl left my throat as I pressed my mouth to hers. She tasted like strawberries and all things forbidden as I slipped my tongue past her lips. Her hands wrapped around the back of my neck, locking me in place. As if I would stop. I wasn't sure I could've at the moment. Not unless she told me to.

I gripped her waist, shifting her against me, letting her *feel* the effect she had on me. A small moan escaped her and I snapped. My kisses became rougher, more demanding, and she met them with equal enthusiasm. My thigh pressed between her legs. Her heat soaked through all the material separating us and I gripped the fabric of her dress at both hips.

My lips moved from Anais' mouth to her neck. She tilted her head to give me better access and trailed her hands down my chest. Slowly, with more patience than I felt, I gathered her skirt a little higher. With each handful I lifted, I expected her to stop me, but, instead, she shifted her hips, allowing the fabric to move easier. And, in the process pressed her core against my leg.

When my fingertips grazed her bare thigh, my body shuttered. "Fuck."

"Please," she moaned, grinding against me.

I eased my leg away and her soft whine filled my ears. "Shh." I took her bottom lip gently between my teeth and tugged. "Anyone could be in the hall."

Letting her gown drop, I led her farther into the room, around the bath and away from the door. Her pupils were blown wide as she looked up at me. The desire in her gaze made my pants uncomfortably tight.

"Sit," I ordered when the lounge was just behind her."

She lowered herself, perching on the very edge of the cushion, then reached for my belt. With one pull, she had it undone.

"Anais," I breathed. This time she didn't correct me. She only slid her hand inside my pants and released my hard length. "Shit."

Her hand felt so good against me. *So damn good.* My head fell back, eyes closed, and she stroked me. Bringing me closer and closer. "Stop," I growled just before I could come all over her. There would be no hiding the stain on her gown.

"But—"

I dropped to my knees in front of her and lifted her skirts again, sliding a hand beneath. The moment my fingers brushed against the wet heat there, her hips jerked. "Look at me," I told her. "I want to watch you fall apart."

Her eyes locked on mine and I slid two fingers across her soaked entrance. Then inside. Her warm walls squeezed my fingers and I felt it all the way to my cock. *Fuck.* I couldn't let it go that far. Things had already gone—

"Saer," she urged, shifting to ride my fingers. "Don't stop."

I pressed my thumb against the bundle of nerves and rubbed in circles as I eased my fingers farther. Pumped her with them until I felt her quiver. I wanted to look down, to see myself inside her, but I wanted to see her expression more.

Her breathing picked up and she lifted herself to meet my fingers. I quickly placed my free hand over her mouth. Not a moment too soon either. A muffled cry of pleasure filled the bathroom as her walls gripped me. Her eyes shut then, hiding what I wanted most, but my cock throbbed so badly with need that I couldn't see straight.

My strokes slowed as her release came to an end and I pulled away. With the same fingers that had just been inside her, I grabbed my cock and pumped, hard and fast. Pleasure built with every stroke. I pictured myself inside her, her legs wrapped around my hips, her back arching, my name on her lips as I buried myself deep. *Fuck.* I exploded hard all over the tile with a low groan.

I rested my head on Anais' knee, utterly spent, and waited for the aftershocks to fade. Once I could speak again, I stood, tucking myself back in my pants.

When she didn't move, didn't speak, I asked, "Are you okay?"

"Yes," she said, voice wobbling.

My gaze snapped to hers immediately. She didn't *sound* okay. "What's wrong?" I took her hands and pulled her to her feet, guiding her around the mess I made. "Did I hurt you? I didn't mean—"

"No. I'm fine, really."

I took her face between my hands. "You're lying. Tell me."

"I… I wish things were different, is all. I don't like sneaking around like this." She pushed my hands away and turned to examine one of the plants. I opened my mouth to ask again what happened but she drew a sharp breath. "I should leave."

Panic banded my chest. "Please—"

"Please what?" she asked when I choked on the rest of my words.

Please don't hate me. Don't be afraid of me. Don't push me away. Though she should do all three. She was going to marry Bastian, unless I revealed her secret. But that would be *worse* than watching her with my best friend. "I'm sorry." I swallowed hard. She'd *wanted* me to kiss her so where did I fuck up? What part of this was too far? "About what we just did. I didn't mean for it to happen. I only wanted to ask you what the duchess knew, but I can't stop wanting you."

Her fingers touched my lips to silence me. "You have to. *We* have to. If anyone found out about this…"

"I've *tried*. Do you think I want to betray Bastian like this? He's all I have in this world, but it's impossible to get you out of my head." I brushed a loosened lock of hair from my face and held back a frustrated scream. The gods hated me, but I couldn't let them win. Everything would be fine—because Anais would be gone soon enough. "I'm going to get you out of here. It's not too late."

She drew in a sharp breath. "I can't leave. My family—"

"I'll take care of them," I promised. Though I didn't know how. "You can't stay here. It's too dangerous." Between the Asters, her fake countess mother, her true identity, and *this*, it was only a matter of time before her fate was sealed.

"And what about you?" Her eyes narrowed. "You know all my secrets, but what of yours? Do I not get to hear them?"

The only sound was my pulse as I considered revealing everything. My whole, sordid truth. But I'd seen the toughest men break during interrogation. She wouldn't stand a chance against the masochists employed by the king, and I wouldn't risk myself. "I can't tell you. Not yet." Maybe one day, if she was safe, and if Bastian was king. He could change the laws.

Allow me a family of my own. But for that to work, the Asters would need to crumble.

"Then how can I trust you?" she asked, matter-of-factly. "You asked if I was afraid of you? I'm not. At least, not how you think. I'm afraid you're not real."

"Not real?" I asked in confusion.

She sighed. "You're the only one here who can hurt me. I don't mean what will happen if anyone finds out I'm not the countess' daughter, but I mean right now, the way things stand. If the prince hates me, I can live with that. It's fine if the court ridicules me and the governors object to my presence. But *you*? I care what you think about me. And that means, if all of this is a lie to find out more information—information I don't have—it won't be fine. *I* won't be."

I furrowed my brow. What was she talking about? Did she think I was using her for information about the countess? There would be easier, less treasonous ways of doing that. "Fuck information. Do you think I would hurt my only friend like this if there wasn't something real between us? I hate myself for it, but I've never felt like this before. It doesn't matter who you are or what you know." I stepped toward her and, when she didn't back away, pulled her into an embrace. "Please understand. I can't risk more than I'm already giving you. And, I know we will have to give up on *us* because you'll either marry Bastian or I'll succeed in getting you far away from here. Know that I am real, though. To you more than anyone else."

Anais wrapped her arms around my torso and sniffled. She said nothing, but she didn't need to. Holding her was enough. But as the minutes stretched on, as we both calmed the other, reality slipped back in. The duchess would be looking for her soon, and I had to wait for the prince to leave the Main Palace.

"Go," I urged, placing a kiss on top of her head. "Return to your room, crawl into bed, and summon a lady's maid. Feign illness or Fransabelle will demand an excuse for how long you've taken."

She nodded. "What about you?"

"I'll clean up in here and leave, unseen."

She hesitated before going, but once she had left the room, I grabbed a towel to wipe the floor. Once the evidence was gone, I knelt there a little longer, trying to stuff the nauseous guilt back into its cage.

SEVENTEEN

Fine mist floated above the pathway as Bastian led the way to the Main Palace. He shrugged his dark blue jacket on as he walked, his rumpled head-servant hurrying behind with his scabbard.

I followed, still fastening my own weapons on, unsure if this crack-of-dawn wakeup was due to an intruder. If that were the case, walking the main paths was incredibly foolish. "Give me that," I told the servant and took Bastian's sword from him. "Bast, what's going on?"

"My father called an emergency meeting about the new governor." He finished his last button and reached for his scabbard. "He's anxious to fill the position and move on."

With both hands now free, I gathered my hair into a bun at the nape of my neck. *But with* this *much urgency?*

They'd barely given us time to dress, and Bastian's crown was braided onto his head with so much haste that it was slightly crooked.

"And—" he slowed his steps slightly "—there's supposed to be an announcement about the wedding."

I stiffened. *The wedding.* I hadn't found out what the Asters' plan for that was yet. Why Anais was pretending to be the countess' daughter and what she was meant to do. She wasn't aware of the particulars, but she would be eventually. At the same time they threatened to expose her secret if she didn't murder Bastian in his sleep.

"She's been well?" the prince asked for what felt like the millionth time since he'd told me to spend time with her. "I shouldn't be concerned?"

The sound of her moans in the bathroom filled my head and I winced. How was I this much of an asshole? "Concerned about what?"

"You know." Bastian shrugged. "We'll get along, won't we?"

I wanted so badly to say no. To tell him she was awful and that he would hate her. But it would be a lie. "Yes."

"You'll see her again today?" the prince pressed.

I opened my mouth to say no, but what would I give as a reason? That I needed to spend the morning figuring out how to get Anais as far from the palace and Ora Et as possible? I didn't want to add to the betrayal with another lie, but if I saw her again... *No.* There could be no repeat of yesterday.

"If you'd like me to," I answered.

"Please." The prince paused outside the entrance to the Main Palace. "And... and tell her that I look forward to seeing her again."

I swallowed hard. "I will."

Bastian smiled warmly and stepped away, toward the gate. "Wish me luck."

Good luck. We'd both need it.

The duchess was alone when I entered the Women's Palace. A velvet couch had been added to the main room where we'd danced the day before. A small table and two matching chairs across from it, and Fransabelle sat, prim and proper, in one of them. Today, her deep red mourning gown stretched up her neck and fanned out just below her chin. I approached slowly so as not to startle her as she stared at nothing. When I was nearly at her side, the duchess blinked.

"You're back," she said stoically.

I nodded. "The prince asked me to deliver a message."

"Did he?" She huffed. "Sit. I need to talk to you."

I perched uncomfortably on the edge of the second chair.

"I've seen the way you look at each other," the duchess said bluntly. "Be careful, Wing."

Heat flashed through my body. She didn't need to elaborate—it was clear what she meant. Me and Anais. I counted myself lucky that *looking* was all she accused me of.

"I don't know what you mean, Duchess."

She leveled a stare in my direction. "You do."

"Duchess, I—"

"I've lived for a long, *long* time so save your breath. You're loyal to the prince, but that won't stop the rumors from spreading. People will see the same thing I do. What will the king do then? If he suspects you're even *thinking* inappropriately about the future queen, he'll have your head."

"I'm Bastian's only Wing," I reasoned. "He needs me."

"Does he? With you gone, King Edric won't have to worry about his son stealing his crown," she said in a lowered voice. "There's a reason Bastian doesn't have a pair of Wings."

Bastian didn't want to steal the crown. He didn't *need* to steal it—it would be his when the king died. But, without a Wing, the king's only heir might not live long enough to inherit anything. "Bastian is his son."

"He can always sire more children," she reminded me. "All he needs is a wife young enough, and he won't have trouble finding one."

"Even King Edric isn't that uncaring," I mumbled, knowing it was a lie. He was ruthless and paranoid. The duchess was right. Any number of women would kill to become queen and birth royal children. History was full of women who poisoned or maimed their way onto the throne.

Fransabelle sighed. "Do what you will with my warning."

"Duchess," came a low female voice. A heavy woman stood in the doorway leading farther into the palace. Scissors poked out of the apron tied at her waist and a long blue ribbon was draped around her shoulders. "Would you like to see the gown?"

"Of course, I want to see it," she snapped. Then, quieter, to me, "What does she think I'm here for? As if the countess bothered to tell her daughter what was needed from an engagement gown."

The soft tinkling of gems preceded Anais' appearance. My heart skipped at the sound, then stopped all together when she stepped into the room. A deep blue gown hugged her torso and flared slightly away from her hips, the fabric cascading down into a short train. Diamonds swirled over the bodice before spreading evenly across the skirts. Strands of the precious stones wrapped around her neck to form a collar, longer ones reaching to swoop over her arms, the longest nearly reaching her elbow. Her hair was pinned haphazardly, likely to get it out of the way for the dressmaker, but the jumbled look with the ball gown hit me like a bolt.

The duchess smacked my shin with her cane before telling Anais, "Turn."

Anais carefully avoided looking at me as she spun slowly. A single strand of diamonds fell straight down her bare spine and ended with a larger teardrop stone at the end.

"It will do," the duchess finally said.

The dressmaker bowed and ushered Anais back through the door.

"*That* look," she hissed at me. "Give me the prince's message and leave. I don't have time for this today."

I cleared my throat and told her that the prince looked forward to seeing Karina again. Then, without another word, I fled the palace and the discerning duchess. My hands shook, my gut churning, as I retreated into the gardens to clear my head. To silence the roar in my ears and the cracking of my heart.

EIGHTEEN

The official engagement announcement of Prince Bastian Alexander Drystan, Duke of Pegia, Lord of the Vargyn Mountains and Lady Karina of House Thiselles felt heavy in my hand. It had been written by expert calligraphers and embellished with gold leaf. Fitting for a royal wedding, especially the first of the new monarchy. Every noble family would receive one and, after the rumors spread, it would be confirmed to the citizens of Eradrist. The entire country would know before the ball, breaking tradition, but that wasn't what concerned me.

If I was going to get Anais out, it had to be now. She was too beautiful for every noble to forget her face. The governors at a dimly-lit dinner, happily sipping on wine, were enough of a risk, but *all of Eradrist* was impossible.

But I still had no idea how to do that safely for both of us. Now that the announcements had gone out, there would be professionals coming to plan the rest of the wedding. Florists, chefs, seamstresses, musicians. The ceremony would take place in the spring which left only four months to prepare a wedding gown, cake, and whatever else was involved in a wedding. Which meant Anais would be constantly surrounded.

A thousand new faces, a thousand potential assassins.

Heat flashed through my body at the thought of her in mortal danger. I couldn't protect her and Bastian at the same time, and he still refused to visit to the Women's Palace. *Nerves* was the only reason I could come up with. But now *I* was the one that had to worry. More so than usual. An image of her in a pool of blood rose, unbidden, to the front of my mind, but I pushed it away, replacing it with the moment she fell through the hedge wall. How she'd felt in my arms when I caught her. The first whiff of wildflowers. Still, my hands began to sweat where I clutched the engagement announcement.

"Are you going to stare at that all day?" the prince asked, turning a page of a book while sitting in his favorite chair.

I flicked the announcement at him, hitting his ear. "That depends. Are you going to read all day?"

Bastian had seemed to earn himself some free time now that the engagement was settled with the governors. The king had resumed some of the duties he'd passed to Bastian, claiming the prince had learned them well enough. A shit excuse for not wanting his own son to become overly influential.

His cheeks turned pink. "One of the maids told me this is Lady Karina's favorite novel. I want to finish it today so we can talk about it when I visit tomorrow."

"Favorite novel?" I snorted, knowing full well it was my jealousy speaking. That he knew something about Anais that I didn't, even though I alone knew her real name. "I wasn't aware she read for enjoyment."

Bastian quirked a brow at me. "Why wouldn't she?"

Because she looked miserable in the library. The material the duchess forced on her wasn't exactly *fun* though. I shrugged and turned my attention to the window. The sky was gray and miserable, the most relatable sort of weather. Who could I trust to help get Anais away from the capital? I could only take her so far myself without being obvious, and the Asters made damn sure that I trusted no one.

"A tailor is coming tomorrow, by the way," Bastian said, flipping a page. "We're both being fitted for the ball."

My eyes snapped to his. "I don't need anything."

He snorted. "Your arms nearly popped the seams of your uniform at dinner with the governors."

Relentless training was to blame for that, but I still didn't want a new uniform. I didn't want anything from Bastian or the crown, unless it was my freedom. Or Anais'.

"He'll likely fit us for the wedding while he's here too."

My heart twisted in my chest. *The wedding.* There would be no fucking wedding if I could help it.

"What's that face for?" Bastian asked.

I relaxed my brows and turned to the window again. "Seems strange to think you'll be married."

He laughed. "Strange, yes, not in a bad way."

That night, after Bastian fell asleep with the book over his face, I snuck into Anais' chambers. I shouldn't have. It was reckless and unnecessary and completely out of my control. If I paced my personal room any longer, I would've gone crazy.

She slept on her side, half-hugging a pillow, with her braided hair curling over her neck. I wanted to kiss her awake, swallow the shocked sound that would surely escape her, but somehow, I gathered enough willpower not to. As gently as possible, I placed a hand over her mouth instead. She jolted awake, and I pressed against her a little harder as she began to flail, clawing at my bracer to no avail.

"Shh," I urged. "It's me."

Anais paused, her hands still clutching my arm, and made an inquisitive, muffled sound. Slowly, I lifted my hand and stepped back. I rubbed my hand on my pants in an attempt to erase the feel of her warm breath.

"What are you doing here, Saer?" she whispered.

"I wanted to see you." I looked away and rubbed the back of my neck. How ridiculous did I sound? Like a— My eyes caught on an open letter on the bedside table. Before she could realize I'd noticed, I snatched

it from the desk and brought it toward the fireplace to
read.

"A letter from your mother?" I said in a tight voice.
The word *Daughter* was scrawled in tight, feminine
writing. "She misses you and hopes you'll invite her to
court soon?"

Anais leapt from the bed. "That's mine."

I held the paper above my head and continued.
"Remember your duty?"

Anais bared her teeth and leapt for the page, her
chest brushing against mine. I felt every inch of her all
the way down to my cock. It wasn't until she leapt
again and I stepped back to avoid her body that I
realized she wore a sheer white nightdress. And,
despite the blazing fireplace, her nipples were hard. I
ripped my gaze away from the dusty pink peaks to her
flushed face. "You should burn this."

She crossed her arms, unknowingly making things
worse as the mounds of her breasts peeked out from
the swoop of her neckline. "Why? It's not
incriminating."

"Everything is incriminating," I said, tossing it into
the fire.

"Not having any correspondence with my mother
is *more* suspicious." She narrowed her eyes. "Why do
you think I left it out on the table?"

I glared at her then, defiance shining in her eyes.
My cock throbbed. *Fuck*. Not acceptable. I grabbed a
blanket from a nearby chair and threw it at her,
perhaps a little too harshly. "Cover yourself."

Anais scowled and let the blanket drop to the floor.
"You may be the Prince's Wing, but you're not mine.
You don't have an obligation to protect me."

I scowled down at her, jealousy and a desperate boldness brimming. "Don't I?"

"You're sworn to protect Prince Bastian above anything and anyone else. Letters from the countess to her daughter aren't something to concern yourself with."

Hearing the prince's given name from her mouth snapped my restraint. Every step I took, she took one back until she hit the wall. With nowhere to go, she looked up at me with wide eyes. It wasn't fear I saw there, but something else. Something primal.

"I will protect Bastian's life with my own." I leaned down to speak in her ear. "But that doesn't mean I can't protect yours in the process."

"And sneaking into my room in the middle of the night is protecting me? What if someone comes to check on me?" she asked in an uneven voice.

I ran the tip of my nose down her bare throat. "Do they often check on you when you're sleeping?"

"If I'm sleeping, how would I know?"

"I don't think they do." I grazed the edge of her shoulder with my teeth and smiled when she shivered. "Your lady's maids are asleep or *occupied* with guards. There is one man in the hall outside, and he's asleep by now too."

Anais placed her hands on my chest as if to push me away but didn't. "How do you know?"

"It's my job to know things, my lady."

She did push me then. Though she wasn't strong enough to move me, I stepped away, and she darted around me. "You shouldn't be here."

"Trust me," I said humorlessly. "I'm aware."

When I turned to face her, she sat on the edge of
the bed, watching me. The firelight danced over her,
drawing me in like a moth. "Bastian will come see you
tomorrow," I forced myself to say, and her eyes fell to
her lap. I trailed a hand over her hair, down her braid,
and lifted the end. "What's your favorite book?"

"What?"

"Your favorite book," I repeated without meeting
her curious gaze. "What is it?"

"I don't have one."

"Are you lying?" I twirled the hair around my
fingers, memorizing the silky feel of it.

She tilted her head. "Why would I lie about that
when you know much more scandalous things about
me?"

I made a low, thoughtful sound. "Bastian was
reading your favorite book today so you could talk
about it tomorrow."

"He was?" she asked, surprised.

A sliver of bitterness worked its way to the surface.
"Does that make you happy? Knowing you'll have a
husband willing to do things like that for you? He'll
treat you well for the rest of your life."

She winced. "But how long will my life *be* if I marry
him?"

Not long. He would find out the truth eventually.
Someone from Port Black could recognize her, an
angry governor would eventually start digging into her
past, or the Red Asters would play their hand. "We'll
never know, because you're leaving before the
wedding."

"Saer, I can't—"

"Trust me." It was asking a lot. More than I was capable of. But I would do whatever necessary to stop this impending disaster from happening.

Anais studied my face for a moment, though I wasn't sure what she was looking for. Then she reached out and grabbed my beltloops. "If I trust you, will you stay?"

"No." I pulled her hands away gently. After what happened in the bathroom—and what she said following it—I had to do better. *Be* better. "The situation hasn't changed which means, if I stay, you'd regret it later."

"Things can be different if I don't marry the prince." She twisted free of my grip and slid across the bed to make room for me. "We can have each other however we want without guilt."

A low growl built in my chest as I leaned one knee onto the mattress. *Fuck.* I wanted what she was offering more than anything else in that moment, but I couldn't. "When I get you out of the palace, we won't see each other again."

She inhaled sharply. "Why?"

"Because if you want to remain safe, you need to stay away." I gripped her ankle and pulled her body closer. Then I swung her legs sideways and flung the covers up over her. "Go to sleep, Anais."

"I'm not tired."

I chuckled, but the humor quickly faded as I hovered over her. My pants grew uncomfortably tight and I fisted her blankets. "Then close your eyes." I lowered myself so my lips hovered just above hers without touching. "Imagine that I stayed. Imagine my hands on your body, my tongue on your skin. And, when I leave and you press your fingers inside yourself, pretend it's me."

"Saer," she breathed.

That was all I could give her. Those words. If I was going to let her go, I couldn't risk my heart more than I already had. And, if I failed to save her, I still wanted to be able to look Bastian in the eye. The small bit of hope that I held onto for happiness was at an end.

"I would make you moan loud enough to wake the entire palace," I promised. Then I placed a brutal kiss to her lips and left through the unlocked window.

Landing quietly on my feet behind a large bush, I checked the area and moved through the shadows all the way back to my room. My cock was so stiff, it hurt. I knew if I did anything about it, I would feel guilty for it after, but I could barely breathe from the want. Before I could stop myself, my hand wrapped around the hard length.

And I pretended too. Pretended that Anais was doing exactly as I told her—fingers inside, imagining they were mine. My name on her lips.

NINETEEN

rrow nocked. String taught. Target area cleared. I took a deep breath and released. The arrowhead pierced the straw man straight through the heart as I reached for another. There were too many soldiers training today to spar. I'd gotten a lecture more than once that showcasing my skills was too distracting for the younger men.

As if *showcasing* was my intent. I only ever wanted to improve and, at the same time, work out my frustrations. The fact that the leaders referred to the men as *younger* was laughable too—I had trained in this very arena while they sat on their mothers' hips. Another arrow left my bow and sank into the target's left eye. Or, what would've been an eye if it were more than straw bound together into a man's silhouette.

Another and another followed, leaving the target utterly vanquished. I set the bow on the table beside me and sighed as the steward ran out to retrieve the arrows. My gaze went to the groups of men. Some ran drills with spears while standing in formation, others used dulled swords in pairs or against more straw men. No one else had dared approach archery while I trained there, not that I was surprised.

The high, stone walls and dirt floor of the arena had seen me humiliated, whipped, and torn down repeatedly through the years. Ostracized from the others due to my position as Wing, and then, later, because I'd defeated both of the King's Wings in a battle meant for show. *Meant to show the King's strength.* Not mine nor, through association, Bastian's.

"My Lord Wing," the steward said, setting the arrows down beside me.

"Thanks," I mumbled.

The group of youths near the entrance suddenly went still, taking a knee. An eerie silence filled the air. No more clashing metal or stomping of feet. I snagged my bow, nocked an arrow, and began to raise it as Bastian stepped into view.

He wore leather training gear instead of his usual embroidered finery but his coronet was still in place. The sun glinted off the silver where it peeked from beneath his braids. I lowered the bow and walked out to meet him with sweaty palms.

Dulled swords and low skillsets didn't mean no one would take a swing at the prince. They would die for it, but if anyone were foolish enough to try, they likely wouldn't give a shit about that. *The Red Asters would remember their bravery!* Idiots. The Red Asters wouldn't give a shit. I narrowed my eyes and scowled at the men around us.

"Your Highness," I said with a bow. "What are you doing here?"

Bastian clapped me on the shoulder. "The meeting finished early and the guards said you were training."

"I would've come to get you." I did my best not to sound like I was scolding the prince in front of everyone, but my nerves were fraying more and more the longer we stood there.

"The prince was worried he'd gotten rusty."

Volney.

I gripped the bow so hard I thought it would snap. The King's Wing had escorted Bastian *here*? We could've trained together at the Prince's Palace or cleared the arena to eliminate any threats.

Bastian lifted his sword, the sheath already unbuckled from his belt. "Should we practice like old times?"

I glowered over his shoulder at Volney. *Fucking bearded prick.* "If you wish, but it might be wiser to go elsewhere."

"Nonsense." Bastian drew his sword and threw the sheath at Volney's face. "Clear a space," he ordered.

Fuck.

I had to let him beat me in front of the men. But, when he did, I would probably be mandated to train harder when Volney reported it back to the king. No one had forced me to train in years. Though I enjoyed it, doing it at my leisure was one of the only choices I had been allowed to make.

"Shall I warm him up for you, Your Highness?" Volney asked.

Bastian shot a curious glance at the Wing and opened his mouth—probably to say no—when I cut him off.

"A rematch?" I forced a laugh. Letting *him* win could earn my way back into the Main Palace. If Volney alone beat me, then surely Volney *and* Nen would be able to keep the king safe from my imagined assassination attempts. "I'd be more than happy to beat you again."

"Saer," Bastian warned.

"It's fine," I assured him and drew the sword at my hip. Then I pointed to two of the most skilled men. "If anything happens to the prince while I fight, it will be your heads."

The order made them bristle. They were older than me and in charge of entire battalions, but not as highly ranked as I was. They flanked Bastian and escorted him toward the wall to better protect his back.

Once I knew he was well guarded, a quick glance told me the soldiers had moved to give us more room. I hadn't even lowered into the proper stance before Volney struck out. The tip of his sword soared straight for my abdomen and I stumbled back a step to avoid it.

He used my poor footing to his advantage and spun with the sword, turning completely around before I could steady myself, and slammed a fist into my jaw. I landed on my ass and rolled, narrowly avoiding a boot to the throat.

Fighting to kill, are we?

I launched myself up. His eyes were on my sword, not on the small dagger I slipped from my bracer. It flew from my fingers, slicing his thigh, before he even knew what happened. Volney's sword flew upward as he howled, catching my blade midair. He glared at me, teeth bared behind his untrimmed beard, and I felt the hate pulse from him

Let him win.

Let him.

It was easier said than done as he swept out a leg, knocking me to the ground. Fucking dirty fighting. I wanted to trace his smirk with my blade, etch it permanently into his features. But instead, I forced myself up. Made a few clumsy swings. Blocked. Countered. Made it look real.

And then, when I got behind him with the intent to land at least one good blow before letting him disarm me, he whirled around at just the right moment. His elbow slammed down hard on my shoulder. I tilted sideways from the force and then the hilt of his sword slammed into my temple.

Stars danced in front of my eyes. The arena spun. Bastian leaned over me, which meant I must've been on the ground, though I didn't recall getting there. His orders to get a medic rang in my ears. I groaned and lifted a hand to my head as the prince mumbled something.

My head throbbed when I woke. Couldn't remember falling asleep either... But I wanted to do it again to avoid dealing with the raging headache.

"Saer?"

I cracked an eye to find Bastian sitting beside a bed in one of the healer's rooms. Shelves of tonics hung behind the prince and a bitter odor lingered in the air. I pushed myself up into a sitting position and touched my head. "Ouch."

"Volney went too far," Bastian seethed.

"It's fine." Or it would be when the room stopped tilting every time I moved my head. "I meant to let him win, but I didn't expect him to finish me quite so hard."

"Why would you let beat you?"

I met Bastian's gaze and held it. Did he really not know? "If I lost to him, that would mean your father's Wings are capable of protecting him against me."

Bastian sat back in a creaky chair and folded his arms. "You mean against me."

"We all know *you're* not going to get through both Volney and Nen," I said dryly.

He huffed. "You know how to wound a man's pride."

"You'll get over it. Maybe now I'll be allowed to go in the Main Palace with you on a regular basis." And avoid the temptation of going to the Women's Palace at the same time.

"You're a damn moron, you know that?" Bastian punched my arm. "You're not sick of me yet? Why do you *want* to sit through tedious meetings?"

A middle-aged man with graying hair opened the door and stepped inside. "Your Highness," he said with a bow. Then he turned to me with studious eyes. "It's good to see you awake, Lord Wing. How do you feel?"

"As you'd expect."

The healer ignored me and went to his wall of glass bottles. Each was filled with brown, yellow, or clear liquid. "You have a concussion. I'll give you something for the pain, but the best thing to do is rest. Two days, if the prince can spare you, or extremely light work if he cannot."

"Light work?" I grumbled. "What do you think my job is?"

"I can spare him." Bastian punched my arm again. "The guards can escort me to the Main Palace. I promise to come right back after and behave so you don't need to worry."

Now that he'd announced his exact plans in front of the healer, *worry* was all I would do. He was probably an Aster. Faramond was going to *love* hearing about this. The rebels could use the situation to kill two birds. First, Bastian as he went to the Main Palace alone on a regular schedule, and then me, when the king blamed me for daring to be injured.

"Two drops, twice a day," the healer said, pressing a cool cylinder into my hand. "Any more than that and you won't wake up again. Understand?"

"Yes," I said through gritted teeth. The healer nodded, bowed to Bastian, then left. I swung my feet off the bed and glared at Bastian. "Rest for two days? Both of you are out of your minds."

"And yet, your mind is the one that just took a blow." Bastian smirked. "It's been a while since you've had a black eye. Do you think your secret lover will find it attractive? I've heard some women do."

I reared back, regretting the sudden movement instantly. "What are you talking about?"

"The noblewoman you met," he prodded.

My heart slammed into my ribcage so hard I thought it would break bones. "We aren't lovers. I was infatuated for a moment, but we both know I can't be with her. Besides… she's engaged."

"Engaged?" Bastian scooted forward in his chair, eyes twinkling as if he just got the clue he needed to discover her identity. And perhaps he had. How many noblewomen were engaged right now? *Fuck.* But his gaze softened. "Sorry. I shouldn't have brought her up."

"Nothing a few nights at the brothel won't fix," I muttered. The thought of touching anyone besides Anais made my skin crawl.

"I thought you gave that up?"

"Gave up fucking?" *Not intentionally.* It had been a while since I visited the royal brothel—a *perk* of my position—but I never enjoyed it. Not really. At first it was curiosity that sent me there, then youthful abandon that quickly turned to self-loathing. I forced myself onto my feet and only swayed slightly. "I'm a Wing, not a eunuch, you bastard. Now move it before the smell of this place makes me throw up."

TWENTY

When I was younger, I always wanted healing to take longer so I could miss days of training. It had been the only time I was allowed a decent night's sleep followed by a day or two in bed. Now, I wished my body still ached to avoid guarding Bastian as he visited the Women's Palace for the first time.

We waited in one of the sitting rooms for a servant to bring Anais, and my stomach churned. The furniture appeared new, either recently purchased or reupholstered with dark blue velvet to match the prince's colors. Two sofas, four chairs, and a low, ivory table at the center, resting on a gray fur rug. A fire burned in the white fireplace behind us.

"She was expecting us," Bastian mumbled.

"Yes." He had asked me to send a note before we left the Prince's Palace, but we had been waiting at least fifteen minutes now. Anais probably ran off again. The thought brought a small smile to my lips. "I'm sure they're simply making sure every hair is in place before she sees you."

"I don't think I'd notice if her hair wasn't perfect," Bastian said. After a short pause, he added, "She's very pretty."

So he'd reminded me. Over and over.

"And if she's as kind as you claim, then…"

"Then you will live happily until your dying day," I finished for him, the words bitter against my tongue. The problem was when that day arrived—and by whose hand.

The door swung open to reveal Anais in a copper gown. Strands of beads crisscrossed from her neck to her waist and draped down her arms from her shoulders. She curtsied low—almost low enough, undoubtedly thanks to the duchess. "Your Highness," she said and breezed into the room.

"Please, call me Bastian," he said, stepping forward to meet her. Immediately, he lifted her hand and placed a kiss to the back of it. The same hand that had been wrapped around my cock days ago. A flash a shame washed over me.

The familiar clack of the Fransabelle's cane preceded her into the room. "I was beginning to think you'd never come visit your fiancée."

"You wound me, Duchess," Bastian said with a laugh.

Fransabelle curtsied as best she could. "Your Wing has kept us company while you stayed away."

"I'm grateful for him." Bastian looked over his shoulder to give me an appreciative nod and I wanted to sink into the floor. "You'll have to forgive me for being absent. Recently, my father allocated more work to me."

"Of course," Anais said, cutting off whatever the duchess was about to say. "Would you care to join us for cards? The duchess told me you enjoy a good game."

"I would love to." Bastian wasted no time leading her to the table near the fireplace. He held out her chair and pushed it in for her before doing the same for Fransabelle. Then he took his own seat. "What do you know how to play?"

Anais began listing what games she knew as a lady's maid delivered a deck to Bastian. I walked up to the window to distance myself from them and stared out at the garden with artistically pruned shrubs. White marble pillars held a small roof up at the center of a pavilion. At its center was a statue of a woman in a flowing dress, holding a shallow basin full of water. Small songbirds fluffed their feathers on the edge of it.

"Saer, are you joining us?" Bastian asked.

I crossed my arms and leaned against the wall without looking away from the window. "No."

"We can't play without an equal number of players," he encouraged.

"We can play something else," Anais suggested. Then, in a softer voice, added, "If he doesn't want to."

"Lord Tufaro has a job to do," Fransabelle said. "Leave him to it."

My nostrils flared. I knew what she was doing—keeping me away from Anais. It made me want to storm over to a chair and tell them to deal me in. But

I wouldn't because the duchess was right to keep me distanced. The sounds Anais had made in the bathroom as she came echoed through my head almost daily. Her silky heat around my fingers, the taste of her on my lips… *Fuck*. I pressed my forehead to the cold glass and focused on the birds.

Anais laughed at something Bastian said. I blurred out the words, forced myself not to listen, but it was difficult given our proximity. No matter how hard I tried to get lost in my own thoughts, they always circled back to Anais. Then she would speak and my ears immediately zeroed in on the sound. For nearly an hour, I huddled against the window, fighting the urge to bolt from the room.

But, as the duchess reminded me, I had a job to do. So I stood and I guarded Bastian even though all of the danger was already in the room. Anais was the Red Aster I needed to protect him from, even if she didn't know it, and she held more power over my future now than I was comfortable with. One word about what happened between us would drive a wedge between the prince and myself. I swayed slightly where I stood, my muscles beginning to ache from how stiff I was.

"Come sit down," Bastian called.

I locked my knees. "I'm fine."

"Saer." His tone hardened, letting me know it wasn't a request. "Sit down before you fall down."

I sighed, my breath fogging the windowpane, and crossed the room to the chair furthest from the group. As soon as I sank down onto the velvet cushion, my body unconsciously relaxed. The cards were stacked on the table in a neat pile, but no one moved to deal another round.

"I'm fine, Your Highness," I said when I felt him staring at me. Anais was too, but I wasn't brave enough to address her under the circumstances. Besides, I wouldn't admit my muscles were sore or that I suffered the beginning twinges of a headache, even if the prince and I were alone.

"Did something happen?" Anais asked.

Before I could stop myself, my eyes lifted to hers and I felt the connection resonate in my bones. "No," I said, and settled my gaze on the deck of cards.

"You have a black eye."

I tilted my head to hide the fading mark. It was yellow now with only a touch of purple. "Training."

The word came out harsher than I meant it, and the room filled with tense silence. The duchess' thoughts were likely spinning with suspicion over my attitude. The fuck if I cared though.

"Lady Karina," Bastian started after a long moment. "Have you met any ladies of the court yet?"

"Not yet," she said, barely a whisper. The dejected sound made me feel like complete shit.

"Still?" He turned his gaze to Duchess Fransabelle. "Surely she's learned enough by now to make an acquaintance or two. You can't teach her how to interact with nobles from a book."

The duchess pursed her lips. "Countess Odelia failed to teach her many things."

Bastian shifted to the edge of his seat. "Would you like to get out of the Women's Palace and explore a bit, my lady?"

"I..." The brush of Anais' eyes as she looked, ever-so-briefly, in my direction made my breath hitch. "I would, yes."

Anais wouldn't find the freedom she craved by meeting other nobles, but it sounded more exciting than constant lessons with the duchess. The problem was making connections—the more people she knew, the more likely it was she would be recognized after I helped her escape. If not right away, then in the future. She could be at a market two years from now and run into a lord or lady. I rubbed my hands down my thighs to avoid making fists and further alerting Bastian to my annoyance.

"Set something up for tomorrow," Bastian told the duchess. "Something small with ladies you think she will genuinely get along with. Work your way up to larger groups if you're concerned."

"Yes, Your Highness," she agreed.

He stood and offered Anais his hand to do the same. "For what it's worth, I think you'll be adored."

"Thank you," she said with a blush.

I bolted to my feet, more than ready to leave as Bastian built-up to our departure. He did the same thing every time he had social calls. I shifted my weight from foot to foot as he made a few more comments to the women and wished them a pleasant afternoon. I didn't offer them any such farewell, only bowing, before following the prince from the palace.

"You need a nap," he whispered, half-joking, once we were on the path back to the Prince's Palace.

"I don't need a *nap*," I grumbled.

He snorted. "Between you leaning into that window like it was the only thing keeping you up and your mood, you need more rest. I don't have many duties over the next few days so I'll keep you company."

"I'm fine," I insisted.

"Of course you are." He clapped a hand on my shoulder. The same one Volney hurt. I winced and jerked away from the touch, which earned me a knowing look. "You were right about her, by the way."

Jealousy slid through my veins like oil. "Lady Karina?"

"She seems genuinely kind. I don't think it will be hard spending my life with her," he said with a sheepish smile.

Except he wouldn't spend his life with her. If I managed to get her far from the capital, there wouldn't even be a wedding. *I'm shit.* I rolled my shoulder, easing some of the dull pain Bastian's touch caused. *No.* I was doing the right thing—saving *two* lives.

TWENTY-ONE

My plan worked. I now spent all day in the Main Palace listening to the governors prattle on until the king snapped and I couldn't even blame him. Each one of them passive-aggressively beat a dead horse for hours. It didn't matter how much sense another governor, the king, or Bastian made in a rebuttal—the governor speaking at the time heard only what they wanted. Words were twisted. Tempers flared. No wonder the country was falling to shit.

But it kept me occupied.

Between guarding Bastian and training myself as hard as possible, I didn't have the energy to seek Anais out again. I'd decided on a location for her to flee to. A small village in the south that herded sheep. Her western accent wouldn't stand out as much there as it would in the northern villages, and it was of such little consequence that no soldiers ever patrolled the area. She could get herself a small house in the mountains there, meet a nice farmer, and live her life. The problem was *how* to get her there.

The king pounded on the table, drawing the eye of everyone in the room. "I will hear no more of it," he snapped at the Governor of Defense.

It was something about pushing to claim an important trade route from our northern neighbors, but it wouldn't happen. Eradrist wasn't ready for a war. So I turned my attention to the window overlooking one of the lavish inner courtyards.

A handful of young women sat around a glass table, picking at their late breakfasts of berries and small scones. My heart somersaulted when my gaze landed on a honey-haired beauty. *Anais* sat at the table, completely oblivious to me watching. The duchess hovered near the entrance to the small area, leaning on her cane.

Bastian had visited her twice more while I had been recovering from my concussion. He was simultaneously smitten and worried. *She won't make friends easily*, he'd claimed. The other women would judge her too harshly and, if they didn't, chances were they wanted to use Karina to advance themselves. She was too naïve to court intrigues to tell the difference. Coming from Bastian, the truth felt wrong. He was supposed to be the positive one while I looked for problems in every crevice.

Anais laughed before plopping a red berry into her mouth. Even though I was too far away to hear the musical sound, I felt it in my bones. Had it really only been two weeks since I was in her room, asking her to think of me as she touched herself?

I shook away the memory. She seemed content around the other women, and whether it was friendship or not, her smile appeared honest. That was good—her being happy.

The wide, wooden doors creaked open and I snapped to attention. A young girl stepped into the meeting room wearing an unadorned dress. She wrung her hands in front of her as she approached the table full of governors. King Edric and Bastian shared a quick look where they sat on a slightly raised dais and I regretted losing focus.

"Speak," the king barked.

The girl blanched. "Thank you for seeing me, Your Majesty."

"What do you want?" Governor Hesby asked.

"I've petitioned to speak here today because Governor Pevran was my aunt. Her final letter wasn't included with her belongings." She lifted her chin in an attempt at seeming brave. "I would like to read it."

"It's evidence of her mortal sin," Governor Hesby said, waving a dismissive hand. "It will remain permanently in the archives."

"She didn't say she wanted to keep it," Bastian spoke up. "If you'd like to read the letter, my Wing will escort you to the archives now."

I stiffened. Was I some sort of errand boy now? *The fuck, Bastian.*

"Thank you, Your Highness," the girl said with a low curtsy.

Bastian nodded at me to go, leaving me with no choice. He was safe in the Main Palace without me, and with Anais also there, I didn't have to worry about losing my inner battle to visit her. It was fine, I told myself. I would take the girl and return.

Once the governor's niece and I were in the hallway, she followed closely at my heel. "Can you read and write?" she asked.

I startled at the question. Did she need me to read her the letter? I wasn't sure I could handle it after being there for Pevran's last moments. "Why?"

"No reason. I would like to make a copy of the letter to take home with me."

I glanced at her from the corners of my eyes. She couldn't be more than fifteen, yet she conquered her fear so well. Though, I doubted any copy she made would be legible with how hard her hands shook.

"I'll instruct the scribes to give you paper and ink," I said.

She nodded and followed me into a large room full of scrolls. Ladders leaned against the walls so scribes could reach the shelves near the high ceilings and thick curtains were drawn to ensure nothing was damaged by the sun. Candles flickered inside glass lanterns to make up for the loss of light. I quickly found a scribe and told him what we were looking for. The man bowed and hurried off to fetch the letter.

"Did you know my aunt well?" the girl asked.

"No." I folded my arms across my chest.

"I'm Cirna, by the way."

I raised a brow as she waited expectantly. "The Prince's Wing."

"You have a name, don't you?" She blushed and looked away. "I'm sorry."

"Lord Saer Tufaro," I said, humoring her. "I didn't realize Governor Pevran had any family."

She chewed her lip. "No one was supposed to know. My parents died of a fever years ago. She said she didn't want anyone kidnapping me for a ransom, so I was raised by my neighbors. She wrote every week though and paid for my upkeep."

The scribe returned and ushered us over to a table with paper, an ink well, and the letter Pevran had pulled from her locked box. Cirna slid into the seat and immediately started poring over the letter. A few minutes later, she began writing it, word for word. When she finished, she sat back and sighed.

"Are you satisfied?" I asked, eager to return to Bastian. And the window that allowed me a forbidden glance at Anais.

"She doesn't mention me," the girl said. "There's nothing personal here at all."

No. If Pevran was hiding her niece, she wouldn't want to reveal the truth as she died. Who would protect the girl, then? It wasn't kidnappers Pevran was worried about but the Asters. "How did you know to come here?"

"I heard she died from the bulletin in town. It was hard convincing anyone that I wasn't lying just to steal her things." Cirna twisted in her chair to look up at me. "I don't think she really killed herself. She was too dedicated to helping people."

I offered a half-hearted smile. Who was I to tell her that wasn't always enough to keep someone alive when they didn't want to be? I'd seen a handful of dead nobles hanging from rafters or with self-inflicted cuts to their wrists. *More* than a handful of commoners in Ora Et. But I didn't think Pevran truly wanted to die. She accepted her fate and, even with her last breath, helped someone. Helped me. By taking the blame for her death and embracing it as her own.

"I'm sorry for your loss," I said, and knelt down to her level. Now that she'd come forward, I feared the Asters would pounce. It would be easy to use the girl. If they threatened to expose her aunt's secrets to the crown, she would undoubtedly do whatever they asked. Even if they sent her on a suicide mission. "If you ever find yourself in trouble, you can ask me for help."

She wrinkled her nose. "Unless you can find me a new place to live, there's nothing you can do."

"Why do you need a new place to live?"

"My aunt paid the family that I'm living with for my expenses. They're amazing people but they can't afford to let me stay." She gathered her copy of the letter and folded it neatly, stuffing it into her skirt pocket.

An idea struck, hard and fast. "How do you feel about the south?"

"The south?"

"It's warm most of the year and there are lovely mountains." I was being rash. This needed more thought. More planning. How could I be sure this really was Pevran's niece? Or that she wasn't an Aster. "A friend of mine is moving there and she needs someone to travel with. It could benefit you both."

Cirna's brow creased in thought. "After I sell my aunt's belongings, I'll think on it. I have no coin at the moment and no prospects in the south, but... maybe."

"I would, of course, pay you to be her companion on the journey. Enough to get you settled, and I'm sure my friend will help you whenever you need it once you arrive." I wasn't sure what Cirna knew how to do—if she could cook and clean, or if she had any useful skills that would make her employable. Anais could help her with any of that. A small price to pay for freedom. "Where are you staying now?"

Cirna narrowed her eyes and stood. "Why?"

"I will come to you for an answer." I rose from the floor and stepped away, trying my best not to intimidate her. "She leaves in a month, so you'll need to make a decision before that."

"The Valewood Inn," she finally said. "But I'm only thinking about it. I could say no."

I nodded, though her tone said differently. The offer of money and a life elsewhere seemed to appealed to her more than she wanted to admit. "Of course. As long as you tell no one, I'll accept whatever answer you give."

Cirna hesitated before saying, "okay."

Leading her back to the gate of the Main Palace, I began to plan. Anais and Cirna had similar enough features to pass for relatives. They could travel as sisters. I could come up with a story to keep them safe on the road—that they're going to see their sick father or to work for their uncle on a farm. Guards would be looking for Anais once everyone realized she was gone—*just* Anais. Not a pair of siblings.

A month wasn't very long, though perhaps it would be to Cirna. I'd have to send money to the inn to cover her stay, otherwise she might be forced to leave. Other arrangements needed to be made, as quickly and quietly as possible. Horses procured. A route to map. My heart gave a sudden ache and I rubbed at my chest. I wasn't sure I was ready to never see her again.

But this was best for Anais. For everyone, really.

TWENTY-TWO

With the entire palace in a whirlwind of activity, my pulse refused to slow. Day after day, I scoured every rooftop, dark corner, and blind spot. Bastian and I couldn't walk more than a handful of steps without me being convinced something was amiss. It happened so often now that the prince had begun to ignore me, which had me constantly two moments away from dragging him back to the Prince's Palace.

And, at night, I surveyed the Women's Palace instead of sleeping. I hadn't gone back inside, but patrolling the wall made me feel better. The perimeter of the palace building itself brought me too close and into the eyeline of guards—not that it stopped me.

It should've. This was dangerous. So fucking dangerous. If anyone even suspected that I planned to help Anais disappear, everything was ruined. But it would all be ruined if Faramond had her murdered too. *No.* He wouldn't. Not when King Edric continued to arrange the engagement ball, and more and more nobles had arrived for the event. Guards had nearly tripled.

Which was why, right now, I wasn't guarding Bastian or Anais. I tugged my hood forward, grateful for the thick wool as a bitter wind swept through the streets of the capital. I was putting a lot of faith in Cirna—a young girl who I didn't know—but what choice did I have?

Valewood Inn was a rundown building, much like others on the street, but slightly worse. Half of a collapsed balcony hung from beneath the second-story windows, all of which were boarded up.

I slipped through the front door and did a quick sweep. No immediate danger, though the gruff, unwashed men were sure to be capable of creating some. Cirna was young and, some might say, pretty. And staying alone. My jaw clenched. If anything happened to her, I'd find the men who did it and gut them. I owed it to Pevran, if nothing else.

"Can I help you?" A heavy woman asked from behind the bar. Her curly, red hair was tied back with a frayed ribbon.

"I'm looking for my friend." I stepped nearer the bar to keep my words private. "Cirna. She should be expecting me."

The woman narrowed her eyes. "Is she now?"

"I'm from the palace." I rested my arm on the bar, letting the craftsmanship of my bracers prove my words. "And I need to speak with her."

"This about her aunt?"

I nodded, a small lie.

"I'll have her meet you in the kitchen," she said after a brief silence. "I've made her safety my personal concern, if you know what I mean."

It didn't matter where Cirna and I spoke so I followed the barkeep to a small, yet efficient-looking kitchen. A stone oven, pots hanging in fireplace, and a flour-coated table at the center. I ignored the large bugs crawling across the surface and perched on a tall stool.

Cirna didn't take long to join me. She wore the same dress as before, but her expression was slightly more haggard. "You paid my bill," she said as a greeting.

"I did." I kept my hood up but raised my chin so she could see my face.

She crossed her arms and looked off to the side. "It hasn't been a month yet."

"I said my friend was *leaving* in a month. It's been three weeks now, and I need to make the final preparations. Which means I need your answer."

"Who is your friend?" she asked.

I hesitated. If Cirna agreed, she would know Anais by name and would think her a simple maid, but if she didn't agree, that knowledge could become a liability. "A woman who works at the palace," I hedged.

"Can't the king secure her passage?"

I snorted. "The king doesn't care if commoners travel safely. Even if he did, he can't be responsible for ensuring everyone in the kingdom has an escort."

Cirna seemed to think on it for a moment. "Fine, I'll do it. But only because you're paying me."

"Thank you." I sighed in relief. "Be ready to leave in eight days. I'll bring my friend here along with two horses. Pack lightly."

"Do I get to keep the horse?" she asked nervously. "Once we get there, I mean."

I hadn't thought that far ahead—or I *had*, but not about the horse. "Sure," I told her.

At that, Cirna smiled for the first time. "Thank you!"

I slipped past her, tapping a knuckle against her forehead. "Keep yourself safe until then."

When King Edric informed Bastian they would be dining privately together tonight, my options were to dine separately with Volney and Nen or fend for myself. It wasn't a hard choice. But it was made even easier because I needed to meet with Anais. To tell her the plan. Nothing more. Still, my heart hammered at the thought of being near her again.

Instead of seeking out dinner, I snuck back into the Women's Palace. Anais wasn't allowed to dine anywhere else in case Bastian chose to eat with her. I hated that she had to sit and wait, eating alone every night when he had to eat with the king, but it wouldn't be for much longer.

When I reached the small, intimate dining area, however, I found it empty. Her dinner plates still sat on the table, the food half gone. Usually, servants would've whisked them away immediately. I continued lingering in the shadows of the room, rapping my fingers on my thigh. Had she choked on dinner again and been rushed to the healer? Or was there an intruder who the guards hadn't been made aware of?

"She's gone *again*?" a woman whispered outside the room.

"The ladies' maids are looking for her now. If they don't find her before the duchess learns of it, we'll be blamed."

"I thought she stopped sneaking off?" the first woman asked, her distress clear.

"Didn't you hear? The prince told the duchess to give her time to herself so she wouldn't become overwhelmed."

The other women replied, but they were too far down the hallway now to understand. With everyone looking for Anais in the Women's Palace without any luck, it was clear she wasn't there. I backed slowly out of the room, retreating the way I came, and raced into the gardens before anyone spotted me. It was stupid to think she would hide in the forgotten corner where we met, but my feet carried me there regardless.

"Saer?" Anais gasped when I stepped through the overgrown grass. She hugged herself where she stood beneath the tree's bare branches, wearing only her thin, black satin gown and red agate beads across her chest.

At the sound of her voice, I crossed to the tree, stepped over the bench, and cupped her face in my hands before she could utter another word. My lips found hers, desperate and hungry. The cool evening air had chilled her skin, but it quickly warmed beneath my touch as she returned the kiss. Anais gripped my bracers, holding me there.

"Lady Karina?" a distant voice called.

Fuck. Right. People were searching for her. I broke the kiss, and traced her cheekbones with my thumbs. "What are you doing here?" I whispered.

"Breathing." Her eyes locked onto mine, searching. "Where have you been?"

I looked up at the now-bare branches of my tree. "Doing my job."

"You're avoiding me." Her grip tightened slightly. "I'm sorry about what I said in the bathroom. I was scared, but I didn't mean—"

"Don't apologize." I pressed a quick kiss to her lips. "You were right. I wish things were different too, but they're not. It's too dangerous to pretend otherwise."

Tears filled her eyes, hovering along her lower lid. "I can't marry him."

I opened my mouth to tell her she wouldn't have to when something about how she clung to me made me pause. Bastian would never hurt her—not intentionally and never physically. But his experience with romancing women was as lacking as my own. "Did something happen between you two?"

"No." She pulled my hands from her face but continued to hold on. "The prince is wonderful and any woman would be lucky to be his wife. That's why I can't do this. I would have to lie to him every day for the rest of my life and… and love someone else when he deserves someone who loves him back."

An ache bloomed in my chest. Bastian did deserve that. He deserved a lot better than he had—a mistrustful father, a deceitful best friend, and a lying fiancée—but that was all the more reason for me to stick to the plan. With Anais safely in the south, he could marry someone else. Someone who could give him their heart and—*wait.* Did she just say she loved me? *Fuck.* I wasn't worthy of that.

"You leave next week," I whispered. "I've secured the horses and prepared a map. You'll go south with Governor Pevran's niece. While she's young and, I suspect, unworldly, she'll offer you protection without knowing it. The two of you will travel as sisters which will help throw off any guards you come across." *As long as Cirna was smart enough not to mention they were traveling from the capital.*

Anais released my arms to grab at my shirt. "Can't *we* go together instead?"

Unlike Cirna, if we both went missing, my presence would only garner more attention. A young couple traveling together, matching our descriptions, would get us caught in no time.

Run, Pevran told me. But how could I? I might be able to avoid the Red Asters for a while, but not the rebels *and* the royals. And definitely not if I was seen to have kidnapped the prince's fiancée.

"If things were different, I would leave with you," I said honestly.

"Please," she said, her quiet voice cracking.

"In eight days, I'll come to your room and sneak you from the palace. I've secured common clothing for you, so only bring anything of sentimental value. You'll have enough money to replace anything else once you reach the south."

Panic flickered across her face. "My family—"

"Would want you to survive. I'll send them whatever they need." I pulled her against my chest and embraced her. "I'm sorry you're in this position, but this is all I can do to save you. If the Asters tell you to do something, even if it's to kill Bastian, you'll have no choice. They'll expose you otherwise." And, either way, the king would kill her as a traitor.

"How do you know?" she asked.

"Know what?"

"That they would threaten to expose me. Have they done it to others?"

I released a deep breath. "Yes. To those he's killed and those he hasn't."

"He's pardoned rebels before?" she asked, sounding a little hopeful.

"No," I said, quickly squashing her optimism. There was no pardon for people like me—disloyal pieces of shit were rewarded with a traitor's death.

"Then—" Anais stiffened and pushed out of my arms. "Are you one of them? Are you a Red Aster?"

I slammed my palm over her mouth, holding her against me with my other arm around her lower back. "Watch what you say," I hissed. When I met her wide eyes, I softened, but not enough to release her. "I have as much say over my life as you do in yours. Did the rebels place me beside the prince when we were children? Yes. Have they been threatening me and coercing me to do horrible things ever since? Yes. But am I one of them? No. My allegiance is to the prince, but I can't protect him if the Asters turn me over to the king, so I have to *keep* doing terrible things. Do you understand? I have no other choice."

When Anais said nothing, when the only sound was my pounding heart and frantic thoughts, I let her go. She couldn't turn me in without risking herself, even if she wanted to now.

"Aren't you going to say anything?" I asked. Her chest heaved as she looked me up and down. My eyes lingered on her mouth, where my hand left a red mark, and I wished I could soothe it away. "Don't tell me you've finally learned when to hold your tongue."

Her eyes slowly lifted to mine. "I understand."

"Do you?" I stepped closer and she held her ground. "Then you'll understand why you need to leave. The countess *is* working with the Asters and they *will* ruin you."

She nodded mutely.

"And…" I looked down at her and sharp pain twisted in my chest. "And you'll understand why I can't leave with you. That I have to protect Bastian."

"Yes." She pushed up onto her toes and brushed her lips against mine. I melted into the kiss, twining my fingers into her hair, but she leaned away far too soon. "If what you said is true about the Asters, you can't stay here either. What if they tell *you* to kill the prince?"

"Then I will fall on my sword," I vowed.

"In eight days, I'll leave. I'll go wherever you send me and do whatever you say, but only if you promise to find me again." She tugged me down by the knotted hair at the base of my neck. "Protect the prince while you can, but when the time comes that you can't, don't stay to die. Find me and live instead."

Emotions clawed at my chest. Guilt, as always, but longing, sadness, and fear also dragged their talons across my heart. And something else. Something I didn't recognize. It made me want to fall at her feet and weep. To make her that promise and mean it. But I couldn't. My fate was to die here, protecting Bastian.

"I'll see you again," I told her. Not in this life, but perhaps the next. "Now, you need to get back to the Women's Palace before someone tells Duchess Fransabelle that you went missing again."

She huffed. "I've been granted liberties."

"Yes, but something tells me they don't extend this far," I said with a smirk. "Go. Before I need to break you out of a dungeon next week."

Anais hesitated, looking from me to the gap in the hedge that would lead her out of our haven. "In case it wasn't clear earlier, I'm in love with you."

My breath caught. "Anais…"

"I don't expect a reply. You just deserved to know." She leapt up to place a chaste kiss on my cheek and raced away. Back to the palace and her maids.

While I… I couldn't move. Love wasn't in the cards for me. I'd known that since childhood that I wasn't allowed to feel the warmth of it. There were no parents to love me, no hope of a wife one day. Bastian and I loved each other as brothers but the burning heat in my chest now was *nothing* like that. Was this what the stories talked about? Could I be in love with her too?

Bastian stood at Anais' side, one hand on her elbow, guiding her arm. She rolled a heavy ball and it smacked against his, knocking it out of the way.

"You did it," he encouraged with a wide smile.

Anais smiled but it was too tight to be real. She'd been avoiding my gaze since we arrived at the Women's Palace so Bastian could teach her how to play different garden games. It was almost too cold to be outside, but he'd purchased her a fur cloak for the occasion. *More like the game was an excuse for the gift.* But what could I say? He was being a good fiancée.

"Good morning, Saer." Duchess Fransabelle came up beside me where I stood at the foot of the palace steps. "They make a handsome couple."

"Yes," I agreed. Very handsome. Very royal. And it was fucking me up inside. Who was I to destroy what could be a happy marriage? *A Wing*, I insisted to myself. Helping Anais get to safety outside the palace had nothing to do with my feelings for her. It was about saving both their lives.

The duchess' eyes were daggers as she scoured me from head to toe. "I'm glad you took my advice."

"Your advice?" I shifted uncomfortably and watched Bastian throw another of his balls at the one Anais just tossed. *Let it go, duchess.*

Fransabelle made a low *hmm* in the back of her throat. "I'm also pleased the prince has visited Lady Karina so often. She seems to be enjoying court as well."

I clenched my jaw. "Wonderful news."

"Her lessons aren't coming along quite as well now that her schedule is busier. Much like your own since you've been welcomed back into the Main Palace."

I narrowed my eyes and looked down at the duchess. She was bundled in her own fur cloak, complete with a matching hat and hand warmer. "Palace life has sorted itself out once again," I said in a low voice.

"Palace life." She turned and looked straight up at me with unnerving focus. "But what about your personal life?"

My lips parted. "My what?"

"Exactly. Keep it that way." She turned without another word and walked back into the warmth of the greenhouse attached to the rear of the Women's Palace.

"So damn observant," I grumbled. It wouldn't matter after tomorrow though. Anais would leave and I would perform my best act yet. The concerned Wing, the dutiful guard, the outraged rebel. To two opposing audiences. While I knew I should feel *some* way about that, only numb resignation existed.

Bastian laughed and I snapped my attention back to their game. Anais looked pleased with herself as he scooped up his final ball. "If I knock yours out of the ring this time, you've lost."

"I'm optimistic, Your Highness."

"What will you give me if I win?"

Anais stiffened. "I'm afraid I don't have anything you'd want."

"A kiss." He said in a higher-than-normal voice and when she paled, he added, "a chaste kiss, on the cheek."

It felt as if someone had kicked me in the chest. I struggled to drag in a breath, my eyes flashing wildly between their faces. The open, hopeful expression on Bastian's face was a stark contrast to Anais' blank stare. *No.* He can't fucking kiss her. She didn't want it any more than I wanted to see it happen.

Anais hesitated, her eyes darting from the balls on the ground to the one in his hand. And then, for the first time, to me. Our gazes caught for the briefest moment, but it felt like I was struck by lightning. A deadly secret hid in that bolt.

"All right," she agreed.

My hands curled into fists. *Fuck this.* Heat flooded through me followed by a wave of cold. What the hell was wrong with me? They were *engaged.* Ashamed, I walked away from them to do a pointless perimeter search of the rear gardens.

I heard the faint *clank* of Bastian's ball hitting another, but that was all I knew as I walked among a row of evergreens. I didn't know if Anais' ball left the ring, if he kissed her cheek—or if *she* was meant to kiss his. And that was exactly how I wanted it.

The crescent moon offered little light to navigate through the forest. Tomorrow there would be a new moon—perfect for Anais' escape. I followed the road that led south from a few yards into the trees, carrying a bag with a change of clothes for her, preserved food, and a canteen. The money I would hand her personally on the off-chance bandits found the brown sack hiding in the branches.

Spotting the perfect tree, I wedged my foot into the forked trunk and climbed until I found a branch thick enough to hold the bag. I slid back down and committed the area to memory. Large fallen tree to the right, a slight incline in the road, minutes from the edge of Ora Et.

Once that was taken care of, I walked back into the capital with lighter steps. All that was left was to check on Cirna and the horses I had stabled *for my employer.* It was close enough to where the rich families lived for it to be believable, and far enough to avoid gossipmongers. Valewood Inn would be busier than last time given the hour, but—

Faramond stood a block away, puffing on a thick cigar outside of the inn. I quickly slunk into the nearest alley and flipped up my hood. *What the fuck is he doing out of his office?* And *here* of all places.

The door swung open and another man stepped out followed by Cirna.

My heart stopped, my mind following suit. Thoughts flickered in and out between waves of utter panic. Faramond knew about Cirna. He found her. She knew who I was. Knew my plan. It wouldn't take much for Faramond to put two and two together once Anais went missing. Alone. Because now Pevran's niece was compromised.

Fuck fuck fuck!

The side of my fist slammed into the brick wall. I should've known better than to trust the girl. No one—*no one*—was trustworthy. Not even me. I planned to make Bastian's fiancée disappear, worked with the Asters, was loyal to the prince. There wasn't a single person who I could say I was completely honest with. Except Anais…

And now it was all going to blow up in my face.

No. Damn it, no. I was going to get Anais out of here now before it was too late. Not to the south, because Cirna would tell Faramond and they would find her. Pevran's warning to *run* coursed through me with each beat of my heart.

So I did. I ran.

Back to the palace instead of away from it.

TWENTY-FOUR

Everything now hinged on what Faramond knew before he took Cirna from the inn and how long it would take the youth to crack when he began questioning her.

My lungs burned as I finally made it back to my personal room. I shut the door quietly and paced the small space. If Faramond didn't know I was planning anything, he might not stumble upon the information right away. His questioning would likely focus on Governor Pevran and the fact that her niece was a secret. It would start with questions about why she was kept hidden instead of enjoying the luxury her aunt could've offered and end when Cirna was excited to help Faramond. Because he offered money or status or whatever else she wanted most. The man had a way of squeezing desires from a person without them even knowing it.

The entire plan was compromised now. Even if Faramond let her return to the inn under the pretense of allowing her to leave Ora Et—*if* that was what she truly wanted—there would be people waiting to ambush Anais and me when I went to collect her. I could fight them off, but it would cause a scene. Too many people would see and they'd be more than happy to turn the information over to a guard for a few coins.

"Fuck," I hissed. We had to leave. Tonight. Now. Anais' bag was already waiting in the woods and I had the money that I intended to hand over the next day.

I flung my trunk open and strapped every weapon possible to my body. A sword on each hip, a bow and quiver over my shoulder, throwing knives tucked into my bracers, daggers in my boots. By the time I was finished, all that remained in the trunk was a chain and a battle axe. I hadn't used either since training with them as both were too heavy for my taste.

After wrapping a second, warmer cloak around my shoulders, I pried up the loose floorboard and grabbed the large coin pouch. The contents clinked softly as I tied it securely onto my belt.

Run.

My reasons not to listen to Pevran were the same as before, except now I *couldn't* stay. Faramond would come for me. And, soon after, the crown. Bastian included. I stopped dead with my hand on the door knob. *Bastian.* He would defend me to his father and the governors only to be proved wrong. Humiliated. Betrayed. Alone.

Because I was, and always had been, the worst thing to ever happen to the prince. I squeezed my eyes shut for a moment to reconcile myself to this final treachery. The truth was always going to come out. At least this way, some good could come from it when Anais escaped.

I tightened my grip on the knob. Perhaps there would be time later to explain things to Bastian, but not if I was dead. Though, I suppose, after this, he wouldn't give me the chance to explain. Not that I deserved any less.

Squeezing my eyes shut, I shook the thoughts from my head. I had to run to save him from whatever Faramond planned with the countess. To save Anais from being their pawn. And, just maybe, myself. I let out a harsh breath and slipped outside.

Sneaking into the Women's Palace was as easy as it was the other times I'd done it, but my pulse raced, insistent that I would be caught. My mind snapped from frantic worry to the forced calm I'd honed over the years. Then back again. And again. It was a miracle I was able to slip into Anais' bedroom without being seen. Thank fuck she was still awake when I passed into her bedroom.

She was curled into the chair near the fire, winding a frayed ribbon through her fingers. The same ribbon I'd seen tucked into the bottom of the ottoman the day I looked through the room. "What's that?" I asked before I could stop myself.

Anais jumped at the sound of my voice and quickly tucked the ribbon into her palm. She was on her bare feet in a second and pushed me toward the door.

"What are you doing here?" she whispered. "You have to leave. My ladies are bringing my tea."

"We have to go. Tonight. *Now.*" I took her wrists to stop her from pushing at my chest as the undeniable clank of dishes came from the room on the other side of the door. "Drink it out there. Quickly. But act normal."

"Act normal?" She looked up at me with wide, concerned eyes. "Why? What's happening?"

"Lady Karina?" A knock came on the door and Anais startled. "Your tea is ready."

Of-fucking-course it was. I nodded at the door and mouthed, *go.*

"I'll take it in the sitting room tonight," she called and turned to me. "Hide under the bed."

She made a show of stomping across the room to cover my soft footfalls and whipped open her wardrobe door as I wedged myself beneath the bed. She glanced at me and wrapped a shawl over her thin nightdress, then pointed to my feet. I scooted up toward the head of the bed so my boots didn't peek out of the end.

"Lady Karina?" the ladies maid called. "Do you need my assistance?"

"No." She quickly slammed the wardrobe shut again and disappeared from my limited viewpoint. With the fireplace burning, I could make out everything from an ankle-high perspective, none of it important.

The door opened and shut. Female voices murmured from the other room. My fingers wrapped around the wooden slats holding Anais' mattress, squeezing, and I closed my eyes. This was an opportunity to compose myself. To think. It would only get us caught if I couldn't manage to calm my own thoughts.

Deep breath in. Deep breath out. Focus. We would escape the palace the same way I had planned for us to leave tomorrow. Retrieve the bag I hid—that I should've grabbed on my return to the palace, if I'd been thinking—then backtrack north. Getting the horses was too risky. I hadn't researched the northern routes like I had the southern, but I'd accompanied Bastian on them enough to know which towns we could safely hide in. The horses were a risk anyway. Too expensive for most commoners to own and too large to hide if we were ambushed in the woods.

The door opened again and I tensed.

"The fire is dying a bit," Anais said. "If you wouldn't mind placing a few more logs in now so I'm not disturbed tonight."

"Of course, my lady."

Two sets of steps crossed the room and I gripped the wood so hard I thought it would splinter. I knew Anais was buying us more time before she was detected as missing, but I hated every second the young woman stoked the fire. Her blue silk skirts swished across the floor, far too close for comfort.

"Are you sure you wouldn't like to speak to the healer?" the girl asked. "Everyone says his sleeping draughts are wonderful and you're such a light sleeper."

"I'm sure, thank you," she said in a strained voice.

The lady's maid poked at the logs until the fire popped, then the clang of metal on metal told me she

replaced the iron poker. "If you change your mind—
"

"I will let you know," Anais assured the woman. "Goodnight."

"Goodnight," she echoed.

My gaze trailed the hem of her skirt as she crossed the room and I held my breath until Anais shut the door behind her. As soon as the bolt clicked into place, I rolled out from my hiding place. *Focus. Calm.* She needed warmer clothes.

Opening her wardrobe without a word, I pulled her warmest looking items out and tossed them onto the bed. None of them were made to survive a true winter's night. Heavy brocades replaced light silk, but the cut of each gown was still meant to accommodate strands of gems. The cloak Bastian gifted her was the warmest thing she had and, while it felt wrong to use it now, there was little choice.

"What are you doing?" Anais asked, suddenly at my side.

"Get dressed." I shoved a pair of wool stockings at her before swiping a pair of fur-lined boots.

Anais stayed at my side, hopping on one foot as she pulled the stockings on. "Something happened. Did someone find out?" her low voice rose into a squeak.

"Not yet." Satisfied, I closed the wardrobe silently and moved to the window. I pulled the heavy curtains aside to gauge where the guards were. "Pevran's niece was taken by the leader of the Asters tonight. It's only a matter of time before he gets enough information from her to piece things together. If we don't leave now, it could mean the end of us both."

The rustle of clothes stopped. "You're coming with me?"

I glanced over my shoulder to find her holding the black and gold gown against her chest. The ties hung loose at her sides. I crossed the room and gathered the ribbons, pulling one row at a time until the bodice hugged her comfortably. Or, at least, I hoped it was comfortable. We had to run—which meant she needed to be able to breathe. Kneeling, I lifted each of her feet, placing them into the boots, and tied them.

"The Asters will kill me once they know my plans to help you." I left my hands on her calves and looked up. It was true—I was a dead man. Whether they caught up to me tonight or a year from now, there was only one way out for me now. There had *always* been only one way. Saving Anais from the same fate would be a final act of selflessness. Heavens knew, between all of my lies, I didn't have many of those. I wouldn't lie to Anais now, but I would tell her only the brighter side of my thoughts. "If I'm going to die, I figured, why not allow myself to be happy first?"

Her chin wobbled. "Saer…"

"You're going to be safe; I swear it." I stood and lifted Bastian's cloak from the bed, settling it on her shoulders. "We have to go now. Any other questions can wait until we're out of Ora Et."

"Okay." She clung to the front of her skirts and lifted her chin like the brave woman she was. "Lead the way."

TWENTY-FIVE

Quiet filled the woods, making my senses more acute. I had expected to hear the hoot of an owl or the rustle of animals in the brush. *Something.* But it was as if all the wildlife were collectively holding their breath, waiting for palace guards to give chase. The farther we ran, the surer I was that a lady's maid had already discovered Anais missing.

My lungs burned with cold, my fingers numb where I clutched her freezing hand. Skeletal trees surrounded us with their leaves blanketing the ground. The moonlight was barely enough to see this deep in the forest, but I kept my eyes fixed straight ahead. I led Anais around fallen trunks and patches of mud to keep our boots dry. There was no time to talk, to slow. We had to put as much space between us and the palace as possible.

"Saer." Anais tugged on my hand. "I need to stop."

I ground to a halt and tugged her against one of the wider trees. "What's wrong?"

She leaned into the trunk, breathing hard, forehead slick with sweat. "It's been hours. I need to rest."

"There isn't time." I scanned the woods, half expecting an Aster assassin to leap from the sky like the one who attacked Bastian and I in the temple. "The king will have men looking for us on horseback. We have to find somewhere safe before dawn."

"They'll think I ran off again," she wheezed. "No one will tell the king I'm missing until they're sure of it."

Her ladies *had* searched frantically for her on numerous occasions. Some of them while she hid in the garden with me. I stared down at her and brushed the loose hair from her face. "I don't have the same excuse to hide behind. Bastian will raise the alarm the minute they say I'm not in my room."

She winced. "I'm sorry. You're doing all of this for me when—"

"Hush." I gave her a small smile, though I felt the guilt twisting my stomach. The truth was, it hadn't been for her at first. Helping her escape was to save Bastian. And it still was. A person can simultaneously have different reasons for what they do. This was saving Bastian, but it was also helping her. It was a big *fuck you* to Faramond and the crown too. They'd used me for too long. But Bastian... My smile slipped. "If I were a stronger man, I would've left a long time ago."

Anais set her cold, stiff hand against my cheek. "You don't have to be stronger. So many men think they do, but you're already strong enough. You're already something much better than that."

I turned my face and kissed her palm. Part of me wanted to ask what she meant, but it didn't matter. I *did* need to be stronger or we wouldn't survive this. "Drink." I slipped the bag I retrieved from the tree off my shoulder and handed her the water sack. "We have to be careful not to dehydrate before we stop for the night."

She pushed off the trunk and swayed slightly.

Damn horses would've helped. But they were loud and conspicuous. Considering how excited Cirna had been to keep her steed, she bring them up to Faramond eventually.

"We're stopping?" she asked, lifting the water to her chapped lips.

I nodded. "If we keep going for another hour, there's a city large enough to blend in."

She wilted a little at that—not that I could blame her. Another hour with already sore feet and aching muscles was a lot to ask, but the alternative was far worse.

The city of Avaalass was smaller than Ora Et but otherwise, the same. Crumbling buildings and gaunt residents. They were like another city too, though. Similar to Port Black, it was highly traveled and full of crime. Also, prostitutes.

"Are you sure this is a good idea?" Anais asked, teeth chattering.

We stood in the alley behind two inns—one that catered to the weary traveler and one that catered to those seeking *companionship*. "They'll be more discreet." I tugged the cloak tighter around her shoulders. "And it will keep anyone inside from thinking we came into town together."

"But what if someone propositions me while you're inside?" She leaned sideways and looked at the girls working across the street. They were hidden in their cloaks too, their hair just as disheveled as Anais' and faces equally pink from the winter air.

"Say you've already been paid for." I slipped the hood over her head. "Stay right here. It will only take a minute to secure a room."

Anais shifted farther into the alley. "Hurry."

I didn't like leaving her there, but it truly wouldn't take long to pay for a room. If she stayed hidden, men looking for a prostitute would likely be too dazzled by the women flaunting themselves.

Inside the less-reputable inn, I was instantly assaulted with the scent of sex mixed with a hint of cinnamon. I swung my gaze around the dim lobby. A single couch sat in the room with a middle-aged man, likely drunk, passed out on the worn cushions. Other than that, and a rather gaudy mirror, there was a half-door with a gangly teen on the other side. He couldn't be more than eighteen which meant this was likely his parent's business.

He grinned when I caught his eye. "Looking for a bit of pleasure, sir?"

"I just need a room—I've already paid for the girl."
I pulled a coin from my pocket, the pouch hidden
safely beneath my cloak. No good would come of
flaunting it. "Will this cover the whole night?"

The teen ran his tongue over yellowed teeth. "We
aren't exactly a *whole night* sort of establishment."

Exactly. I smirked. "I'm in the mood to take my
time. Nothing worse than being interrupted in the
middle of fucking a woman."

"Alright." He barked a laugh. "The night's almost
over and we aren't going to turn away good coin. One
whore staining the sheets is a lot easier to clean up
after than ten."

The teen held out his palm and I dropped the coin
into it. *Don't punch him.* That would imprint my face in
his mind for a long while and we needed the opposite
of that. Pocketing the money, he tossed a key at my
chest and busied himself with folding sheets. At least
Anais and I could expect clean ones. I paused halfway
to the door.

Oh fuck.

This was a hotel that rented rooms for quick
pleasure. Not comfort. We might have clean sheets—
but they would only be on *one* bed. A man laughed
outside, shaking the thought away, and I raced back
into the night.

Anais was where I had left her, huddled into her
cloak, shaking from cold. I paused a few feet from her
and took her in for the first time since we stopped in
the forest. She looked like she had in the gardens.
Unbridled and slightly ruffled. Her gaze cut to mine
and she released a heavy breath.

"Ready?" I asked and held out my hand.

She took it with a smile and let me pull her in. "We'll have to make it look believable," she said as she leaned into my side.

I wasn't sure if it was for the shared warmth or the ruse, but either way, it sent a different kind of shiver up my spine. "That won't be a problem," I whispered, wrapping my arm around her shoulders, and steered us back to the door of the inn.

Stepping inside first, I placed a hand low on her back and ushered her into the warmth. Two women clung to a portly man who spoke to the inn keeper in a lowered voice. Seeing the opportunity, I shut the door quietly and guided Anais across the room, hand on her ass in case anyone looked over. I leaned down and nuzzled her neck for good measure. From an outside perspective, it had to appear I was overly eager and her less than thrilled.

The staircase leading up to the second floor was wide and appeared newly redone with unfinished wood. Moans and creaks filled the air from shut doors. The sound of a sharp slap made Anais jump, but it was followed by a deeper groan. She looked over her shoulder at me and giggled.

I grinned back at her and pointed to the next to last door in the hallway. She slipped into the dark room. I followed, bolting us safely inside as she struck a match that sat on the table just inside the door. The half-used candle flickered to life when she touched the match to the wick, but it wasn't nearly enough light to see the room for what it was.

What I could see was a wide bed with what passed for clean blankets and a thin, moth-eaten curtain slung across the only window. It wasn't fit for a lady of the court, but it was relatively safe which mattered more.

"One bed," she said so quietly that I barely understood.

I shrugged off my cloak and hung it on a hook attached to the wall. "I'll sleep on the floor," I offered.

"I wasn't complaining," she said quickly. "Besides, you'll freeze down there."

When I turned to tell her it didn't matter, she was already laying her cloak on top of the blankets covering the bed. The bodice's ribbons that I'd tied earlier had loosened, showing slivers of bare skin between them. I'd seen her back with rows of gemstones draped across it, but this was different. It was a *hint* of flesh and it made me desperate to press my fingers against it. To loosen the ties and kiss my way down her spine.

Anais looked over her shoulder at me and paused. Then straightened slowly, pulling her hair to one side. "Do you want to help me with them again?"

My gaze flew from her back to her eyes. The gleam there told me she knew *exactly* where my thoughts had wandered and that she... She *liked* it. There was nothing stopping us now. No ladies' maids who could catch us or guards to accidentally pass by. But I'd betrayed Bastian so much already. At least I could say I didn't betray him *this* way.

"We should rest for a few hours and get back on the road," I grumbled.

Her eyes flicked to the floor. "If you want me to wear the clothes you packed, I'll need help getting this one off."

Right. The other clothes. I'd have to bury her current dress—selling it was too risky and there was no fireplace in the room to burn it. But that didn't mean she had to wear the other clothes right now. In fact, it would be better if she didn't. Start tomorrow fresh. I winced, acknowledging to myself what a horrible excuse it was. Still, I said, "you can change in the morning."

She rolled her eyes. "I'm not sleeping in this muddy thing. Please help me."

It was the *please* that had me taking a single step to close the distance between us. My hands shook as I unlaced her bodice, the fabric dropping lower with each row. When I got to the final row, the ribbon slipped from its hook on either side, and Anais did nothing to stop the dress from pooling at her feet. Leaving her in nothing more than an underskirt, stockings, and boots.

My heart skipped a beat. I'd seen her back. Seen her in a thin night dress. But this had a different affect. It was more intimate. Heavier. And it was fucking destroying me. "Anais," I warned.

She turned, baring her chest to me, and tugged on the front of my shirt. "You said they'll kill you, but they'll kill me too."

"They won't find you," I promised, circling her wrists with my fingers. *Damn.* It was hard not to look down. Not to take in what she was showing me.

"We can only hope they won't find either of us, but there's a good chance they will. So, for now, I want to be happy, like you said in my room." She licked her lips and I felt it in my cock. "Even if it's just for tonight."

How was I going to say no to that? I wanted her more than anyone *ever* and she very clearly wanted me. This could be our only chance.

Fuck the Red Asters.

Fuck the king.

Fuck living for everyone else.

Tonight, I wasn't the Prince's Wing and she wasn't Lady Karina. We were Saer and Anais.

I swooped down and captured her mouth. Her lips were still cold from our escape and tasted the way winter smelled. My hands landed on her back, sliding over smooth skin, soaking in the feel. Memorizing her as she worked the buckle holding my swords to my waist. The metal hit the floor with a clunk.

"Wait," I breathed, pulling back. She gave a soft whimper as I stepped away from her. "I have a lot of sharp objects on me right now so before you hurt yourself…"

She watched every move I made as I pulled out all the hidden weapons and piled them in the corner. "It looks like you were expecting to go to war."

I smirked and tugged off my bracers, tossing them into the pile. "I was."

When I jerked the hem of my shirt from my pants, she motioned me forward. I obeyed. Her hands gripped the fabric and I bent so she could pull it over my head. When I stood again, her sharp intake made me tense. Did she hear something outside that I hadn't? I made one step to the window and she grabbed my arm.

"You're remarkable," she explained, eyes roving the hard lines of muscle on my abdomen.

Taking her careful perusal as permission to do the same, I allowed my gaze to drop to her breasts. The soft globes rose and fell with each of her breaths while the chilled air had hardened both light pink nipples. I swallowed hard at the desire to suck them into my mouth.

"Touch me," she breathed, almost begging.

One calloused hand dove into her hair, gripping her head near the base of her neck, while the other grazed up her stomach to cup her breast. I stole the small noise of pleasure she made as I gently pinched her nipple. The sound urged me forward, my cock leading the way.

I dragged my lips from hers to trail over the column of her neck. Then lower. I fell to my knees in front of her and took the other peak into my mouth, rolling it with the tip of my tongue.

"Saer," she gasped.

"I want you," I said as the last bit of control fled my mind.

Her fingers stroked through my hair. "You have me."

"No." I nipped the swell of her breast. "I want *all* of you."

"Then take me."

It was all I needed. I bunched her skirts up to her waist, too impatient to untie it, and ran a finger through her sex. Looking up at her, both our breaths ragged, I pushed two fingers inside the wet heat and growled a low, instinctual sound. She threw her head back and held onto my hair as I slid them out slowly.

"Wait," she said as I slipped them back in. "Wait, I don't want that."

I immediately withdrew and stood. Had I misread the situation? She—

"I want *this*." She skimmed a hand over my pants, gripping my hard length through the fabric. "We can do the rest later."

My mind went blank for a moment as desire flared bright. I wanted to touch her, taste her, please her. But I also wanted to slip my throbbing cock inside her and make her scream. My belt was gone before I realized I was unbuckling it. My pants hit the floor next.

Anais' lips parted as she took in my considerable size, both in length and width. "I forgot how big it was," she said, sounding slightly nervous.

I chuckled. "It will fit, if that's what you're worried about."

She backed into the bed, eyes lingering on my length, making it harder and harder. She sat on the edge of the bed and hiked her skirt up. "Prove it," she dared. And opened her legs.

My gaze narrowed on the slickness coating her thighs. Her sex. *For me.* I prowled to the bed and put one knee between her legs. I leaned forward, a hand on either side of her head, and licked along her lower lip.

"If you want it." I sucked her lip between my teeth and gave a gentle tug. "Take it."

Her back arched at the words, her breasts brushing against my chest. I brought my other leg onto the bed and inched closer. Close enough for her to reach my already-slick head. Her fingers wrapped around the girth and lined it up with her entrance.

"Please," she urged, rubbing the tip up and down through the wetness.

I pressed forward just enough to breach her entrance and stopped as light flashed behind my eyelids. *Fuck.* This was going to be so good. I slipped in another inch and her walls clamped down, drawing out a low moan.

A brief moment of clarity followed the wave of pleasure. Leaning down, I ran my tongue over the edge of her ear. "I want to hear you scream my name," I rumbled. "But someone might hear."

"Saer," she practically whined, shifting her hips beneath me.

"Exactly." I nipped at her lobe. "Promise you won't say it again, and I'll make you explode."

"I won't," she breathed.

Not the words any man wanted to hear, but the ones I *needed* to. I took her lips with my own and our tongues clashed. Her hands moved around my back and nails dug in, silently urging me to move.

So I did.

With one more thrust, I was fully inside her. Moving. Driving a steady pace. Dragging perfect sounds from her throat. When I took a hand from the mattress to rub against her bundle of nerves, she moaned so loud that I knew everyone else in the building heard. *Good.* Let them hear her. Let them desire what was happening between the two strangers in this room. Because it *was* enviable. The way she moved with me, the way she responded. How my heart raced for more than the utter bliss I felt while inside her.

Anais squeezed around my cock with a wordless scream. Her pleasure tightened my balls, but I held back until she relaxed beneath me. Then my thrusts became more erratic until I was forced to pull out. As soon as I did, my own release fired all over the outside of her sex.

I dropped my head to the mattress beside hers and gasped for air. One of Anais' hands trailed up the back of my arm—the one still holding my weight off her—and I shivered.

"Are you okay?" I asked, too tired to move just yet.

"I'm amazing." She kissed my shoulder, then nudged me. "But maybe you're not."

I lifted my head enough to see where she was looking. Long red scratches marked where she had just kissed. "I'll wear them with honor," I said and rolled off her.

Anais immediately snuggled closer and I lifted my arm to let her in. We would clean ourselves up later. But, after running from the palace and losing ourselves in each other, we were both too exhausted to care.

TWENTY-SIX

My eyes snapped open on a sharp inhale. Panic clawed at my chest as I surveyed the unknown room. There were no wooden beams on the ceiling. Beneath me, the mattress was hard. My body tensed, poised to strike out at the unseen danger. Something moved against my side and I lunged, pinning them down with my forearm to their throat.

A startled gasp hit my ears. "Saer?"

Reality pushed through the dream-like haze and I blinked down at Anais. Her honey hair spread across the pillow, her eyes wide, lips parted in shock.

I reared back. "Sorry." I ran my hands over my face. "I'm sorry."

"It's okay." She sat up, pulling the sheet to cover her chest, and reached out to touch my arm. "Was it a nightmare?"

A nightmare? No. It was… life. Real life, coming to bite me in the ass. All the years I'd spent looking for danger, expecting it, made sleeping hard, but now that danger was inevitable. And the strike would come soon. I felt it in my core. But from where? And who? Would Bastian be there when they found us? Would he swing his sword against me?

I wouldn't blame him if he did. After stealing his fiancée, after all the lies I'd told, it was fair. A quick glance at the orange-tinted sky through one of the large holes in the curtain told me dawn was breaking. He would know Anais and I were missing by now. My stomach rolled at the thought of him piecing together the betrayal. Years of trust, shattered. It felt like something inside me died, stealing my next breath.

"Are you okay?" Anais pressed when I forced in a ragged breath.

I squeezed my eyes shut and willed away the pain in my chest. We should leave now before the city woke for the day. Avoid the extra witnesses and put more distance behind us. "Are you rested enough to leave?" I asked, opening my eyes again.

"Is something wrong?" she insisted.

Everything was wrong, starting with how dishonorable I was. But, with her looking at me with those wide, imploring eyes, I couldn't regret what happened the night before. The way our bodies moved against each other, the sound of her coming apart beneath me. I'd never felt a connection like the one we shared—it was almost as if a string tied our hearts together. We had taken our shot at happiness and I would carry it with me for the rest of my life. The warmth. The weightlessness of it.

I leaned in and cupped her cheeks, kissing her lightly on the lips. "Nothing more than was wrong last night," I told her. "We aren't safe yet."

She studied me for a moment, a line between her brows, before nodding. "I'll get dressed."

Together we fumbled through the room to put our clothes on. Anais had no elaborate ribbons to tie this time so, as she buttoned her own thick jacket, I stuffed the black and gold dress into the now-empty bag. The bread and dried meat I'd included inside was now spread out on the bed.

"Eat something before we go," I urged. We'd used a lot of energy the night before and we would need to replenish it before doing the same today.

Anais lifted the loaf of bread and tore off the heel, holding it out to me. "You too."

I smirked and bent over her hand, taking a bite without breaking eye contact. She blushed. "If we were anywhere else, I would give you a more fitting breakfast."

"This is perfect." She chewed a piece of bread and started collecting the rest of the food to repack with her brocade dress. "All that fancy food the countess fed me in the mornings was too heavy."

"What do you prefer to eat if not a royal spread?" I asked, curious.

She shrugged. "An egg or two, maybe. With something warm to drink. What about you?"

I paused. There wasn't a time I could remember eating anything that *wasn't* from the palace. "I don't know. I suppose I eat because I have to, but I've never really enjoyed it. Whatever fills my stomach."

"What?" She gaped at me. "You don't have any favorite meals? What about treats? Sugar candy or fruit?"

A smirk grew on my face as I gazed at her lush lips, her eyes bright. "I enjoyed you."

"Oh, my goodness." She covered her flaming cheeks with both hands. "That is *not* what I meant."

I chuckled and dipped my head to kiss her again. "If we didn't have to rush, I would have you again this morning."

Desire flashed through her eyes. She abandoned the food to turn toward me fully. "We have a *little* time, don't we?"

A door banged open across the hall and someone released a loud belch. My head snapped to the door, all thoughts of devouring Anais' sweetness gone. "Later," I promised. *If there was a later.*

Our pace was slower, the day barely warmer than night. The trees all looked the same, skeletal branches blending together, sky gray. Each footstep crumbled through a thin layer of ice over the blanket of leaves. We couldn't continue on foot much longer in this weather, especially since it would only get colder the more north we were. We also needed to find shelter—an inn, a cave, anywhere to block the wind and make a fire. As the sun rose and set, it was all I could think of.

That and Bastian. What happened when he realized we were missing? Were the guards close to finding us? Did Faramond know? *Of course he knew.* One of the Asters in the palace must've told him—probably before the king even knew.

"Where are we stopping tonight?" Anais asked, voice shaking nearly as hard as her body.

I squeezed her hand in mine, trying to warm her. There would be another town eventually, but I wasn't sure the distance. Another large city, one busy enough to get lost in, was at least three more days if I remembered correctly. Given that we were traveling through the woods, keeping away from the roads… "I'm not sure."

A soft whimper escaped her. "Can we sit for a minute then?"

I slowed, coming to a stop at a fallen tree, and we both sat to rest our aching muscles. The trunk was slick with ice but I barely felt it, my legs already frozen. Flinging my cloak aside, I tugged Anais against my side and wrapped the fabric around us both.

"We'll find somewhere soon," I promised.

Anais nodded and rested her head on my shoulder. I rubbed my hand against her back in slow circles. Both to heat her up and because I couldn't stop touching her. I held her hand all day, twirled her hair between my fingers when we stopped, and snuck a handful of kisses after we ate. My mind should've solely been on our escape, but she consumed me. Pushed out all rational thought.

"Are you warm enough?" I asked.

She laughed. "Perfectly toasty."

"Alright." I groaned as I stood. "Let's get going before we freeze to the log."

A twig snapped nearby in the silent forest. I twisted, my hand immediately going to the hilt of my sword. Pain lanced through my shoulder blade before I could remove the weapon. Then a sharp sting across my side. An arrow slammed into the fallen tree, right beside Anais' thigh.

"Get down," I shouted, and shoved her backward over the log.

I didn't get the chance to see if she stayed hidden behind it before another arrow pierced my back. A strangled growl left my throat as I stumbled. Another arrow. I fell to my knees. Vision blinking in and out. I'd been shot before—stabbed and whipped and broken—but the next arrow hit with a *thunk* that reverberated through every cell of my body. I fell forward, holding myself up with one arm, and coughed. Blood splattered the brown and yellow leaves.

"Anais," I said, and tasted the metallic hint of blood in my mouth. "Run."

A boot slammed into my side and I toppled over. "Hello, Wing," a royal guard sneered. Then, louder, he called, "get the girl."

"No!" I jerked up and was met with a fist to my cheek. Pain exploded, stars dancing in my vision. I tried desperately to blink them away, to see, but the pressure behind my eye made the assailant blurry.

"Try to keep him alive until we get back to the palace," someone said. "The king wants to talk to him."

The guard looming over me scowled. "Not sure we can guarantee that."

I withdrew a dagger from beneath my bracer and threw it. The blade landed in his throat and he stumbled back, gurgling. I smiled as he tumbled over his own feet. Smiled for the small bit of satisfaction it gave. For the distraction it caused. I hoped Anais saw the opening as a dozen guards raced forward to help him.

"Fucker," one of them shouted. Right before driving their boot into my face.

TWENTY-SEVEN

All I knew was pain. Sharp bursts of agony raged through me, a barrage of biting aches. But mostly heat. Ungodly heat radiating from my back. I attempted to lower my arms to ease some of the warmth but they wouldn't budge.

I cracked my eyes open to a dark room. The only light came through the semi-circle barred window at the top of the wall in front of me. On the other side stood a pair of muddy guard's boots. I exhaled, the sound trembling, the breath a visible cloud in front of my face.

The dungeon.

This was the dungeon at the palace.

Memories flooded through me. Leaving Ora Et, the woods, arrows, Anais—I jerked forward at her name. A strangled shout tore from my throat. Chains

252

held my arms over the top of a thick wooden beam and the movement speared through my shoulders. They were undoubtedly dislocated on top of having arrow wounds. My vision blinked in and out as my body continued to throb in time with my pulse.

In the distance, a metal door creaked open followed by footsteps. I hung my head, willing the dizziness away. This was always going to be my fate so, as the footsteps neared, I calmly resigned myself to whatever came for me. I had always thought I'd fight against dying even if I accepted the truth of it, but now I only felt… Guilt. For all those years lying to Bastian. Betraying him even though I loved him. And for not getting Anais away quickly enough. Wherever she was right now, I hoped her fate wasn't as bleak as my own. A yawning darkness opened in my chest, threatening to pull me in. I knew if I allowed myself to fall to the inky pit, all the horrible things I'd done, every lie and misleading remark, would torment me just as my body would be tortured soon. I deserved it, but I wasn't prepared for more suffering. Whoever questioned me would send my mind spiraling in that direction soon enough.

The boots that stopped in front of me weren't the well-worn leather of a guard but gleaming black. My head whipped up, expecting Bastian, but instead, I found King Edric. "You caused quite the ruckus," he said in a flat voice and picked off a glove one finger at a time. He handed it over his shoulder to one of his Wings—I couldn't tell them apart in the dim light. They were both hulking masses that blurred in and out in my peripheral.

"Where's Anais?" I rasped.

"Worried about your whore?" King Edric sneered as he removed the second glove and handed that over as well. The second Wing—Nen, I thought, when my vision cleared for a moment—held out a coiled rope. *Not a rope.* The king let the whip trail down to the stone floor and gave it a practice flick. It gave a light *tsk* against the stone floor, but I knew from experience that it wouldn't sound so innocent against flesh. The king moved his gaze up my body before settling on my eyes. "Worry about yourself."

Then he lashed out. Hard and fast. The crack of the whip against my stomach pulled out a startled cry. Before I could recover, a second lash landed on my upper chest, the tip curling over my shoulder. The third intersected both. But I held my screams then. Swallowed them as the king rained pain down on my torso.

The burning, stinging pain in my back now matched the front as the hits blended together. I felt the blood ooze from where the arrow had struck my shoulder blade, but the whip marks were too close together to notice if one bled or they all did.

My vision tunneled as the king continued his assault. I heard the cracks. Felt the agony of the whip landing in some distant recess of my mind. *Crack, crack, crack.* I dragged in a wet breath. *Gods have mercy and let me die.*

The gods did in fact have mercy—just not the kind I'd wanted. I'd lost consciousness at some point, but I was still alive. If that was what this was considered. I slumped against the restraints, unable to hold myself up, and the wooden beam brought all my weight down onto my shoulders.

"You're awake," came a familiar voice.

I lifted my head enough to see the outline of Bastian. Someone had lit two torches on either side of the window since I was awake last. Hours? Days?

"Bast?" I croaked. My throat was dry, tongue thick. "What are you doing here?"

He stepped closer, wringing his hands together in front of him. Dark circles painted the skin beneath his eyes, but it was the dead look in them that drove a nail through my chest. "Is it true?" he asked in a rough, quiet voice.

"Is what true?" Although I was sure the answer would be yes.

"You're with the Red Asters? You were placed at my side to spy on me?"

I let my head drop back down to avoid his gaze. "I was a child—I wasn't given a choice."

Bastian swallowed hard. "Not then, no. But you grew up."

"Yes. I grew up." I squeezed my eyes shut against the pain growing in my chest. Somehow it was worse than the arrows and the whip. "But what would you have done if I told you when I was ten? When I was twenty? By then, I'd already been a traitor for so long that the truth would've gotten me killed. And, if by some miracle, your father pardoned me, the Asters would've sent an assassin."

"I would've protected you," he said with conviction.

Pressure built behind my eyes, threatening tears for the first time in over a decade. He would've tried and knowing that was what mattered to me. "It was *my* job to protect *you*. That's why I didn't tell you. How could I save you from the rebels if I was dead?"

He was silent for a moment. "Was that why you became my friend? For them?"

My head snapped up and I winced. "If I wasn't your friend, I wouldn't have lived my life like this. Decades spent walking the knife's edge. Worried you would find out. The *king* would find out. Or the Asters would ask something of me that I wasn't willing to do and perish for it. Every day of my life has been a lie and I hate myself for it. I deserve my fate, but I need you to know…" I blinked away the tears threatening to fill my eyes. It hurt my chest to talk this much, both from the wounds and the explosive guilt, but I was about to die. This could be my last chance to explain everything. "You need to know that I never betrayed you to them."

Bastian locked eyes with me and cocked his head. "Until now."

I flinched. "Anais?"

A crease formed between his brows. "What?"

"Nothing." *Fuck.* I'd just exposed her name when *Karina* could possibly be the only thing keeping her alive. It was too late to pull the word back in—all I could do was distract him from insisting on an answer. "Don't blame Karina. Please. If you still have a shred of love for me, don't kill her. It was my idea to run."

His chest rose and fell in harsh breaths. "I don't know how to feel, Saer. I want to pretend this is all a nightmare and go back to how things were. But I *can't.*

So, I need you to explain *why* you thought having an affair with my fiancée was something a friend would do."

"It's not what you think." *Mostly.* I struggled to get my feet beneath me. If I told him Anais' secret, she was equally as fucked as me.

"She's set to stand trial in three days, but you and I know what the verdict will be so don't martyr yourself for her. Explain. You owe me that."

I sucked in a strangled breath. Hadn't I given him everything? Always? But he was right—I owed him the whole truth. And, finally, I could give it to him. If Anais was set to stand trial instead of being quietly sequestered, she wouldn't be found innocent. The governors disapproved of her *before* she committed a crime against the crown. I released a defeated sigh, unable to summon the ability to lie. "I was trying to save you."

"From Karina?" he scoffed, turning his back on me to pace.

"Yes," I wheezed. "Question the countess—you'll learn her child died a few years after your father took the throne."

Bastian whirled on me. "What?"

"The real Karina is dead. Anais is someone the countess bought to act the part. She had no choice but to play along for her family's sake, but she had no idea the countess was working with the Red Asters. I don't know what they planned to use her for, but they *would* use her." My boots slipped in the blood pooling at my feet and the weight of my body twisted my arms higher. I threw my head back with gritted teeth. "Believe me," I forced out. "If they ordered her to kill you, she couldn't refuse. The Asters would've made sure your father knew her secret just like they told you mine when I ruined their plans by running." He didn't need to tell me how he knew I was an Aster. Faramond threatened to expose me and he did. "Denying the rebels is a death sentence. Leaving was the only way to save you both."

Bastian worked his jaw. "I'll have the countess questioned before the trial."

"You'll condemn Anais to death if anyone finds out."

Bastian gave a humorless laugh. "You say you ran for my sake, but it sounds like more than that."

Because it was. I could've let Anais' secret slip in a way that wouldn't implicate me and neutralized the problem weeks ago. *Fuck it.* I was about to die. Without being told, I knew that there would be no trial for me. Might as well go out having said it aloud once. Even if it wasn't to the right person.

"I love her." I closed my eyes and let my head roll where it may. There wasn't enough strength left in me to do anything else. However Bastian felt about Anais, I was convinced he didn't love her, not like I did. One day, perhaps, they would've grown to love each other and I stole that from him. I hated myself for it, but I couldn't regret it either. "It started when I met her in the garden. Once I found out who she was, I tried to stop but I just… couldn't. I'm sorry, Bast. So damn sorry."

Warm hands gripped my cheeks, tilting my face up. I expected a punch to follow. Bastian's hands to lower to my throat and finish me. Instead, he looked at me with a mix of shock and sadness. "She's the noblewoman you talked about?"

"Yes," I breathed.

His grip on my face tightened. I closed my eyes, ready for it all to end. Fitting that he would be the one to do it. It was better this way. For him and me.

Bastian's forehead landed on mine and he snarled. "Fuck."

I opened my mouth to apologize again, but he was gone. Practically running from the dungeon. I released a defeated sigh as a traitorous tear slid down my cheek. Had I helped Anais escape death? Did Bastian have enough answers to give him peace? I was too exhausted to sort any of it out. But I knew with certainty that I wouldn't see my friend again. I'd be lucky to see the sun rise.

"Goodbye," I whispered to his back as the sound of the creaky door filled the cell.

My last thought was that I hoped he would stay safe before I allowed myself to find oblivion again.

TWENTY-EIGHT

The thick scent of herbs woke me as someone gently touched my chest. I pried my heavy lids open to find the royal healer standing in front of me, rubbing a healing balm into the raw lashes. *Why?* Was I to go through the charade of a trial after all? They would need me alive and coherent. Unless King Edric simply wanted to keep me alive to torment me longer.

"He's awake," the healer said over his shoulder.

I lifted my head a little higher, groaning as the pain radiated from my back. My chest was blissfully numb. Bastian leaned against the wall behind the healer with his arms crossed. At the sight of him, I tried to push to my feet, but my legs shook too much to manage it. The healer set his salve-covered hand on my shoulder to steady me.

"Hold still," he admonished.

"Your Highness," I croaked. Not only because of the audience, but I wasn't sure if I was allowed to use his given name anymore.

"Relax and let the man work." The prince scuffed the floor with the toe of his shoe. "He needs to return before someone notices him missing."

"If we could undo his chains now," the healer suggested.

Bastian nodded and stepped forward with the key to unlock the chains around the wooden beam. "I wasn't sure if you'd wake up fighting if we took them off before," he explained quietly as the chains clinked, loosening. "The whole plan hinges on us going unnoticed."

The chains slid to the ground and my body slumped to the side, legs unable to hold me up on their own. Bastian caught me with an arm across my chest. He slowly lowered me to the floor and helped the healer remove my tattered shirt.

"What plan?" I wheezed.

"Did you think I'd let you die?" Bastian braced my shoulder, letting my forehead rest on his collarbone as the healer gently moved one of my arms.

Without warning, the old man popped my shoulder back into place. I immediately wretched from the pain, my mouth flooding with saliva. The healer repeated the motion to my other shoulder before I had a chance to recover. The room tilted, sight and sound unfocused. Sweat beaded on my skin and I clutched onto Bastian like an anchor.

"Hold on," Bastian urged.

The healer began treating the wounds from the arrows next. I hissed in pain at the first touch of his ointment, my clarity rushing back, but then a cooling tingle spread from the wounds.

"I still don't know how to feel about everything that happened," Bastian continued despite the healer's presence. "I'm furious with you now but I… I understand. At least, I want to. If I let my father kill you, I'd regret it when the anger fades."

I huffed a laugh. "Wouldn't want you to regret it."

"You know what I mean," he mumbled. "When you're all stitched up, I've got a coach ready to take you to the Summer Palace. You can stay there until you heal enough to forge your own path."

"I can't leave you here alone." I winced at the first prick of the healer's needle.

"You can stay and die, or leave and live, but both options leave me without a Wing."

The sorrow in his voice echoed what I felt in my chest. "It's my duty to die protecting you."

"Your duty is what I say it is." He squeezed my shoulder where he still held me steady for the healer. "Now hold still."

That wasn't true. Everyone had drilled it into me since I'd arrived at the palace: *protect the prince or die trying.* But I was in no position to argue. The state of my body left me with no choice but to obey. As the healer worked, I thought about the times I spent with Bastian at the Summer Palace. Carefree summers where we would explore the woods and, when we got older, learned to hunt. Now I would be the prey, though. Hunted by anyone and everyone that wasn't Bastian as the price on my head was bound to be enormous.

"All finished, Your Highness." The final snip of the healer's scissors left the last hole stitched shut. "I have some medication for him to take over the next few days to ward off infection."

"Thank you," Bastian said and stood. I fell forward, catching myself with my hands and my elbows trembled with the weight. A clink of coin exchanging hands filled my ears. "Alright," he said to me once the healer departed. "Let's get you up."

"I don't think I can walk," I admitted.

"You've been stuck on the post for two days without food and water. Even if you weren't beat to hell, I wouldn't expect you to."

Bastian grabbed one of my arms while another pair of hands gripped the other. My gaze flew to the side to find Volney slipping his head beneath my elbow to better carry my weight.

"What the fuck?" I growled. Where the hell had he come from? Was he here the entire time?

"You let me win," he replied. "If you're dead, I won't get a rematch."

"Horrible excuse to commit *treason*," I shot back. "How did you even get involved in something like this?"

"Saer." Bastian grunted under my weight. "Shut up."

The healer stood at the entrance to the dungeons, waving us forward. Bastian and Volney dragged me through the dark tunnel, toward the breaking dawn. There would be a change of guards soon at the main entrance to the palace, which had to be the reason for the rush.

"Hurry," the healer urged.

Bastian exited into the graveled courtyard first, paused, then nodded to Volney. A carriage was already there with a pair of horses hitched. *My* horses. The ones I'd bought for Anais' escape.

"You knew?" I asked Bastian.

"Fuck no. *He* did." He bobbed his head toward the King's Wing.

"I followed you to the library with Governor Pevran's niece," he admitted. "Then I put civilian eyes on you. The horses were about the only thing of value I could find which takes talent."

"You didn't tell the king?"

He shrugged. "I told the prince."

"Yesterday," he mumbled. "After it was of any use."

"It's useful now, isn't it? No royal horses are missing from the stable."

Bastian shifted my arm around his shoulders as a driver jumped down from the outside bench. It wasn't anyone I recognized—a boy, likely from Ora Et, paid in enough gold to ensure his silence. He swung the door open and Volney all but threw me inside.

A pair of small hands circled my upper arm when I landed in front of the padded seat. My gaze lifted to find Anais huddled into her cloak. Time seemed to stop as she offered me a tentative smile.

I scrambled to my knees and turned back to Bastian just as the driver swung the door shut again. My hand flew to the handle, ready to fling it open and demand an explanation from Bastian. This wasn't right… I wasn't supposed to be alive, let alone given a chance at happiness outside of the palace. After everything I'd done, I didn't deserve it.

"Bast," I shouted as the carriage jerked forward.

My entire life was spent as his Wing. Everything before the palace never existed in my mind—even my parents' faces were lost to time. My earliest memory was meeting Bastian in the place and sharing his blocks. A test to see if we—at three and four years old—were compatible before they threw me in front of the king for approval. He was the only one that was kind to me, even then. A lonely prince and an even lonelier orphan quickly became family.

Bastian raised his hand halfway in a silent farewell and it summoned echoes of our shared childhood. Of the pain and the laughter. When he turned his back on the carriage, I could hardly breathe. Volney walked at the prince's side as they disappeared around the side of the stone building.

"No. Bastian!" I slammed my palms against the carriage window. There had to be another option for us. "Wait!"

"Saer," Anais whispered, touching my bare back with cool fingers. "You'll rip your stitches."

"Fuck the stitches," I growled.

She tugged on my arm. "Sit down before someone sees you."

Let them see me. Let them alert the guards and get me thrown back into the dungeon where I belonged for being such a shit human.

"*Please.*"

The desperate word cracked something in my chest and I dragged myself from the window to sit beside her. "How are you here?" I rasped.

"The prince came to see me last night." Anais rifled through a leather satchel and pulled out one of my shirts. "Put this on before you freeze."

I took the linen from her and gingerly tugged it over my head as she picked up a folded cloak from the bench beside her. Without the energy to shift to wear it properly, I arranged it over myself like a blanket instead. "What did he say?"

"That he talked to you and…"

When she busied herself with tucking the cloak around me instead of finishing her sentence, I asked, "And what?"

"He had me promise to make you happy." She bit her lower lip. "Once you're healed, we'll talk about what that means. If you don't want me, then he's given me enough coin to make it on my own, but I won't leave you until you're better."

My hand darted out from beneath the cloak to grab hers. Dizziness returned at the thought of losing her and Bastian all at once. I wouldn't survive it. "I want you, Anais."

Tears filled her eyes at the same time a real smile spread across her face. She leaned in and kissed me tenderly. And all too briefly. "I thought you were dead," she whispered when she pulled back.

"I'm not dead." I shifted in my seat to take the pressure off my wounds and set my head on her shoulder. "Let me rest here awhile?"

"Of course." She inched closer and squeezed my hand. "Rest. I'll wake you when we get to the Summer Palace."

I closed my eyes without telling her it would be three days before we arrived. My mind was collapsing in on itself almost as quickly as my body wilted. There was too much to process. Too much pain blocking any of it from making sense. Too many questions I would never have answers to now that Bastian and I were permanently separated. The *whys* and *hows* I'd never get to ask. But I was leaving Ora Et and Anais was with me…

Perhaps I *had* died after all.

TWENTY-NINE

Days blurred together at the Summer Palace. All of the furniture was covered in white sheets, the cupboards bare. I would've gone hunting for something to eat but my body ached with a fever. Joints stiff. Head murky. Anais stayed by my side as the infection raged, ready with a cool cloth and a dose of the healer's medication. It tasted like sour dirt.

It was nearly a week before I could sit up without getting dizzy. Another day before I had the strength to stand. Anais had done her best to feed us. Between stretching out the supplies Bastian sent with the carriage, her foraging for winter berries, and the discovery of canned peaches, we hadn't been in danger of starving. But the supplies were dwindling now.

"I wish you wouldn't do this." Anais followed me outside on the third day after my fever broke. "I can walk to town and buy something instead."

"Town is too far and it's too cold," I said, slinging a bow over my shoulder. Luckily the hunter's cabin on the outskirts of the land was still stocked. Bastian had packed two daggers into our bag, but nothing long-range. "I'll be quick. Stay inside, just in case anyone passes by."

When she shut the door behind me, I headed into the woods. Frost clung to the top of matted grass, so each step *crunched*. It was good to be outside again, free of the stale palace with its shuttered windows and covered furniture. Without Bastian, it felt wrong to be here. Anais and I stayed in the cook's room beside the kitchen for easier access to the exit, if needed, but all I could see whenever I left the bedroom were memories.

When Bastian and I summered here, we would steal dessert before dinner. The cook would've given it to him—he *was* the prince—but it was more fun that way. To snatch a jelly bun and run. Hiding behind curtains or in alcoves to eat it. Learning from the cook how to roll out a perfect crust. Her allowing us to keep the extra pieces so we could sprinkle them with sugar and bake them alongside her pie. Having fun with him was worth whatever scolding we received. I wished we could go back to those days. Everything seemed simpler then.

An hour later, I returned with two dead rabbits. *Please, Gods, let Anais know how to skin them.* She'd grown up in Port Black so fish were more of a sure thing than mammals, but I'd overdone it with hunting. I'd felt well enough earlier. Now I just wanted to rest. *Needed* to.

Anais swung the door open when I passed into the courtyard and rushed out to meet me. "Poor rabbits," she said, taking them by their ears.

I leaned in and kissed her on top of her head. "Do you know what to do with them?"

"Yes," she admitted a little reluctantly.

Practically falling onto the stool in front of the large kitchen worktable, I let the bow clatter to the ground. "I'm sorry. I should do it."

"Are you okay?" The rabbits landed on the table and she knelt in front of me. "You didn't get hurt out there, did you?"

I stared down at her with her wide, concerned eyes and my heart skipped. So many times, I'd woken from a fever dream to find her beside me, and each time I thought I was still asleep. *Still dreaming.* I tucked a piece of hair behind her ear and gave her a smile. "I'm not hurt."

"Tired then?"

"Tired," I agreed. "I'm sorry."

Anais set her hand on my thigh. "Don't be sorry."

I set one arm on the table and laid my head on it. With my free hand, I stroked her soft golden hair. I was perpetually sorry—to her, to Bastian. We sat like that for a long time before I drummed up the courage to ask, "What happened to you when I was in the dungeon?"

"Nothing."

"Nothing?" I repeated in disbelief.

"They locked me in my rooms without visitors, except the prince. I was set to stand trial the day we left, so I imagine whatever horrible thing they had planned for me would've come soon enough."

Bastian hadn't told the king her identity then. Not that I was entirely surprised given how he smuggled us out of the capital. I couldn't help wonder what he told his father about our disappearance. Were we thought dead or fugitives again? It would help to know where we stood so when we left, we could take proper precautions.

Tomorrow I would go to the library and search the maps of Eradrist. We were close enough to go south, to the same place I'd found for Anais. Pevran's niece never knew the name of the town, just the direction of it. A meadow would complement Anais' free spirit. I would build us a small house on a hill. Perhaps purchase a few sheep. I could already see the sun kissing her face.

I closed my eyes to better imagine it, and when I opened them again, Anais was plating chunks of cooked rabbit. "That smells amazing," I said, peering up at her.

She jumped and spun around, smiling. "Thanks."

We ate in silence, the meat a little dry but still hitting the spot. My appetite appeared to be back as I got myself a second helping. I cleared the dishes once we had both finished and threw another log on the fire.

"We should talk about what we're going to do next," Anais said when I sat on the edge of the table beside her. She was still on her stool, tracing a knot in the tabletop.

"South," I said with certainty.

She furrowed her brows. "South what?"

"We'll go south, together, and make whatever life we can with this second chance."

Anais chewed her bottom lip.

"You don't like the south?" I asked, leaning toward her and lifting her chin. "Or you don't want to go with me?"

"I want to go with you," she said quickly.

"Then what's wrong?"

"It's not important."

"Tell me anyway," I urged. Important or not, if it bothered her, I wanted to know.

She took a deep breath and let it out. "When we go *together*, what does that mean?"

I lowered my brows. "I don't understand."

"You never planned to come with me originally and, when we ran, you weren't going to *stay* with me. We slept together when we thought it could be our only chance so I suppose I'm wondering—"

I closed the distance between us, silencing her with a kiss. Her tongue darted out to meet mine and she pushed onto her toes so I didn't have to lean over as far. Without breaking the kiss, she sidestepped to stand between my legs.

My hands snaked around her waist, pulling her closer. I slid my lips across her cheek, down her neck, and back up again. "Anais," I breathed against her mouth. "Look at me."

She brought her head back enough to meet my gaze. Desire swirled in her eyes, tainted with uncertainty. I didn't want her to question this. To question me. The thought of leaving her before was hard, but now? Impossible.

"Saer?" she asked, her hands landing tentatively on my thighs.

"I love you." I moved one hand to her cheek and ran my thumb along her cheekbone. "I think I've loved you this whole time, but I was…" *Trying not to.* "I'm sorry for leaving you uncertain. I'll never let you doubt my feelings for you again."

She smiled and pressed a finger against the crease between my brows. "I love you too."

I kissed her nose. Her forehead. Each cheek. I rained them upon her face until my lips found hers again. This time the kiss was deeper. The sensation of her tongue against mine coursed through my entire body, lighting me up. My cock stiffened in my pants and I was suddenly desperate to feel her around me.

I stood and spun her so she was the one sitting on the table. Her hands found the base of my neck and tugged me back to her. My hands shook as I gathered her skirts around her waist. When my knuckle grazed her slick opening, she gasped.

"Please," she whispered.

"Lay back," I told her in a rough voice. "Let me watch you."

She shook her head. "Later. I want more than your fingers."

"That's what you said last time," I teased. But the eagerness to oblige had me untying my pants with the pull of a string, and I shoved them down. Anais watched me line my hard length up to her entrance and licked her lips. I slipped my tip through her wetness, reveling in the fact that it was for *me*.

"Saer, *please.*"

"You're mine," I said, pressing into her entrance slightly. "And I'm yours."

"Yes." She shifted her hips in an attempt to take me in deeper.

Instead, I lifted her up and sank to the stone floor with her on top. Her knees landed on either side of my hips, straddling me, and I devoured her mouth, hands in her hair. "Use me," I whispered, pulling away only long enough to say the words.

"What?" She pulled away and looked nervously at where our bodies connected. Her skirt had draped over my cock, separating me from her heat. "I've never done that before."

I tugged the fabric out of the way and lined myself up with her entrance. "Do whatever feels good."

She bit her lip and settled her hands on my shoulders before lowering herself. Her walls slowly sucked me in deep. When she was fully seated, my head fell back with a groan and her hands tightened. "Oh my gods," she hissed.

I smirked, knowing the angle would make her feel fuller, and gripped her hips. "Fuck me." Anais shifted her weight uncertainly so I guided her hips up and down. "Like this."

Anais groaned as I continued to guide her movements, setting the pace until her breaths became heavy. I leaned up on my elbows and held her skirts aside so I could watch myself disappear inside her. Over and over. Her movements quickly became more erratic. She leaned forward and I laid back fully so she had space to continue moving.

"Saer," she breathed. "I'm going to…"

She gripped my shirt, rubbing the fabric over the sensitive, newly-healed marks. I winced but then she arched her back, her walls quivering. A spike of heat rushed straight to my cock. *Fuck.* I grabbed her hips again to still her and drove myself up. She threw her head back with a moan, emboldening me. I drove into her again and again until she squeezed around me, screaming as she came. I followed her over the edge, emptying myself into her with a strangled cry.

We laid on the floor, breathing heavily, until she shifted off me. "My knees are cold," she said as she got up and held her hands out to me. "And your ass must be frozen."

I let out a husky laugh. My ass *was* frozen, but it was worth every second of it. "It is." I took her hands and got off the floor. "But I know a way to warm it up."

Anais glanced down at my length and it stiffened again. "Is that even possible?"

"It absolutely is," I growled, and led her to the bedroom.

THIRTY

Anais and I wore our cloaks tight as we rode into the city nearest the Summer Palace. After this, we would avoid villages of any size as much as possible, but I needed to know what we should expect on the trip. We also needed to fill our saddlebags with provisions and I had to acquire a warmer shirt to wear over the one Bastian gave me.

"Keep your head down," I warned Anais. The chance that anyone here would recognize us was low, but not impossible.

We tied our horses in front of a tailor shop where I quickly purchased a wool tunic and gloves for both of us. The young woman working there appeared completely oblivious to who we were so either the crown never released our sketches or they hadn't arrived here yet.

"Better?" Anais asked once I'd refastened my cloak.

"Much." I smirked and stole a quick kiss before leading her farther into town. We passed a bakery, the scent of freshly baked bread making my mouth water. We'd get a loaf on the way back to the horses so we could eat it while it was still warm. My stomach rumbled as we approached a stand with a small selection of winter fruit instead.

"Plums!" Anais pointed to a basket of small purple fruit. "They're my favorite."

I stared at her smiling face. Something as little as a piece of fruit had given her the brightest smile, brighter than I'd ever seen it at the palace. In time, I hoped she would smile like that every day.

"What?" she asked when she noticed me looking.

"Nothing." I placed a hand on her back. "Get as many as you'd like."

Anais nodded to the man at the stall and he began filling a paper sack. "Any apples?" he asked.

Anais looked up at me for an answer. "Six," I said. They would help stretch our food between now and the next stop.

"Long journey ahead?" the man asked conversationally.

I gave a low *mmm* of affirmation and looked around. There was no one nearby to eavesdrop or spy, but that seemed off. It was nearly midday in the center of town and there were only a handful of citizens around. "It's quiet here today."

"The rebels swept through yesterday on the way to the capital. Took everyone they could with them and most people smart enough not to join them have holed themselves up. Bad for business, I tell you." He held a bulging bag out to Anais. "Six silver."

"Rebels?" My pulse jumped. I counted out the coins from my pouch and handed them over while trying not to show any emotion. "Why are they going to Ora Et?"

He raised a brow. "Been living in a cave, have you?"

"Long journey," I grumbled. "What's going on in the capital?"

"The Red Asters are attacking the palace. It's been under siege for days."

Under siege for days. Bastian was alone… at the worst possible time. It was my job to protect him, but I was what? Buying fruit in some unknown village.

"Thank you," Anais told the man and elbowed me in the side.

I guided her away from the fruit stand and passed by the bakery without stopping. My vision tunneled to our horses at the end of the street. What triggered Faramond to attack? Was it our disappearance? The countess had to be losing her mind over Anais vanishing and what it meant for her return to court. Or…

Fuck.

What if this was because Bastian had her questioned? What if she gave Faramond up to protect herself and started an all-out war in the process?

"This is my fault," I mumbled and took the fruit from Anais, dumping it into the saddlebag. "I did this."

"You didn't do anything," she assured me.

"I've done plenty." I moved between our horses and untied their reins with jerky movements. "Faramond attacking the palace now can't be a coincidence."

"Who?"

"The Aster leader," I snapped. "He's using what's happened as an opportunity to take the throne."

"And do what with it?" Anais asked in a quiet voice, casting a look over her shoulder. "There's no one left of the old royal family."

"He'll probably sit on the damn thing himself." My voice shook, each breath coming too fast, too hard.

"Saer, calm down." She placed her hands over mine as I fisted the reins. "This isn't your fault. The rebels have been around forever and you said they were going to use me for something. Maybe it's this. Maybe it's my fault."

"As if they knew I would fall in love with you and leave the prince unprotected? No. This is something else." Something unplanned if Asters were recruiting openly in the streets. They were always more cunning than that. I turned and led my horse back toward the road.

"You should go," she called after me.

I stopped in my tracks. "What?"

The slow clop of her horse's hooves filled my head as she came to my side. "This is about the prince, right? You're worried about him."

My chest tightened, forcing out a harsh breath. "They'll kill him."

"Then go. I'll wait for you at the Summer Palace."

I looked down at her and the image of our future turned to dust. My heart crumbled along with it. If I went back, I would never leave the palace again. Even if I saved Bastian, there would be no escaping my treason charge. But if I *didn't* go back... If Bastian died because I was too much of a coward, how would I scrape any sort of happiness from life knowing that I abandoned my best friend in his greatest time of need?

"If anyone comes while I'm gone, hide," I told her and pressed the sack of coins into her hands. If I told her I wouldn't return, she would insist on coming or change her mind about my leaving, but I didn't want her waiting for someone who would never come back either. "And if I'm not back in a week, leave. Go south and I'll find you."

She nodded. "Go."

There was no other choice but to return, but... I pulled her in and kissed her deeply, praying it wasn't our last. If this was our final moment together, I would take comfort in knowing what we had was real. "I love you."

"I love you too," she whispered.

Fighting every desire to stay, I mounted my horse and bolted from the city. The urge to look back, to get one more glimpse of Anais, nearly overwhelmed me, but I kept my gaze fixed in the direction of the capital for fear of changing my mind. Anais was free now but Bastian still needed me.

The three-day carriage ride from Ora Et to the Summer Palace took half that on horseback. By the time I reached the edge of the capital, my horse was covered in sweat with foam dripping from his mouth, but I was calm. Focused.

When I saw smoke billowing into the night sky from multiple points through the city, I dismounted and crept into the woods. My body slipped into old, practiced movements. My steps were light as I crept past groups of rebels, most of which were calmly sitting around fires, laughing. As if holding the palace under siege was a good thing. To them, it was.

None of them saw me as I stuck to the shadows, using the thick trees and dark sky to my full advantage. It wasn't until I reached the palace wall that I had to stop and wait. There were too many guards on the wall to slip past unseen and all of my usual access points for sneaking in and out were barred.

Except one.

I slipped over a piece of low, crumbling wall leading straight into my forgotten garden. Heart in my throat, I navigated straight to the Prince's Palace. No one stood guard outside the gate and, inside, the lawn had been trampled, papers scattered.

I can't be too late.

Just because Bastian was clearly not here didn't mean the worst. He was probably holed up in the Main Palace, but I wouldn't be of much use without weapons.

Entering my room again felt surreal. Everything had been overturned, which I should've expected, but seeing it was different. Pain pinched my chest. My bed had been hacked in half, my axe still lodged in one of the posts. Feathers littered the floor from my pillow and mattress, and my clothes were in small pieces all over the room. I closed my eyes against it for a moment before regaining focus. *Bastian.* Ripping the axe from the post, I turned for the door again.

An explosion rocked the ground. I stumbled into the doorframe, my ears ringing. In the distance, men shouted, a chorus of agonized cries and panicked orders. I shook my head and raced toward the Main Palace to find the prince.

No one stopped me. They didn't even offer me a second glance. There was too much dust in the air to tell friend from foe and too many of each.

The Red Asters stormed through a new hole in the palace wall and collided with guards. But there were too many of them. The guards were spread out over the entire wall but it seemed like every rebel had suddenly converged. I swung my axe as one man ran straight for me despite my not wearing a royal uniform. The axe only severed his arm, but it gave me the chance to slip around the chaos.

Guards swarmed the entrance to the gates of the Main Palace, and I didn't have time to fight them all. "Move," I shouted.

One of them—a younger man that had a usual post at Bastian's palace—shoved another guard out of the way. "Let him through!"

"He's a traitor," someone else yelled. "Don't let him near the king!"

Fuck. I barreled straight into the group. "I'm here to save the prince," I growled, throwing only defensive blows. Striking them wouldn't earn any trust.

"He's in the north tower," the first guard called.

My eyes flicked to the tall spire rising from the northern side of the palace. Archers leaned out of the windows, bows at the ready. I ground my teeth together, knowing they could shoot me on the spiral staircase as easily as they could shoot any of the Asters.

It didn't matter. I had no choice. My feet barely hit the ground as I raced into the palace, dodging blows from guards.

At the base of the tower, three men guarded a thick wooden door. "I need to save the prince," I said, taking a defensive position. They'd surely heard I was a traitor by now and with the rebels attacking, it was only natural for them to assume I—

The older man on the left pounded on the door. "Open for the Wing!" As wood scraped against wood on the other side, he turned to me. "You're a fucking dead man when this is over."

"You can get in line," I told him.

He lifted his sword to point at my chest. "I've watched the two of you grow up and I believe you have genuine affection for the prince."

I swallowed hard. That was a lot of trust to put into someone he didn't know. Even if he had seen Bastian and I grow up together, I'd committed the worst kind of betrayal.

The door inched open and I slipped by the guards, into the dark stairwell. Torches glowed at even intervals going up, leading me straight past the archers who didn't even blink at my presence. Based on the mob I saw now pushing through the gate, I understood why.

My pulse pounded harder the higher I climbed. I dreaded what I would find at the top, but more-so what was coming behind me. We had to get out of there but if Bastian was injured… No. I'd carry him out if I had to.

A blur met me at the top of the steps, slamming me into the wall. The back of my head cracked against the stone and my vision faded for a moment.

"What the fuck are you doing here?" Volney hissed. "After everything we did to get you out."

"I'm here for Bastian, you prick. Get off me." I shoved at his chest with one hand, the other gripping the axe tighter.

"Volney," Bastian called. "Stop."

He bared his teeth, shoving me farther into the stone, and backed away. I swung my gaze to Bastian. He wore his crown, strands of hair hanging free of the braids around it, and dried blood splattered his pale face.

"Are you hurt?" I asked.

He shook his head. "How did you get in here?"

"It doesn't matter how I got in. We need to get *out*. Now." I rushed to the window to see rebels already at the doors. *Fuck*. "There isn't much time. You don't have enough guards in the palace to stop them."

Bastian hung his head and sighed. "This is the safest place to be right now."

"Like hell it is." I turned and my boot landed in something tacky. I froze, my eyes moving slowly to the floor. And the lifeless body of the king. "What the fuck?"

"He's been dead for hours," Volney said. "Nen died too."

Which made Bastian king. The Red Asters would come for him that much harder now. Another pretender to the throne for Faramond to defeat. I scanned the room for unseen threats, panic humming beneath my skin. "We need to *go*."

"No." Bastian began pacing. "We need to stay. The army is hiding throughout every building within the palace walls, waiting for the signal to attack."

"So give the signal." I pointed my axe to the window. "They can't hold the door forever."

"I want to kill as many of the bastards as I can." Bastian met my gaze and held it. "So we have to wait."

The bastards. The *rebels.* Me.

"They're breaking through the door now. I'll go light the sphere," Volney said, tacking on "my king" after a brief pause.

"Fine." Bastian conceded. "Let's end this."

When Volney was gone, I approached the prince, leaving six feet between us. "Bast, what the hell happened?"

"What happened?" His laugh held no humor. "You made my father look weak when you ran, then I told everyone you were dead which made *me* look weak. While you were gone, I questioned the countess and had a guard follow her. She went right to her rebel contact who decided to…" He motioned with his hands to imply an explosion.

A flash of green light came from outside the windows. *The sphere.* A new roar rose over the rebels. Metal clanged. Men shouted a battle cry. The army. How long had Bastian known the rebels would attack in order to get so many men in place?

"You shouldn't have come back," Bastian said quietly. "I have everything under control."

"But—"

"Saer." He closed his eyes and shook his head. "You weren't the only Wing working with the Asters.

Nen killed my father and Volney threw him out the window. Anyone in this tower could be the enemy."

"I'm sorry," I whispered. "About your father."

Bastian winced. "Nothing I can do about it now, is there? Nothing except rule Eradrist and pray no one else stabs me in the back."

I sucked in a sharp breath. What could I say? Apologize again? He knew I was sorry, but that wasn't always enough. Sometimes forgiveness took time, and sometimes it didn't come at all.

"Sit," Bastian said and motioned to a bench on the far wall. Right before plopping down on it himself.

I obeyed with jerky movements. My body was telling me to get him out of there, to rush him to safety, or at least fight the rebels outside. But I was in no position to push him. All I could do now was sit and wait. Then, if the Asters came through the door, die swinging my axe at their heads.

"No snacks this time," Bastian mumbled as I sat.

My brow creased. "What?"

"It's a siege." He set his head back onto the wall. "All the snacks I had *squirreled away* are gone."

Suddenly, I could almost taste the dried fruit he'd tried to give me that day we were attacked in the temple. Back before everything began spiraling out of control. I would've done almost anything to go back to those days.

"I don't have any nuts with me today. Maybe next time," I told him with a half-smile.

Volney stepped back into the room. "They've got the rebels surrounded. We'll be out of here within the hour."

"Thank you," he said. Then, to me, "You need to run before everyone finds out I lied."

"Enough people saw me coming here that my survival will be common knowledge soon enough."

"If they're still alive." He rubbed a hand down his face and turned toward me. "You're my brother, Saer. I need you to stay alive so one day, after I've earned the trust of the governors and the people, I can bring you home."

My breath caught. "What are you saying?"

"I'm saying you need to get the hell out of Ora Et, find Anais, and enjoy your freedom while you can. One day, I'll drag you both back here."

An explosion boomed below, shaking the walls. Archers shouted, one guttural death cry rising above the rest. I raised my axe and rushed to the top of the staircase and an arrow whizzed by my head. Civilian men stumbled over the bloodied body of a guard. *Rebel* men.

Led by Faramond himself.

He didn't stumble when our eyes met, didn't blanch at the sight. Instead, he *smiled*. Blood stained the entire front of his tunic, his graying hair falling in his face. But his look of triumph drew up every ounce of hatred I'd grown for him.

All the years of manipulation and fear he'd put me through. Forcing me to kill men and women in Bastian's defense simply to fuck with King Edric's head. The beatings I'd endured. My entire life spent feeling isolated and alone. All for the *betterment of Eradrist* when, in truth, it was all for Faramond's desire for power.

My senses honed in on him, and only him, as the rebels behind him quickly fell to whatever forces Volney had summoned. The Aster leader was two steps away when he launched himself at me. I sidestepped him, forcing him into the room. He swung his curved blade at me on the way past, using the strength of his impending fall to rip the axe from my hand.

His mistake was thinking I *needed* a weapon to kill him. I leapt onto his back when he hit the floor, gripped his hair, and slammed his face into the stone ground. Again. *Again.* Bones crunched. His grip loosening on the blade.

"Saer, stop," Bastian said in a low, even voice.

My head jerked up to find him standing over me. "He made me… *this*," I said, feeling the despair in my own voice.

Bastian's gaze flicked between us. "I need to question him."

"Question anyone else. Just let me kill him." I tightened my grip on Faramond's hair and he made a pitiful groan.

"He's their leader," Bastian said matter-of-factly and my eyes widened. "Yes, I know who he is. A lot of hidden Asters talked after the siege began and *incentives* were given."

Incentives. He promised to give them quick deaths or to spare their children in exchange for information. But there was someone who would be poised to take Faramond's place. Someone I didn't know and couldn't give two shits about. As long as the man that ruined me died by my hand.

"Saer," Bastian said again, harsher this time.

I growled and threw Faramond's face down one final time. How could I defy the prince—*the king?* Volney slowly crouched and dragged Faramond away from me. With the heavy cling of armor racing up the steps, I knew the rebels were subdued. Which meant I had no purpose here.

"He's why I let the rebels get this far," Bastian explained.

"I understand." I did. Even if I hated it.

Bastian swallowed hard as the army came closer. "You should go. Use the hidden entrance."

Leave now before the army could kill me. Or arrest me for multiple counts of treason, leaving Bastian in a position where he couldn't save me a second time. "Where?" I asked about the entrance.

Bastian pointed to the wooden bench we'd been sitting on. "Lift the seat. There's a long drop, so be careful."

A long drop so people could easily escape the tower, but no one could easily sneak in. But I wasn't quite ready to say goodbye again. Everything in me screamed to stay and protect him. Stay and *help* in whatever way I could. I swallowed hard, forcing down the fear and sorrow. "Bast…"

"Fucking *go*," Volney said, wrenching the bench open.

The army was seconds away from discovering me. It was now or never. So I jumped into the hole, landing six feet down in a musty tunnel.

I stayed long enough to hear the men arrive. I held my breath as I imagined them taking in the body of Bastian's father. Then released it as a group of voices called "long live the king".

Bastian. A true ruler with a true heart. I swallowed, forcing down the lump in my throat, and whispered, "long live the king." Not daring to linger any longer in case someone checked the passageway for rebels, I slunk through the tunnel. My ankle ached with each step, but I ignored it. Pushed past the slight pain.

Bastian was king. Every guard answered to him now—he would be safe. Especially if Volney was at his side. But there was someone else counting on me now. Someone with hair the color of honey and a smile brighter than any sun. I smiled to myself as snippets of our future rose from the dust.

EPILOGUE

Two Years Later

The sound of Faramond's face breaking against stone echoed through the room. His laugh accompanied it. An evil fucking sound that sent chills down my spine. I slammed his head down harder. Felt the hot blood splash against my face. Heard Bastian telling me to stop.

But I couldn't stop. Faramond needed to die for everyone's sake. And I deserved to kill the bastard. Crack crack crack. Like broken glass under a boot. Harder. Faster. I howled my rage, fed it to the stone floor—

"Saer."

I paused. Listened. My hands still clutching Faramond's head.

"Saer." Gentle hands shook my shoulders. "Wake up."

I lurched up with a gasp. Anais sat back on her heels, long hair mussed with sleep. Morning light seeped into our little home and the lazy bleat of sheep filtered inside. *A dream.* The same dream I'd had every night since I left Bastian in the tower. Left Faramond alive. Those two things had haunted me ever since.

Anais was the only reason I hadn't perished at the Summer Palace. After returning for her, I slept for days. Then, when I woke, it was only because I needed to take care of her that I dragged myself from bed. For her that I made the long journey south, built a home, and bought a field to farm. Without her, I had nothing and no one.

"I'm sorry," I muttered, shaking off the last remnants of the dream.

She brushed the hair from my face. "Are you okay?"

I forced a small smile for her sake and hid my shaking hands beneath the blanket. "I'd be better if you kissed me."

"Oh?" She lifted the hem of her white nightdress in order to creep closer. "If I kissed you here?" She placed her lips on my cheek. "Or here?" My neck. "Or…" Her fingers trailed down my bare chest, over the scars there.

Goosebumps rose beneath her touch. Even after all this time, she calmed me and made my pulse race all at once. "Perhaps a little lower," I proposed, raising a brow suggestively.

A loud bang on the door interrupted the serene morning. "Open up!"

I leapt out of bed, shoving Anais behind me where she still knelt on the bed. None of our neighbors would act like this—not even the authorities. Though Anais and I had mostly kept to ourselves, we'd been friendly with the entire town.

"Who's there?" I yelled.

"I bring a message from the king," the man boomed.

The king? My heart slammed into my chest. Something was wrong—it had to be. Why else would Bastian send a messenger after all this time? I pulled the dagger from beneath my pillow and pushed it into Anais' hand, just in case it was a lie.

When I cracked the door open, a man in a deep blue uniform stood on the stoop. Bastian's colors. Bastian's messenger. I didn't dare think on what the message could be, didn't dare hope…

"Lord Saer Tufaro, you've been summoned to Ora Et immediately along with Lady Anais."

"Let me get dressed." I slammed the door in his face and turned to Anais. To our humble, one-room home. The kitchen where Anais cooked our meals, the fireplace that had warmed us in the winter, and the bed where we made love many, *many* times. A sudden wave of fear washed over me as I realized we were at risk of losing it all. If Bastian had changed his mind about pardoning us… *no.* He wouldn't. Would he?

"I'm not a lady," Anais said, eyes narrowed. "Do you believe him? What if it's a trick to get us to return?"

My dreams weren't the only ones haunted. While mine was always the same, hers were always different with one thing in common: both of us being caught by the crown. It didn't matter how much I assured her that we were safe, that Bastian wouldn't have let us go just to change his mind all this time later, she clung to the idea.

"Trust me." Just like I had to trust Bastian. I took her face gently between my hands and kissed her.

The palace was larger than I remembered. When the carriage passed through the outer palace wall, I took note of the second layer of stone and higher parapets. Every building we passed had work done to it—lighter bricks against darker, a new center fountain, fresh gravel on the pathways. I gave up a small prayer that we didn't have to pass the Prince's Palace on the way to the Main Palace. Seeing it again would make me feel too many things.

Once we stopped outside the Main Palace gates, I gave Anais' hand a squeeze. My nerves were frayed over the idea of returning, but now that we arrived, I was barely holding onto my sanity. And to see Bastian again, to enter his court, dressed as we were…

Anais wore a brown linen dress with soft pink buttons down the bodice while I wore black pants and a deep red tunic. Nothing at all suitable to meet royalty. I hoped it would be a private meeting because we wouldn't gain any respect from the court like this. If that was even his intention.

One of the servants opened the carriage door and bowed while we exited. The sun was too warm on my face, the scent of roses from newly planted bushes overwhelming. I took a shaky breath anyway and

Anais offered me an encouraging smile even though this was her worst nightmare. Not mine.

"It'll be fine," I whispered to her.

Volney waited at the entrance, arms crossed, when we followed the servant through the courtyard. "Took you long enough to get here."

My eyes flicked to the silver wing on his chest. "Lord Wing," I murmured in greeting.

He snorted. "Follow me."

I held tight to Anais' hand as we entered the golden entryway and headed straight into the throne room. Blue banners hung along the wall now, showcasing Bastian's color, and on either side of the matching aisle carpet were dozens of nobles. The room was utterly silent except for the soft tinkle of gemstones on the women. But none of the décor or the gawking people mattered.

Bastian rose from his throne at the other end of the room. His auburn hair was braided around a larger crown than he wore as prince but otherwise, he looked exactly the same in white clothes with gold embroidery. Anais and I walked toward him slowly, my eyes darting around the room in an unconscious search for danger. No one moved. Not the guards, not the nobles. When Volney strode past us, I startled, and he shot me a look from the corner of his eyes.

"Lord Tufaro and Lady Anais," he said, unnecessarily, to Bastian.

We made it to the foot of his dais and gave low bows. My heart thundered as I waited for Bastian to speak. I wanted to embrace him, to tell him about our farm and ask him about everything he'd accomplished in the last two years. He'd already brought Ora Et out of poverty by temporarily eliminating most of the taxes, and there was an influx of foreign traders seeking to do business with Eradrist now. He was doing good things, just like he'd always wanted.

"Get up," he said in a soft voice, right before grabbing my upper arms and pulling me into a fierce hug.

I stood in shock for a moment before returning it with equal force. "This doesn't appear very kingly," I joked, fully aware of the nobles behind us.

"Like I give a shit." He pulled back and cast a glare at the governors sitting along the side wall, almost daring them to speak.

"You look the same," I told him.

He looked me up and down. "You look different. A bit of color in your wardrobe does you justice."

I laughed as relief flooded through me. He wasn't angry with me—at least not as angry as before—and he hadn't changed his mind. Then, did that mean… "It's good to see you," I said, sobering.

"There's time for all that later." His eyes slid to Anais and he bowed slightly. "My lady."

"Your Majesty," she whispered.

Bastian stepped back to his throne and cleared his throat. "Volney, if you please."

Volney unrolled a scroll and shot me a bored look. "By order of his Royal Majesty, King Bastian the First, Lord Saer Tufaro and Lady Anais are pardoned for their crimes of treason against the crown."

Anais shuttered beside me and I took her hand again.

"Furthermore, Lord Saer Tufaro is to be immediately reinstated as a Wing to His Royal Highness."

I sucked in a breath, my lungs feeling too full. *Wing.* Did I want to return to the palace? Anais and I had carved out a peaceful life for ourselves. We'd been *safe.* Besides, it was too high of an honor and I'd been too long out of practice. Bastian told me in the tower that he would bring me back, but I never imagined like this.

Anais leaned into my side and I felt her trembling. *Shit.* If I became a Wing again, I would have to let her go. *Absolutely fucking not.* "Your Majesty, I—"

Bastian held up a hand to silence me.

Volney rolled the scroll back up and pulled a second one from inside his jacket. He took his time, seeming to revel in the suspense. "By order of his Royal Majesty, King Bastian the First, from this day forth, all royal Wings will be allowed to take a wife." He flipped the page over to show how long the new law was. "And so on and so forth."

My head spun as I looked at Bastian. This seemed impossible. I knew he'd been changing things. Making new laws, tweaking old ones, but this didn't serve Eradrist. It only served Volney and… and *me.* He must've fought the governors tooth and nail for them to accept a law like this.

I glanced down at Anais who searched my face, trying to read my reaction there. Whatever she saw, her face lit up. "You're a Wing again."

"Not if you want to go home," I vowed quietly so only she could hear.

"*You* are my home. Not a place. Besides, you've missed him for too long already."

I dragged in a rough breath. "And you can see your family if we live here."

"Something tells me that we won't have to wait long for the wedding," Bastian said with a grin. He stepped forward and clasped my shoulder. "Your uniform is waiting in your rooms."

"I…" I cleared the lump from my throat. "I don't know what to say."

"Then say nothing." He embraced me again, this time with more restraint. "Welcome home, brother."

THE END

Also by Amber R. Duell

Young Adult Novels
The Dark Dreamer Trilogy
Dream Keeper, 1
Dark Consort, 2
Night Warden, 3

When Stars Are Bright

Adult Novels
Forgotten Gods
Fragile Chaos

Faeries of Oz
co-authored with Candace Robinson
Lion, 0.5
Tin, 1
Crow, 2
Ozma, 3
Tik-Tok, 4

Vampires of Wonderland
co-authored with Candace Robinson
Rav, 0.5
Maddie, 1
Chess, 2
Knave, 3

Once Upon A Wicked Villain
co-authored with Candace Robinson
Spindle of Sin
Tower of Shadows

Acknowledgements

2020 was *a year*. Then, the weekend before Thanksgiving, my apartment building caught fire. It started on the first floor and quickly engulfed the entire stairwell. (We were on the top/third floor.) Thankfully, everyone got out okay! But we lost everything we owned. The bright side of things? Our faith in humanity was restored. The number of people and the sheer size of their generosity left me, and my entire family, in awe. So many things arrived at our new apartment without a note letting us know who sent it so, if you sent something and I didn't reach out, please know we appreciate you! This book is for all of you wonderful people who gave me, my husband, and our kids our lives back!

2021 has been a bit of a roller coaster too. Between moving from Mississippi to Massachusetts six months after the fire, our household delivery taking almost seven weeks to arrive, and starting a full-time temp job, I've been a bit scatterbrained. Thank you to everyone who has put up with me and kept me sane while I try to settle in!

All my love to my family, Lindsay, Candace, Loretta, the Saltmates, Elle, Amber, Donna, KM, Jessica, Angela, Melissa, .

Finally, thank *you* for reading!

About the Author

Amber R. Duell was born and raised in a small town in Central New York. After constantly moving with her husband and two sons as a military wife, she's finally returned home. When Amber isn't writing, she's wrangling her two young sons. In her downtime, she can be found curling up with a good book and a cat or two.

FOR MORE, VISIT:
WWW.AMBERRDUELL.COM

www.ingramcontent.com/pod-product-compliance
Lightning Source LLC
Chambersburg PA
CBHW032348310726
48973CB00007B/1903